THE BUTCHER'S WIFE

By RJ Law

Chapter 1

Carol spread out a blanket and sat amid the spring grass, a fresh breeze tickling her bare arms as they warmed beneath the comforting sun. To her left, the river gurgled against the rocky shoreline, a trickling murmur like something from a dream.

She closed her eyes and filled her lungs, a magical scent dancing on the air. It was a faint hint of sweetness she couldn't quite place. Perhaps the smell of new honeysuckle in the offing? Or was it some colorful little ground flowers budding somewhere unseen? She didn't know and it didn't matter. Nothing mattered now but the easy smile on her face.

"Carol!"

She popped one eye open and saw her husband wrestling with his fishing pole.

"I got one!"

"Good for you, hon," she said as she closed her eyes and returned to her waking dream.

"Damn it!" he yelled. "I lost it."

Carol kept her eyes shut, her breathing deep and slow, senses alive, embracing everything.

"I can't fucking believe that," her husband said. "Brand new fucking line and it breaks on the fifth cast."

Carol's eyelids snapped open.

"Do you mind? I'm trying to meditate."

Her husband looked at her and frowned.

"How many sandwiches did you bring?"

Carol gestured toward the basket.

"Look for yourself and leave me be."

He threw down his pole and stomped over.

"Fucking 20-dollar line," he muttered as he bent over.

Carol sighed and shook her head, her pulse rate ticking up despite her practiced patience.

"Bologna?" her husband whined. "That's all you brought?"

Carol's eyes shot open again and she climbed to her feet.

"And what did you bring, Robert?"

Robert put his hands on his hips and started to say something but stopped when he saw the old man watching them from the road.

"Can I help you with something?" he asked with some heat in his words.

The old man gestured upriver.

"That your dog over there?"

Carol looked all around, but Buddy wasn't there.

"Shit," she muttered.

Robert scratched his head.

"Is it a Shephard?"

The old man nodded.

"Yessir," he said. "He don't look too friendly neither."

Carol frowned.

"He's very friendly," she said.

The old man bent over and spat.

"Not to my eye."

Robert shook his head.

"I'll go get him."

He stomped off and Carol followed, the old man watching with a sour look on his weathered face.

There were prickles in the grass, and they jabbed at her bare feet as she trotted up behind her husband, little curses leaking from between her lips with every step.

"Why weren't you watching him?" asked Robert as he stormed up the river.

Carol began a wicked retort, but it faltered when she heard the scream.

They stopped and listened, each looking at the other through wide, uncertain eyes. The wind licked the leaves and grasshoppers buzzed in the breeze.

Another scream.

"What the hell?" said Robert as he broke into a run.

"Robert!" cried Carol as she hurried behind him. "Wait!"

Robert ran through a patch of woods and popped out along the shoreline, where a small group of people had gathered at the water's edge. He slowed and approached, his eyes straining to see around them, heart throbbing within his chest.

"What's he got?" asked a fat woman with a green visor.

Robert pushed through them and looked downriver, where a German Shepherd pawed at the wet bank.

"Buddy!" Carol yelled as she caught up to him.

The dog continued its work, his head low, back turned.

"Buddy!" yelled Robert.

The dog turned and ran a few steps toward them, his face marred with blood and gore.

"Oh my God," said Carol.

Robert took a step toward the dog, and it growled.

"Buddy!" he yelled again, but there was a catch in his voice.

He took another step toward the dog, and it turned back toward the river, racing back to its original place where it appeared to be guarding a prize.

Robert approached and the little crowd followed, all of their faces painted with a medley of wonder and deep concern.

As they approached, the dog began growling again, his eyes fully dilated, mind possessed by feral thoughts.

"Oh my God!" cried the woman with the visor. "Is that a foot?"

Carol screamed and Robert clutched his stomach while Buddy laid down and gnawed at a toe.

Chapter 2

Jimmy sat behind the wheel of his car, eyes trained on the comings and goings at the nightclub across the street. There was a long line now, and the bouncer was turning people away. Lots of guys shook their heads in frustration as the big man moved all the scantily clad girls ahead and inside.

"Hey," the rejects yelled. "Come on. Give us a fucking break."

The bouncer looked at them and shrugged, a "what-do-you-expect" look on his face while all the pretty girls rushed inside.

"You, you and you," said the bouncer, his shoulders thrown back, a little snarl on his lips.

Jimmy looked the man over from afar. He had a bushy black beard and wore sunglasses at night. He stood probably six-foot-four, and his biceps were oiled. Jimmy squinted. Big, yes, but strong? Hard to say. More fat than muscle? Maybe, maybe not. Jimmy couldn't really tell from this distance anymore.

He squinted harder as he watched each gorgeous girl rush inside, the routine winners of the great genetic lottery that is life. Each one absolutely beautiful. Every bit special in her own little way.

For now, Jimmy thought as he spat out the window onto the street. Give them ten more years and we'll see.

Someone approached his car door, but he kept staring at the bouncer.

"Hey doll," said a craggy voice.

"Move along," said Jimmy, his eyes peering through the neon-lit night.

The hooker leaned over and propped her arm against his open window.

"What's the matter?" she asked. "You don't like gettin head?"

Jimmy pulled away from the stink of her mouth.

"I appreciate the offer," he said dryly. "But no thanks."

The woman stood back and spat on the pavement.

"Whatever," she said. "I don't want your old ass dick in my mouth anyways."

Jimmy watched her stumble away with a drug-addled gait. He sighed through his nose and squinted at the bouncer.

"Well," he said to himself as he opened his car door.

He stepped outside into the night and stood, a creak in his spine as he straightened his back. He grunted and rubbed at the fire in his hip. That young doctor said he'd need a replacement sooner rather than later. But at some point, it's like putting new tires on a broken-down Chevy, at least in Jimmy's mind.

He grunted a little and shifted his weight until his footing felt right. Then he took out his gun and closed the car door.

He slid the piece into his rear waistband beneath his jacket, the cold of the steel stinging his sweaty skin. As he trotted across the street, the organized crowd grew restless, each frowning in turn as he approached the front of the line.

"Hey," said a young man with slick curly hair. "Where the fuck do you think you're going? The line starts back there."

Jimmy kept walking.

"Hey," said the man as he stepped forward.

Without stopping, Jimmy palmed his face and pushed him backward.

"What the hell?" shouted one of the others as the curly-headed man fell backward against the sidewalk.

The bouncer watched all this with mute indifference, his true feelings concealed behind his ridiculous nighttime sunglasses and tangles of facial hair.

"What's your deal, pops?" he asked as Jimmy approached.

Jimmy slowed and looked up at the man who now seemed to loom twice as large in the clarity of the moment.

"Move aside," said Jimmy. "I got business with Vincent."

The bouncer frowned.

"You got business with the boss, you don't come this way. Go around back and talk to his boys."

Jimmy sighed and scratched his forehead.

"It's a bit of a walk and I got this thing with my leg."

The bouncer chuckled.

"Alright, old man," he said as he put his hand on Jimmy's shoulder. "It's time to go."

The line of rejects had molded into a little mob during the interchange and now they gasped in horror as Jimmy broke the bouncer's arm with a swift and sudden motion.

"My arm!" screamed the big man as he tumbled to the ground.

Jimmy watched the man with a bored, disinterested expression, the only one he owned.

"Pardon me," he said as he stepped around his writhing body and entered the club.

Inside, it was all noise and flashing lights, people screaming at each other over the music, drinks sloshing in their hands. Jimmy stood at the entryway and took it all in. A tangle of young bodies throbbed atop a huge dance floor, while a potpourri of contrasting perfumes and musk colognes stabbed up into his nostrils.

Just steps away from where he stood, lightly clad servers flashed by, their breasts pushed together, false rabbit ears bouncing atop their heads. A drunk lurched backward from a pool table and one of the girls screeched to a stop, the beer on her tray tipping forward as she struggled to dodge him. She fumbled helplessly as the bottle flipped from its perch and tumbled to the ground.

"Fuck!" she yelped as the drunk turned to view the damage.

"Oh," he said. "I'm sorry—"

Before he could finish, a large man in a suit swept in from the shadows and dragged him away, while his drinking mates watched through startled eyes.

"Goddammit," said the girl as she bent over to retrieve the spilled bottle.

Jimmy watched her bend, the bottom of her skirt sliding up over her buttocks.

"Jimmy!" said a skinny man with hollow cheeks and red cocaine eyes.

He slapped Jimmy on the back and smiled.

"What's with all the action out front?" he said. "You know you ain't gotta do that shit. Just come through the back. We'll take you right in."

Jimmy grunted.

"Sure," he said as he looked the man up and down.

He wore an ill-fitting suit that looked to have been made when he was twenty pounds heavier, and the polyester fibers shone wetly under the red strobing lights.

"What do you need?" asked the man as he rubbed at the burn in his nose.

Jimmy frowned.

"I need to talk to Vincent."

The skinny man snorted a few times and smiled.

"Naw, you need to tell me what you need, and then I can decide if it's worth the boss's time."

Jimmy narrowed his eyes and the man's smile faltered.

"Where's Vincent?" he asked.

The skinny man flexed his jaw muscles and leaned in close.

"Listen, we're all paid up with Mario."

Jimmy shook his head.

"This ain't about that."

The man pulled back and nodded.

"Alright," he said. "Stay here a second."

He turned and disappeared into the mass of people gyrating beneath the smoky red lights. Moments later, he returned with another at his side, this man taller and much more well-fed.

"This way," said the skinny man.

He turned and forced his way through the crowd, Jimmy following, the large man trailing a few steps behind. They reached the other side of the club and trotted up a narrow set of stairs that led to a long balcony that overlooked the entire floor, a mass of arms and legs, of drinking, dancing bodies. There stood another large man, his eyes cast downward at the people below.

"Yeah?" he muttered without looking up.

"He's here to see the boss," said the skinny man.

The man raised a thumb over his shoulder at a black steel door behind him.

"Go ahead."

The skinny man approached the door and knocked a couple of times. Then he gave the doorknob a twist and Jimmy followed him inside.

Before them at a broad oak desk, sat a bald man in a pink dress shirt, the collar open, a tailored gray suit vest over his muscled chest. A pale white scar ran the length of one cheek and down into a neatly trimmed beard, where a few gray threads sprouted out between a thick forest of dark black bristles.

"Uh, boss?" started the skinny man, but Vincent shut him up with one raised finger.

"Gimme a second," he muttered as he looked over a stack of papers. His eyes squinted through a pair of cheap reading glasses that were much too small for his face.

They waited several minutes, the skinny man pulling at his collar, Jimmy looking bored as ever. At last, Vincent finished with his papers and peered up over his glasses.

"Ah," he said with a smile. "Jimmy."

He tore the glasses from his face and sat back in his chair.

"To what do I owe the pleasure?"

Jimmy looked at the skinny man.

"I'd prefer to speak alone if that's alright."

Vincent snapped his fingers.

"Out," he said.

The skinny man rubbed his nose and stepped back.

"Yes, sir."

He rushed out of the office and closed the door behind him.

"Now," said Vincent. "What are you doing here? You know we're all paid up?"

Jimmy nodded.

"This isn't about that."

Vincent scratched the scar on his cheek.

"Alright, then, what's it about?"

Jimmy cleared his throat and swallowed.

"I need a favor."

Vincent's eyes widened.

"A favor?" He chuckled. "Well now, ain't that some shit?"

He shook his head and leaned forward.

"What can I do for you, Jimmy?" he said with false concern.

Jimmy frowned.

"I need to find someone."

Vincent propped his forearms against his desk.

"Who exactly are we talking about?"

Jimmy reached into his pocket and withdrew a folded sheet of paper.

"Name's Miles Francesa."

He passed the paper over to Vincent, who eyed the black and white mugshot with a frown.

"You know him?" asked Jimmy.

Vincent tossed the paper down onto his desk.

"Maybe," he said. "What's this for?"

Jimmy shrugged.

"He's a bail jumper."

Vincent shook his head and laughed.

"You got to be fuckin kidding me," he said. "You're still doing this kind of small-time shit for that crooked attorney?"

Jimmy shrugged.

"Gotta make ends meet somehow."

Vincent's face hardened.

"What's the problem? Mario not paying you enough?"

"I didn't say that," said Jimmy.

"But if he were, you wouldn't have to be doing this pathetic side work, ain't that right? Or is it that you got debts? Maybe that's the problem."

Jimmy stared forward with his even expression.

"Don't worry about me," he said flatly.

Vincent leaned back in his chair and eyed Jimmy from head to toe.

"You know, you ought to come work for me. A man with your talents, old as you are. There's still time to make some real money."

Jimmy looked at him, his eyelids lazy, always heavy, always low.

"I appreciate the offer, but I'm all set."

Vincent's face soured.

"What, you're too good to work for me?" he asked. "You'll shake people down for Mario, but you won't take drug money, is that it?"

Jimmy sighed.

"I don't judge anybody for how they make a living," he said. "It just ain't for me. Now, do you know this guy or don't you?"

Vincent nodded.

"Of course, I know him. I know everybody."

"Well," said Jimmy. "Do you know where I can find him?"

Vincent sucked at his teeth.

"What's it worth to you Jimmy? You willing to owe me a favor for this?"

Jimmy shrugged.

"Something proportional," he said. "That's all."

Vincent smiled.

"That's all I'd expect."

He reached into a desk drawer and took out a pen.

"He's hiding out here." He flipped the paper over and jotted an address on the back. "He's been there a couple days."

Jimmy watched him write.

"He work for you or something?"

Vincent shook his head.

"Nah, I don't know him, but he's tight with one of my boys. Old friends, I guess. Came to him in a rough state, begging for cover. So, my guy put him up in his basement."

He passed the paper over to Jimmy.

"And what about your man?" he said. "He gonna give me trouble?"

Vincent shook his head.

"I'll give him a call and tell him to stand aside. He won't like it, but he'll damn well do it."

Vincent nodded.

"I appreciate it."

Vincent scratched his beard.

"Of course, Jimmy," he said. "With all the crazy shit going on, guys like us gotta stick together."

Jimmy grunted and turned toward the door.

"And Jimmy," said Vincent. "Keep your hands off my guys, ok? I got a reputation to uphold. I can't have you manhandling my boys."

Jimmy opened the door without speaking.

"Remember, Jimmy," said Vincent as Jimmy shut the door behind him. "Even guys like you ain't immune to accidents."

Hours later, Jimmy sat behind his steering wheel outside a rundown house on a potholed road. In this decaying part of town, a large stinking refinery loomed large, smokestacks seeding the sky with a billowing smog of noxious air.

He opened the car door and stepped out amid the sharp stench of burning petroleum. He slipped his pistol into his rear waistband and trotted across the street, the clap of his shoes drowned away by the faint sound of sirens and highway traffic.

He stepped onto the gravel driveway and made his way toward the structure, a one-story shithole with a peeling shingled roof. Six crumbling concrete steps led up to a cracked front porch, where fat roaches scuttled amid the low porch light.

Jimmy scaled the steps and banged on the front door, a slight give beneath his shoe as he crunched one of the roaches down.

Heavy boot steps slammed down inside, and the door swung open.

"Yeah?"

It was a big man in a dirty wife-beater, his arms latticed with tattoos. He stared hard at Jimmy through another set of red cocaine eyes.

"I'm looking for Miles," said Jimmy.

The man kept staring.

"You Vincent's guy?" Jimmy asked.

The man firmed his mouth.

"Maybe," he said.

Jimmy sighed.

"Well," he said. "Is he here or not?"

The man snorted and stepped back.

"Yeah, he's here."

Jimmy stepped through the entryway and looked around.

The living room was a filthy place adorned with lawn furniture and pizza boxes. There was a stink on the air, unwashed flesh and spoiling food, a urine-soaked bathroom, and what was that other thing? A hamster cage maybe? Who could guess? Who would want to?

Jimmy looked down at the floor, where more roaches scurried about.

"Nice place you have here."

"Eat me," said the man as he brushed past him.

Jimmy followed him inside and put his hands in his pockets, the noxious refinery smell a happy memory now.

"Miles!" yelled the man, his voice rattling a framed photo against its crooked nail.

The man fell into a soiled recliner and leaned backward, the footrest popping up with a sickly squeal. Jimmy pushed his bottom lip out and tapped a shoe.

"You want a beer or something?" asked the man.

Jimmy started to answer but stopped when Miles skulked into the room.

"You Jimmy?" he asked, his face pointed toward the ground.

He had a sick look in his eyes but not in a drug-addled way.

"I am," Jimmy said.

Miles nodded.

"I'm ready."

The other man sat up fast and Jimmy almost went for his gun.

"Fuck this," he said. "You tell him what you seen."

Miles snapped his head around.

"Shut up, Tony," he said.

Jimmy watched them both, his eyelids relaxed, pulse the same.

"Well," he said. "We best be getting on."

Tony jumped up from his seat.

"You don't even care what he's got to say?"

Jimmy looked from one to the other.

"Not particularly," he said with his flat, disinterested voice.

He turned toward the door while Miles and Tony said their goodbyes.

Outside, huge flames danced atop the refinery stacks, the towering fires flaring brightly as they burned off excess gas. Jimmy watched them through lazy eyes, his lungs taking in the noxious output, a growing nausea in his gut.

"Hurry up," he called.

Seconds later, Miles stood beside him.

"You ready?" Jimmy asked.

Miles nodded and they moved down the porch, pain firing through Jimmy's bad hip with every downward step. When they got to the car, he stopped and looked at the young man.

"You're not gonna give me any trouble, are you?"

Miles shook his head.

"No, sir," he said. "I know who you are."

Jimmy nodded.

"Alright then."

They opened their doors and got inside.

"Go ahead and put your seatbelt on," said Jimmy as he cranked the engine.

Miles put his seatbelt on and sat back in his seat.

About 30 minutes later, Jimmy pulled the car up in front of a big brick house with a for-sale sign on the lawn.

"What is this?" asked Miles. "I thought you were taking me to the cops."

Jimmy shook his head.

"No, you're gonna stay here tonight with a babysitter. Your lawyer will make arrangements with the cops tomorrow."

Miles looked confused.

"Why?"

Jimmy shrugged.

"I'm not a lawyer," he said. "From what I understand, though, it's better this way. You stay here tonight. Let your attorney arrange your surrender. Might be able to swing something in your favor that way. I wouldn't count on it though."

Miles nodded.

"Fair enough."

He reached for the door handle.

"Hey," said Jimmy. "Let me ask you something. If you don't mind."

Miles shrugged.

"Alright."

Jimmy scratched his jaw.

"Who do you work for exactly? I mean, the shit they arrested you for, that ain't all you. No offense, but somebody big is behind it."

Miles looked at his lap and shook his head.

"You wouldn't know them."

Jimmy pinched his eyebrows together.

"I know everyone in this city," he said. "Everyone worth knowing anyway."

Miles looked at him, a strange glint in his eyes, almost like pity.

"Not them," he said.

Jimmy thought about that for a moment.

"How do you know I don't?"

Miles shrugged.

"Because if you knew who they were, you'd either be working for them, or you wouldn't be alive."

He wrenched the door open and stepped out of the car.

"Thanks for the ride," he said.

The young man shut the door and walked toward the brick house, where a big black man stood waiting in front of the open front door.

"Anytime," muttered Jimmy though Miles was much too far to hear.

An hour later, Jimmy pulled up to his place, a nothing little house he rented from an old lady with glaucoma in one eye. He parked his car in the driveway and got out, rubbing his leg and cursing his age. He unlocked the door and stepped inside, no movement or sound, just quiet throughout.

"Barney," he called out into the darkness.

A slow shuffling broke the quiet and a yellow retriever crept into the room, his old face weakly lit by the pale moonlight filtering through the window shade. Jimmy flipped on the kitchen light and the dog limped forward.

"Hey," whispered Jimmy as he knelt. "Come here."

The dog came closer, and Jimmy rubbed his ear.

"You hungry?"

He shut the door behind him and walked across the room. He opened the pantry and took out a large can of dog food. He worked it open with an old-school handheld can opener and shook the stubborn contents out with a wet shloomp into an empty metal bowl. The dog sniffed the food and ate. Jimmy scratched the dog's ear and opened the refrigerator door.

He made a bologna sandwich and tossed potato chips onto his plate. Then he went into the little living room and sat in his old, tattered recliner. He grabbed the remote and flipped on the television, the newsman prattling on about the economy and political polls, gas prices and whatnot.

"... and economists expect the consumer price index to increase in the short term with the recent events abroad," said a handsome man with a clean haircut.

Jimmy bit into his sandwich and chewed.

"And in local news," said a perky young woman with blinding-white teeth, "more human remains were recovered in the East River this evening, as police continue to investigate an alarming string of related killings."

"That's right, Kim," said the handsome man, a dazzling gleam in his deep blue eyes. "Police are investigating what may, in fact, be an apparent set of serial murders. To date, there have been at least a dozen victims, all identified only by partial remains."

Jimmy chewed and swallowed.

"But what does it all mean?" the newsman continued. "Is a serial killer at large in the greater metropolitan area? Doug Mathews is on the scene."

Jimmy bit into his sandwich again and chewed slowly as the camera panned the river, its dark water giving back the moonlight amid the ink-black night.

"A foot, a hand, a dozen more of the same," said Doug Mathews with his deep broadcaster voice. "These are the ghoulish treasures of a morbid exposition into the murky depths of the East River."

"Get back!" yelled a policeman at a line of frenzied reporters.

"What began as a tragic mystery has evolved into an ongoing crisis. Police have more questions than answers, but they do know one thing: This isn't normal."

"About ten bodies a year," said a broad-chested man in a decorated police uniform. "That's what we usually pull from the river on average."

"Ten bodies," said Doug Mathews. "A startling number. Tragic, disturbing, and yet paltry compared to what's happened in the past six months."

"Based on what we've seen," said the police chief, "we're investigating the possibility of a serial offender."

Jimmy turned as Barney nudged against his arm.

"Alright," he muttered.

He fingered loose a piece of bologna and passed it over. As the dog chewed, the TV kept screaming.

"But why only feet and hands?" asked Doug Mathews. "Where are the heads? Where are the torsos?"

Jimmy changed the station and rubbed Barney's head.

"It's a sick fucking world," he said to the dog as it whined for more bologna.

He tore off another slice and passed it over, while Andy Griffith grinned amid the black-and-white reruns of a simpler time.

Chapter 3

"It affects the juiciness, texture, tenderness and flavor," said Marcus as he gazed out the passenger window. "Without it, you got nothin."

Hiroto sat quietly behind the steering wheel, his dead eyes fixated on the loading docks, where the workers moved about beneath the moonlight, their bodies silhouetted as they wheeled crates on and off the bobbing boats.

"See, lean muscle has a high frequency of thin, evenly distributed flecks of fat," Marcus continued. "This all melts during cooking and that's what adds the juiciness and tenderness throughout the meat. That's what fine marbling is. That's why it's so important."

He looked at Hiroto and shrugged.

"That's why everyone wants your guys' shit," he said. "That Japanese shit, the Kobe, Wagyu beef. If you like beef, which I don't, but the principle's the same. It's fat that brings the flavor."

Hiroto stared forward.

"Now, with medium marbling, that's just larger, less evenly distributed flecks of fat," he said. "But that ain't near as good. You see, larger pieces of fat will take longer to render and ultimately liquefy. As such, when you cook a medium-marbled cut of meat rare or medium-rare, that fat just isn't going to have enough time to render, and the meat won't be as tender or juicy. This will also leave behind little flecks of fat that negatively impact what I like to call mouthfeel."

He paused and looked at Hiroto, but the cold, hard Japanese man remained a statue of focus.

"Now, coarse marbling is even worse," he went on. "You see, with this—"

"Please," said Hiroto in his bad English. "Be quiet and listen."

Marcus started to protest but stopped when he heard the banging.

"Awe damn it," he said.

He popped open the glove box and took out a little black box. He opened the car door and stepped outside. While the loaders worked the docks, he walked to the back of the car and opened the trunk. Inside, a fat man wriggled against his restraints, eyes peeking out from the bottom of a black hood he had somehow worked up over his nose.

"Please," he muttered. "Please let me go. I won't tell nobody."

Marcus shook his head and opened the black box. He removed a syringe filled with milky white fluid and gave it a tap. He jammed his thumb against the plunger until the little air bubble pushed out. Then, he forced it into the fat man's neck and emptied the contents with a practiced hand.

"Pleeease," said the man as he drifted away.

Marcus pulled the hood back over the man's head and closed the trunk.

"Too much drug," said Hiroto as Marcus got back into the car.

"Yeah," he said. "Well, what are you gonna do?"

They waited in the dark for a while, Marcus tapping his hand against his knee, Hiroto's eyes darting all around, nerves electric.

"Relax," said Marcus. "I've done this a hundred—"

Someone knocked at the passenger window and Marcus jumped.

"Jesus," he yelped as he fumbled for his gun.

"It's alright," said a man outside the window. "We're ready for you now."

Marcus squinted out the window, his eyes blinded by the longshoreman's flashlight.

"Relax," said Hiroto with his awkward accent.

Marcus looked at him and grunted.

"Just pop the trunk."

They waited while the longshoreman went to gather his men.

"Now, see with the Kobe beef," said Marcus. "That's a special breed of cow with some world-class marbling. But it ain't just the breed that counts. What really makes the difference is how they raise them from babies."

Hiroto watched in his rearview mirror while the longshoreman hoisted up the fat man and dumped him into a large wheelbarrow.

"First, they give them beer to induce appetite," said Marcus. "Then they massage them daily in place of exercise. Hell, they even play classical music to help them relax at feeding time, all to make them as fat as they can possibly get."

The trunk closed and the car bobbed a little. Marcus watched the longshoreman approach through the rearview glass.

"You got your punch card?" asked the man, a wet stocking cap pulled low over his brow.

Marcus fished around in the glove box and handed it over.

"That's worth two," he said. "He's at least 260."

The longshoreman took out a little metal hole punch and stabbed it into the card twice.

"Here you go," he said.

Marcus took the card and looked it over.

"Thanks," he said as he slipped it back into the glove box.

The longshoreman nodded and gestured to his men, who followed him toward the docks with the wheelbarrow. Hiroto started the engine and they backed away.

"Now, with your wild game—" Marcus started, but Hiroto closed his hand over his left arm like a vice.

"Radio," he said.

Marcus swallowed.

"Alright," he said as Hiroto released him. "No need to get antsy."

He turned up the radio and they pulled away, the sun growing larger as it breached the great liquid horizon.

Chapter 4

Jimmy's car squealed into the parking lot and grumbled to a clattering stop. While his engine idled, a dozen eyes followed the harsh sounds to their source, birds fleeing their places on overhead power lines while people shook their heads and hurried past.
As the engine skittered to a quiet, he pinched his fingers around the bridge of his nose and rubbed. His headache throbbed as the morning sunlight glinted off all the chrome bumpers and stabbed through the windows into his squinting eyes.
"Shit," he thought as he leveraged the door open.
It was much too early for a man like him, which was saying something, considering it was 11 a.m. With his usual grunt and grimace, he climbed to his feet and crossed the parking lot, a deep frown warning away any potential nods of courtesy from even the friendliest of people-persons.
With a forceful shove, he pushed the door open and stepped into the little law office. A tiny bell tinkled as the door stretched open. He glanced up at it and rubbed his head, while a little old woman with glasses blinked at him over the reception desk.
"Hello, Jimmy," she said with a warm smile.
Jimmy looked around the waiting room. There was a tattooed man with a neck brace and a pregnant woman with an arm cast. Each one regarded him with brief glances and then returned to whatever they were reading.

"Hello, Madeline," Jimmy said as he approached.
He raised his eyebrows.
"How are you feeling?"
Madeline shrugged.
"I'm old," she said.
Jimmy nodded.
"I hear ya."
Madeline scoffed and shook her head.
"You're not old," she said. "You'll see."
He grunted.
"I can hardly wait."
Madeline gave a soft smile, and wrinkles spidered out as it touched her eyes.
"He said to send you right in when you arrived."
Jimmy nodded.
"Thank you, dear," he said as he approached Howard's office.
When he approached the door, the people in the waiting room glared as if he had jumped the line at the world's most popular amusement park. The tattooed man slapped his magazine down against his knee. The woman pursed her lips and sighed through her nose. With a little shrug, Jimmy turned the doorknob and entered the office, his hip catching a little as he made his way inside.
"Jimmy," Howard said as he half stood from behind his desk. "How you doing, buddy?"
Jimmy shut the door and limped into the room, his hard weathered face doing little to mis-advertise his age.
"I'm tired, Howard."
The lawyer sat back down in his seat and nodded.
"Sure," he said. "It's a little early for night owls."
Jimmy crossed the room and sat down on a little beige sofa with faint floral designs. The furniture squeaked as he sat but the sound was overpowered by the grunt from Jimmy's mouth.
"Why am I here, Howard?" he asked as he stretched out his bad leg.
Howard ran his hand over his receding hairline and sighed.
"Well, I need a little favor."
Jimmy scratched at a scab on his knuckles.
"You got some work for me?"
Howard folded his hands on his desk and nodded.
"I do," he said.

Jimmy frowned.

"How bad is it?"

Howard shrugged.

"Well, to be honest, I don't know yet."

Jimmy sat back in his seat and took in a deep breath. He looked at Howard and frowned.

"But bad enough you called me."

Howard leaned back in his own seat and tapped his fingers against his desk.

"Well, let's just say it could be bad. Actually, it could be really bad. But hopefully not."

Jimmy scratched his whiskered jaw, his face pinched thoughtfully.

"Well, lay it on me."

Howard picked up a pen and held it at both ends, his head slightly bowed as if he were preparing to confess some humiliating indiscretion.

"I have a client," he said. "Well, two clients, really. A husband and a wife. I mostly deal with the wife. I've been representing her for several years. She just married this guy not too long ago. Nice enough guy. A little pretentious."

Jimmy looked bored.

"I don't tail adulterers, Howard."

Howard shook his head.

"No, no," he said. "Believe me, I wouldn't waste your time."

Jimmy folded his arms.

"Well, let's get on to the point."

Howard nodded.

"Fair enough," he said. "Alright then, here's the deal. The wife visits me and says the husband came home one night with blood on his hands. Blames it on a deer. No visible damage to the car, but he explains that away by saying it was another car and he was helping."

Jimmy grunted.

"Does that sound suspicious to you?" asked Howard.

"Just keep going," said Jimmy.

"Well, if you do think that sounds suspicious, you're going to love this. It happens again a couple weeks later. But this time, he's got scratch marks on his back."

Jimmy still looked bored.

"So what? She thinks it's hooker blood or something? He's a serial killer?"

Howard frowned.

"Well, she doesn't know what to think."

Jimmy looked around Howard's office, a simple enough place. Way too simple for a man of his worth, especially with the billboards and TV ads. Where the hell was all his money going? Jimmy thought for a moment and decided that was a question he didn't want answered. He shook his head and frowned.

"What is it, Howard?" he asked. "You got a thing for this girl? She the one that got away?"

Howard swallowed.

"Look, Jimmy, I just need you to look into this guy, tail him a little, make sure he's on the up-and-up."

Jimmy sucked his teeth.

"I don't know," he said. "This is some light duty compared to the stuff you usually have me doing."

Howard nodded.

"I understand that," he said. "I'll make it worth your while. Just do me this favor. You're still a P.I., aren't you? Even if it is only part-time."

Jimmy stood up and flattened the wrinkles on his pants.

"I want everything in advance. Plus expenses. All in cash."

Howard nodded.

"Whatever you need."

Jimmy approached the desk.

"And if this guy is up to something, what then?" he asked. "I won't be making any statements to the police."

Howard shook his head.

"No, of course not," he said. "If you find anything, just let me know. I'll take care of it."

Jimmy eyed him through a pair of narrow slits.

"What's this guy's name?"

"Michael Patterson," said Howard. "He works at Viox Genomics."

"And the wife?"

"Robin."

Jimmy nodded and turned for the door.

"Is that all?" asked Howard as he stood up from his desk. "You need more details?"

"Nope," said Jimmy as he walked out the door.

Chapter 5

Robin Patterson walked amid the uptown fashion district, where the biggest luxury brands hawked the latest eye-catching ensembles. At her side, a pair of well-to-do ladies giggled and chatted as they window shopped, each already wearing the trendiest of trends.

As the three walked in their perfumed little clique, some moved aside as if making way for royalty. Still others offered up subtle sneers, minor acts of defiance with the slight twist of the lip. One of the three women, a startlingly beautiful thing with endless eyelashes, noticed and threw a hand over her chest.

"What was her problem?" she asked, her long pale fingers fondling a fat emerald pendant.

The other two women turned and followed her eyes.

"What?" asked Robin.

The breathtaking woman put her hands on her hips.

"She sneered at us."

"Just ignore them, Stacia," said the other woman, her neck wreathed with a diamond necklace that threw off blinding flashes of fire beneath the afternoon sun.

"Yeah," said Robin. "We're having fun!"

They all turned their attention back to the store side of the street, where expansive windows beckoned them indoors with all sorts of fineries.

Among these affluent sophisticates, Robin looked every bit the part, her posture flawlessly refined, dress embarrassingly expensive.

But even as she laughed and gossiped, something tore at her attention. It was a man lingering several blocks back, suspicious for no other reason than the way he stirred her guts.

He was gruff looking, even at a distance, and he seemed to be there always, each and every time she turned her head.

"What are you looking at?" asked Stacia, her eyes squinting as she peered down the street.

Robin frowned.

"That man," she said.

They all looked at the man who seemed small and harmless at such a distance.

"What about him?" asked Stacia.

Robin shrugged.

"I noticed him before," she said. "I think maybe he's following us."

They all watched with low eyebrows and bated breath as the man flagged a cab. Robin frowned as he got inside and sped away in the opposite direction.

"Well, there you go," said Stacia as she elbowed the other woman. "Someone's a little paranoid."

Robin looked at them through low eyelids.

"You can never be too safe."

The other women giggled, and they all continued moving up the street, the passersby greeting them with space and sneers.

About two hours later, they all sat in a fine restaurant, their stomachs gurgling as they digested a slurry of what had once been sumptuous meals.

"Will there be anything else?" asked the waiter, his face neither warm nor kind.

"No," said Robin.

She passed over a credit card.

"Very good," said the waiter with a bow as he snapped up the card and walked away.

"Thank you so much for lunch," said Stacia.

"Yes," said the other woman. "I'll treat, next time. We'll go ... someplace nice."

Robin's eye twitched as she smiled politely.

"Sounds wonderful."

Thirty minutes later, the other woman was gone, and Robin sat listening to Stacia drone on about her husband's failings.

"I mean, I know he's a lot older than me, but why can't we ever do anything I want to do?"

Robin nodded, her face pinched with empathy.

"Have you tried asking?"

Stacia looked at her as if she'd suggested anal sex.

"I shouldn't have to," she whined.

Robin took a deep breath and nodded.

"Ok," she said. "And how is—"

"And the sex," Stacia interrupted. "It's nonexistent. I mean, you should have seen this little thing I put on the other night. It made my body look incredible. I mean, of course, I have a beautiful body, but this thing, it brought out my full essence. But did it make a difference? Of course not. Nothing ever does. All he cares about is the fucking Guild."

Robin's face turned stern.

"No," she said softly. "No."

Stacia swallowed.

"Yes," she said, a hint of fear on her face. "Of course. You're right."

The waiter brought Robin's card.

"Thank you," said Robin.

She took the card and nodded her thanks.

"Um," said Stacia. "I think I'll go now."

Robin assumed a false look of hurt.

"Oh," she said. "Are you sure?"

Stacia nodded and stood up.

"You won't repeat this, will you?" she asked. "About what I said?"

Robin looked confused.

"What did you say?" she said. "I'm sorry, I wasn't really listening."

Stacia swallowed and looked down.

"Ok," she said. "I'll see you at the party."

Robin smiled.

"I can't wait."

They exchanged happy little nods, and Stacia walked away. Robin watched her leave and then shook her head. Then she slipped her credit card into her Louis Vuitton wallet and started thumbing through her phone.

"This seat taken?" said a gravelly voice.

Robin looked up to see a middle-aged man in a cheap suit.

"Actually—" she started, but he had already started to sit.

"Hey—" she began, but now he was talking.

"Never eaten at this place," he said as he sat with some discomfort. "The burgers any good?"

Robin cocked her head.

"Do I know you?"

The man shrugged.

"I doubt it."

She assessed him quietly, her face surprisingly relaxed.

"Well," he said as he looked at her through a set of lazy eyes. "Don't you want to know my name?"

She frowned as if disappointed by some internal revelation.

"I'm assuming it's Jimmy."

Jimmy sat back in the chair and lowered his eyebrows.

"And what makes you say that?"

Robin shrugged.

"Howard told me I might see you."

Jimmy grunted.

"Of course, he did."

She eyed him with muted curiosity as if she were sizing up an applicant for a job.

"What?" he asked.

"You're not what I expected," she said as she looked him over.

He had a big bald head and a jaw covered with coarse gray whiskers. His cheeks were slightly pock-marked, and his nose was more than a little off-center. He was 50 at least, maybe 55, but none of that stole from his imposing size.

"Oh yeah?" he asked. "Is it my sideburns?"

She pursed her lips.

"I thought you'd be younger."

Jimmy shrugged.

"Well," he said. "The first 50 years of childhood are the toughest."

Now came the waiter, his face showing a strange sort of concern.

"Will you be ordering something else?" he asked.

Robin looked up at him and smiled.

"Just some coffee, maybe."

Jimmy kept his eyes on Robin.

"The same," he said.

The waiter nodded and walked away.

Robin watched him leave and turned toward Jimmy.

"Well," she said. "Do you need some information from me?"

Jimmy frowned and looked her over. She was pretty but not beautiful. Pale but in a good way. Not unhealthy. More of a subtle look, he supposed. Cute but mature. Youth with a hint of wisdom, Jimmy thought. Not a bad combination, at least from his point of view. Eyes framed in the little crow's feet that would get worse before she expected.

"Oh," he said. "I just thought we might have a little talk."

Robin gave a closed-lip smile, which Jimmy assessed. Then she inhaled slowly, which Jimmy also assessed. Always assessing. Everyone, everything, all the time.

"Well," she said. "What would you like to talk about?"

Jimmy took a slow deep breath.

"Well, why don't we start with your husband?"

Robin rubbed her forehead.

"I really wish you would get your information from Howard. If I knew it would get this complicated, I wouldn't have asked him for help."

Jimmy turned his palms up.

"Nothing complicated about this at all," he said. "Except your husband and his bloody clothes."

Robin shot him a look, but Jimmy couldn't discern its meaning.

"What do you want?" she asked.

Jimmy shrugged.

"I want to know what I'm getting into before I get into it," he said in a matter-of-fact tone. "It's how I got to be this age."

Robin sighed and looked at the table.

"I don't know what you're getting into," she said. "I don't know anything except what I told Howard."

The waiter approached and set a pair of steaming coffee cups under their noses.

"Anything else?"

Jimmy stared at Robin as she regarded the man.

"No," she said. "We're fine for now."

The waiter nodded and walked away.

"Look," said Robin. "I just freaked out, alright? I wanted to know if I'm being paranoid or not."

Jimmy leaned forward and scratched at a sticky spot on the table.

"You know," he said. "At a place like this, you'd think they'd clean the tables better."

He looked up at her.

"Too busy, I guess. Maybe it's just laziness, though."

She pinched her face.

"What?"

Jimmy shrugged.

"What do you think?" he said. "Where would you put your money?"

Robin just looked at him, her mouth half-open.

"You see," said Jimmy. "That's kind of what I have to do in my line of work. Make judgments on things you can't really judge."

He lifted his coffee cup to his lips and slurped loud enough to draw glances from neighboring tables.

"Now," he said as he licked his lips. "Your husband came home with something on his shirt, and the news is having a field day filling people's heads with all kinds of craziness. Stirring up a shit storm so they can get more eyes on their advertisers. And it's working. Hell, I have a friend at the police station. He tells me they get a thousand calls a day. So-called tips. People saying they saw their neighbor drag a rolled-up rug to the trash. Had to be a body. Couldn't just be a rug."

Jimmy shook his head.

"No, Mrs. Patterson, most times, almost every time, it's just a fucking rug."

Robin looked at him and he looked back, her expression difficult to parse. Was he losing his touch?

"Mr. Jimmy," she said with a calm, even tone. "I can appreciate what you're saying. And I believe you are probably correct. But I just married this man, and I want to know if I've made a mistake. I didn't go to you. I went to my friend, Howard. I asked for his help, not yours. If you don't want to help me, you don't have to."

Jimmy nodded and they sat for a moment without talking.

"No," he said. "I'll find out what's going on." He took another sip of coffee. "But I doubt it'll be anything that interesting. Save for an affair."

He watched her as he said the last sentence, but her plain expression held firm.

"But he can't know," she said. "He can't find out that you're watching him."

Jimmy gave her a polite smile.

"He hasn't so far."

Robin swallowed and nodded.

"Thank you," she said.

Jimmy downed the last of his coffee and stood up.

"Thank Howard," he said. "He's the one paying for this."

He gave a little nod.

"Thanks for the coffee," he said. "Enjoy your day."

With that, he turned and left the restaurant. Robin watched him through the window, her eyes tracking his movements as he limped his way down the sidewalk and disappeared into the flowing mob.

Chapter 6

The trucker sat in Howard's office, his fat head protruding from a foam collar. Rolls of jaw flesh overflowed over the neck brace as he struggled to sit straight, high-pitched squeals leaking from his nose with every breath.

"It really doesn't even hurt that bad," he said. "I don't think I even need it."

Howard frowned as the man tugged at the great collar.

"No, you need to keep it on," he said. "The insurance company will have people watching you. If they see you without it, they'll snap a few photos, and our goose will be cooked."

The trucker frowned.

"It sure itches, though."

Howard nodded.

"Yeah, well, itch now, get paid later."

The trucker looked as if he'd just received a terminal diagnosis.

"Yeah, I guess you're right."

Howard gave an affable smile.

"Of course, I am," he said as he stood up from his desk. "Just go home and rest. Watch some TV. Leave everything to me."

The trucker hooked a finger up beneath the neck brace and scratched.

"It just itches somethin fierce."

Howard walked around the desk and slapped him on his shoulder.

"Yes," he said. "Well, maybe we can get you something to help with that."

The trucker stood, and Howard guided him out of his office.

"Madeline," he said.

The old woman looked up from the reception desk, eyes peering up over a set of narrow glasses.

"Can you put in a call to Dr. Geathers?" he asked. "See if we can get some mild sedatives for Mr. Walker here."

Madeline nodded.

"Of course," she said.

Howard slapped the trucker on the back.

"I will call you as soon as I hear back from the insurance company," he said.

He flashed a trademark smile and retreated into his office.

"You keep that brace on, you hear me? We don't want to slip up this close to the finish line."

The trucker started to answer, but Howard was already shutting the door.

"Yes," Madeline was saying into the phone as the door closed. "This is Madeline Collins calling on behalf of Howard Newberry ...."

Inside his office, Howard was already on to the next thing, something with that big drug company, Viox Genomics. This one had big class-action potential, lots of sick clients, a good chance for a fat settlement.

He hurried to his desk, flipped open a folder and spent the next couple hours reading and jotting down notes.

There was some good stuff here, he thought, as he flipped through the documents. Experimental drugs rushed through trials. Rapid approvals by the FDA. An incredible amount of people with troubling symptoms. The perfect recipe for a huge haul.

He pushed the folder away and sat back in his chair. He'd need help on this one. Someone with money and relationships with experts. Tom Bookings, maybe? No, Hellen Gallagher! She was a tiger, that one. Hell, he thought, why not both? There was more than enough money to go around, and he needed the manpower to handle this many clients.

Before he knew it, the sun had crept below the horizon, and darkness had claimed the exterior world.

"Howard," said Madeline. "As she cracked open the door."

Howard looked up.

"I'm headed home," said the old woman. "Will you need anything else before I go?"

Howard sat back in his chair and rubbed his eyes.

"No, Maddie, you go on. I'm just gonna finish up a couple of things here."

She nodded.

"Well, good night then," she said as she shut the door behind her.

Howard waited until her headlights popped on and her car pulled away from his office window. Then he reached into his desk and removed a bottle of scotch. He poured a half-glass and swirled it around, his mouth salivating in anticipation. He downed it all in two big swallows and lifted the bottle for another pour.

There was a slight noise outside his office door, and he paused, the bottle in mid-air leveled above the empty glass. He strained to listen, but nothing came, so he tipped the bottle and more liquor splashed into the glass. He raised it to his lips and paused again.

There was another noise. This time louder. A straining creak in the floor just outside his office door.

He swallowed hard and set the glass down. Without taking his eye from the door, he opened his desk drawer and slipped his hand inside. His fingers fumbled over pens and paper clips until they found the little pistol, a silly precaution, almost forgotten amid the stacks of ordinary days. He removed the weapon with a trembling hand, his heart picking up as his imagination filled the silence with all sorts of terrifying potentials. An angry husband? A bad cop he'd humiliated on the witness stand?

He waited for something to happen, his shaky gun pointed at the office door. Then, he had a horrifying vision of his gun firing into Madeline and her frail elderly body, or worse, Robin, bloody on the floor, hands clutching her stomach, thick, beautiful lips mouthing, "why?"

He shook the thoughts away and stood up from his chair, lowering the pistol as he crept toward the door.

"Hello?" he called out. "Identify yourself. I have a gun."

He stood by the door and waited, but it was quiet except for his screaming thoughts. He swallowed and grasped the doorknob, the cold steel of the gun foreign in his soft attorney hands. He gave it a twist and pulled it open. He poked his head out and looked around.

With embarrassing ease, a hand swept in and snatched the gun away. Howard yanked his arm back as if he'd touched a hot stove and stumbled backward into his office.

"Just relax," said a husky voice.

Howard peered into the darkness outside his office, and from that darkness stepped a broad-shouldered white man with an apologetic smile. Just behind him, a tall, thin Japanese man followed, a little sneer on his face that exposed a perfect set of white teeth interrupted by a single gold crown.

"Please," said the broad white man. "Stay calm. We just want to ask you a couple of questions."

Howard moved backward until his ass met the front of his desk. He glanced at his phone, which sat a few inches from his dangling fingers.

"No, no," said the white man. "Let's not anger my friend here."

Howard's eyes flicked over to the Japanese man, who now held Howard's gun at his side.

"Please," said the white man. "Have a seat."

Howard glanced at the gun once more and then moved behind his desk. He sat down and swallowed as the men spread out before him.

"Your office is kind of small," said the white man as he looked around. "I've seen your face on the bus stop benches and a couple billboards. Thought you were big time."

Howard took a bumpy breath and gave a meager shrug.

"I, uh," he started, but the man put a hand up to silence him.

"Not important right now," he said. "What is important is what I'm getting ready to ask you. And what's even more important than that is what you tell me in return."

He pulled up a chair in front of Howard's desk and plopped down.

"Now," he said. "Why are you asking questions about Viox Genomics?"

Howard started to say something, but the man put a finger up.

"Or," he said. "More specifically, why are you asking questions about Michael Patterson?"

Howard glanced up at the tall Japanese man, who stared down at him without emotion, eyes entirely pupil, depthless in the low light.

"I, uh," he said, his voice cracking slightly. "It's just a case I'm working on. Just standard investigative stuff. Basic lawyering."

The man frowned.

"No," he said in a calm, even tone. "The case you're working on is a class-action lawsuit involving a bunch of sick people who took a drug. That ain't got nothin to do with Michael Patterson."

He leaned forward and propped his thick forearms against his thighs.

"So, I'm gonna ask you again, why are you asking questions about Michael Patterson?"

Howard swallowed and looked at the Japanese man again.

"Don't look at him," said the white man. "Look at me."

Howard's eyes darted back to the man's face.

"Look," he said. "It's no big deal."

The white man sat up and looked back over his shoulder.

"Hold him down."

Howard scrunched back in his chair as the Japanese man stepped forward from the shadows, his thin frame seeming to grow taller with every step.

"Listen," said Howard, his voice cracking as the man rounded the desk. "You don't have to do this."

The white man put a finger to his lips.

"Shh," he said as the Japanese man stood behind Howard and viced his arm beneath the lawyer's jaw. "Save your energy. This is gonna be the longest night of your life."

The white man removed a knife from inside his jacket, the glint of the metal summoning Howard's eyes.

"No," Howard gasped. "Please."

The man took hold of Howard's right hand and stretched out his arm.

"Now," he said as he leveled the knife at the tip of Howard's index finger. "I'm gonna ask you again, and this time I want a straight answer."

Howard opened his mouth to speak, but the knife was already sliding its way beneath his fingernail. He gasped in horror as he watched the metal enter his body.

"Why," said the man as he stared up into the lawyer's widening eyes, "are you asking questions about Michael Patterson?"

Screams boiled from Howard's mouth as the blade tore deeper, blood spurting out onto the desk as his fingernail lifted from the flesh.

"His wife asked me to! His wife asked me to!"

The white man nodded.

"And are you fucking her?"

Howard's face froze mid-scream and his eyes flicked up toward the man.

"Awe," he said. "Look, Hiroto, I think we're onto something here."

The Japanese man scowled.

"No use name," he said.

The white man rolled his eyes.

"It doesn't matter."

The Japanese man showed his teeth.

"Ok, Mal-cus," he said with a hiss.

Marcus frowned and turned his attention back to Howard.

"Well?" he asked.

He twisted the knife slightly and the fingernail broke loose on one side, popping upward like the hood of a tiny car.

Tea-kettle shrieks erupted from between Howard's lips, and slobber poured out the corner of his mouth.

"Yes! Yes!" he shouted. "A couple times, yes!"

Marcus nodded as Howard began to hyperventilate.

"Ok, lawyer," he said. "Calm down now."

Howard began to weep, and Marcus shushed him.

"It's alright," he said quietly. "Just one more question."

He looked into Howard's eyes and gave the knife the slightest twist.

"Have you told anyone about this?"

Low moans of agony filled the room as Marcus pushed the knife deeper.

Chapter 7

Robin sat alone at a small table by the window, a glass of white wine in her hand, flickers of fire leaping from the great diamond on her ring finger. All around her, delightful odors danced in the air, as the waiters delivered a medley of steaming meats and vegetables to eager-faced guests. She inhaled deeply amid the low chatter, her stomach rumbling with anticipation. She lifted the menu and looked over the entrées, her eyes flicking over the seafood and sandwiches, the pastas and soups, the pale, milk-fed veal, the tender, succulent Wagyu beef.

Her stomach gurgled as she checked the time. He was late again, but that was nothing new.

She looked across the room and ensnared a waiter with her eyes. The slim balding man smiled politely and approached.

"Can I get you something?" he asked.

Robin raised her eyebrows and pointed toward one of the appetizers.

"I'm waiting on someone," she said. "Could I just get a half-order of these?"

The waiter's eyes followed her finger to the menu item. He frowned.

"I'm sorry," he said. "We don't do half-orders."

Robin looked up at him.

"I'm not asking for a discount."

The waiter gave a closed-lip smile.

"Of course not," he said.

Robin looked at him, but he said nothing.

"So, you're saying you can't bring me a half-order?"

The waiter gave a nod.

"Yes," he said. "I'm afraid so."

Robin pinched her eyebrows together.

"Why can't you just charge the full amount but only bring half?" she asked. "Is that too complicated?"

The waiter frowned.

"It's simply the restaurant's policy. I can bring you the full order, and you can eat half if that is what you wish."

Robin took in a slow breath.

"Why don't you just charge me for the full order, cook the whole order and throw half of it in the trash?"

The waiter looked confused.

"I'm afraid—" he started, but Robin cut him off.

"Never mind," she said as she looked past him toward the door.

The waiter followed her eyes again and saw the man approaching.

"Yes," he said. "I'll give you some more time."

He gave a little bow and turned away just as Jimmy approached the table.

"What are you doing here?" Robin asked. "Do you realize I'm meeting my husband for lunch? He will walk through those doors any moment."

She watched as he sat down across from her.

"Oh, really?" he said. "Great. I'd love to meet him."

Robin looked over his shoulder at the door, but no one was there.

"Why are you here?"

Jimmy sat up in his chair.

"Well, I wanted to update you on how things are going."

He raised his hand and flagged down a waiter while Robin watched through anxious eyes.

"Couldn't we do this another time?" she said.

Jimmy frowned.

"I tried," he said. "This seems like the easiest way to get in touch with you."

The waiter arrived with a forced smile.

"Will there be something else?" he asked.

Jimmy ordered a black coffee while Robin eyed an old couple entering the front of the restaurant.

"Fine," she said. "Let's do this fast. What have you learned?"

Jimmy shrugged.

"Not much," he said.

Robin watched him with silent confusion, but Jimmy just sat quietly, his finger tapping the tabletop.

"Not much?" asked Robin.

Jimmy scratched his chin.

"I mean, your husband's a tidy guy for the most part," he said. "Real predictable. Goes to work. Plays some golf. Comes home. No real outside life that I can see. At least so far. Doesn't necessarily mean there aren't any secrets. But if there are, I haven't seen anything yet."

She shook her head in disbelief.

"Why are you telling me this?" she hissed. "Why am I even meeting with you? Shouldn't you be telling all this to Howard?"

Jimmy raised his eyebrows.

"Well, that would be difficult considering that Howard's gone missing."

He watched her from beneath his low eyelids.

"What do you mean missing?" she asked.

Jimmy shrugged.

"I mean missing. He hasn't been to work in a couple days. His secretary doesn't know where he is. He's got cases. He's got clients. They're all in the lurch. He's not on vacation. He didn't elope. He's missing."

Robin put a hand to her forehead.

"Oh my God," she said softly.

Jimmy said nothing, his eyes watching her.

"Do you think this has something to do with my husband?"

Jimmy shrugged.

"Maybe," he said. "Probably not. Howard's a good guy, but he's always been into shady things. What lawyer isn't?"

Robin swallowed.

"But you think he's in trouble?"

Jimmy shrugged again.

"I don't know," he said. "If he had gotten on the wrong side of some bad people, I would probably have caught wind of it."

Robin pinched her eyebrows together.

"How?"

Jimmy shook his head.

"Well, let's just say I've been around a while, and I have a lot of connections. Anyway, he could have skipped town. For all I know, he's being investigated by the feds. Howard's a private guy. We've been friends a long time, but I've never pried into his business, and he's never pried into mine."

Robin shook her head and stared down at the table while the waiter brought Jimmy's coffee.

"Ah," said Jimmy. "I appreciate it."

The man gave a false smile and walked away. Robin waited until he was gone and then leaned in closer to Jimmy.

"I think if Howard is really gone, we should stop this," she said. "I wish I hadn't come to him with it in the first place."

Jimmy shook his head.

"Howard's already paid me. And once I start a job, I finish it."

Robin looked up at him.

"What if I want you to stop?"

Jimmy looked at her.

"Even still."

They sat in silence for several moments, the sound of voices all around them, people talking about this and that amid the sound of dish clatter.

"Robin?" said a deep voice from across the room.

"Shit," Robin muttered under her breath.

Jimmy turned to see a tall, athletic-looking man approaching, his eyes pinched with a confused sort of interest. Jimmy watched as Robin's face lit up with a 1000-watt smile.

"Hello, dear," she said.

The man approached the table and looked at each of them in turn.

"I'm sorry for being late," he said. "And even sorrier to say I can't stay."

Robin formed her mouth into a subtle pout.

"No?" she asked. "Something with work?"

"Yes," he said, his eyes flicking toward Jimmy as he spoke. "And who is this?"

Robin gave a casual gesture toward Jimmy.

"This is Jim," she said. "An old friend. He happened to be eating here."

She smiled at Jimmy.

"Jim," she said. "This is my husband, Michael."

Michael stepped forward and put his hand out. Jimmy stood and reached out to take it.

"Good to meet you," he said.

Michael squeezed his hand like he was trying to wring water from a damp rag.

Jimmy looked down at his hand and frowned.

"Whoa," he said. "Quite a grip you got there."

Michael released, and Jimmy shook his hand as if it had just been zapped by a live wire.

"I'm sorry," said Michael. "My father taught me the merits of a firm grip. Said you can tell a lot about a man by the way he greets you."

Jimmy shrugged as he retook his seat.

"Can't argue with him there."

Michael smiled, but it was less like a smile and more like a man showing his teeth.

"Of course," he said.

Jimmy looked him over. He had dark hair and an oddly small nose. He wore an expensive suit tailored to hug his muscled frame, and his eyebrows hung low over a set of live eyes that seemed to consume the world with an eager, covetous appetite.

"And how do you two know each other?" Michael said as he put a hand on Robin's shoulder.

Jimmy started to say something, but Robin was faster.

"He was a friend of my father," she said.

Michael's eyebrows shot up.

"Oh, wow," he said. "Really? A friend of Donald's."

Jimmy nodded.

"Oh, yeah," he said. "We go way back." He chuckled and shook his head. "The things I could tell you about old Donny Boy."

Robin flexed her jaw, and Michael frowned.

"Donny Boy?" he said. "I've never heard anyone refer to Donald like that. You two must have been close."

"Well," Jimmy started, but Robin cut in.

"Jim was just leaving," she said.

Michael raised his eyebrows.

"Oh?"

Jimmy shrugged and started to stand.

"Yeah," he said. "Things to do, people to see."

Michael smiled.

"Well, how disappointing. Perhaps we'll have a chance to talk again sometime."

Jimmy nodded.

"Yeah," he said. "I can't wait."

Michael stuck out his hand again, and Jimmy looked at it. With an undetectable sigh, he reached out and let Michael snatch it up like a carnivorous plant.

"Tell you what," said Michael as he gripped Jimmy's hand. "We're having a little get-together this Saturday. Just a handful of friends for a light dinner. Why don't you come?"

Robin reached out and put her hand on Michael's arm.

"Oh, Michael, I'm sure he already has plans."

Michael looked down at her hand and then up to her face.

"Nonsense," he said. "What could be more important than catching up with an old friend?"

Jimmy raised his eyebrows.

"Well, I rarely turn down free food."

Michael grinned.

"Excellent," he said as he released Jimmy's hand. "Then it's decided. It's a casual affair. I'll let Robin fill you in on the details."

He checked his watch.

"Well, I have to be going. I'm so sorry, dear."

He pecked Robin on the cheek and nodded to Jimmy.

"We'll see you Saturday."

He gave another sneer-smile and walked away.

Robin looked up at Jimmy, who stood watching Michael leave the restaurant.

"What the hell are you doing?" she asked.

Jimmy shrugged.

"Just trying to get to the bottom of things."

Robin put her fingers against her temples and rubbed.

"You can't come to that dinner party."

Jimmy frowned.

"No?"

"No," Robin hissed at him. "That almost gave me a heart attack. I can't lie like that for a whole evening."

Jimmy raised his eyebrows.

"Don't sell yourself short. You're a natural."

Robin took a deep breath and looked off to the side, where a young child watched them both with wide, uncomprehending eyes.

"Listen," she said as she turned back to Jimmy. "If you want to keep digging around a little. That's fine. As long as you're not causing me any trouble. I don't want my life disrupted. I don't want to see you anymore. Not unless you have something meaningful to tell me. My agreement was with Howard. Not you."

Jimmy nodded.

"Sure," he said. "I understand."

He gathered his coffee cup and took one last swallow.

"I'll be in touch," he said.

He gave a slight nod and turned away, his limp seeming worse to Robin's eyes as he hobbled out of the restaurant.

Chapter 8

Light music purred from the speakers as Robin chopped carrots, her lips humming along to an old familiar tune. To her left, the skillet crackled on the stovetop, little fingers of steam filling the kitchen with the fragrance of spiced broth. As the last of the sun boiled red on the horizon, a fresh evening breeze filtered its way through the window screen, tickling the little curtains as it poured into the room. Robin breathed deeply and smiled. It was going to be a wonderful night.

The clock on the wall said 6:30. She glanced at it and frowned. Michael was running late again, but this gave her more time to make things perfect. She tossed some vegetables into the skillet and gave it a stir. Then she turned the heat down low and pulled her apron loose.

As birds whistled the last of their evening cries, she rushed past the open windows in her living room, stepped over the sleeping dog, and made her way to the bathroom. She stood before the mirror and frowned. Though lovely enough, she was definitely looking her age. She opened the drawer and plunged her hand inside. There was still time to make it right. She dabbed and powdered, a little more blush, an extra layer of lipstick. Everything seamless and subtle, years of practice, a thousand times refined.

The front door creaked open in the other room, and she heard the dog emote with excited little whines. She assessed herself in the mirror one last time and hurried out of the bathroom.

"What kept you?" she asked as she turned the corner.

But the answer was obvious.

"Oh, Michael," she said.

Her husband was removing his jacket.

"Calm down," he said as he raised a hand.

Robin looked at the blood smears on his shirt.

"Of all nights, you pick tonight to show up like this?"

She looked out the window to make sure none of the guests were arriving early. He followed her eyes to the window.

"Must we do this now, Robin?" our guests will be arriving within the hour."

She put her hands on her hips and shook her head.

"Well, strip everything off and shower. I'll take care of it."

He stripped down to his underwear, a colorful pair of bikini briefs that flattered his muscular physique. Then he handed everything over to his wife and made his way to the bathroom.

"It smells wonderful in here," he said over his shoulder as he disappeared around a corner.

Without responding, she gathered up the clothing and tossed it into a small basket. She rushed across the dining room and hurried down the stairs to the little laundry room tucked discreetly at the corner of the expansive finished basement.

The sound of the shower gushed above as she jammed all the clothing into the washing machine. She added a generous dose of detergent, the color-safe type with bleach that had proven its worth over the past couple months. She slammed the door shut, set the dial to medium-sized load and started the cycle. Then she hurried upstairs.

Now, the kitchen was fogged with smoke, the skillet snapping violently as its contents ran dry.

"Shit!" she yelled as she hurried over.

She took hold of the handle and moved it to a cool burner, her eyes just catching the streak of blood on her forearm.

"Shit!" she yelled again as she moved to the sink.

She turned on the tap, and clean water spilled down onto the congealing smudge. She scrubbed at it with a yellow sponge, which quickly turned scarlet as she ran it over her skin. When the smear was clean, she rinsed the sponge until it took on a salmon color. Then she gave up and threw it in the trash.

Over the next hour, she slaved in the kitchen, preparing light fare for their small party of guests, which arrived right on time.

One by one, Robin greeted them with her sunniest smile, a practiced thing, so flawlessly unvaried, like something stored on a shelf alongside coats and dresses and summer hats.

Outside among the flowers and the gurgling water features, they chatted in two- and three-person circles, sophisticated conversations about politics, playful banter about golf.

"No, see," Michael said to a tall bald man as he bent slightly at the waist. "You're drifting in your backswing."

Robin watched him over the shoulder of a fat woman with dark circles of rouge on her pale, wrinkled cheeks.

"Your azaleas have come in beautifully this spring," said the woman as she snorted the fragrant air. "And they smell wonderful."

Robin took a sip from her wine glass and put a hand over her chest.

"Thank you," she said. "But I can't really take credit. We have a man, of course. He's quite skilled."

The woman's eyes widened.

"Yes," she said. "We've been quite disappointed with our man of late. Perhaps you could give me the name of yours."

Robin frowned on the inside.

"Yes," she said. "You know, I can't recall it this very moment. Let me check with Michael when he has a minute."

"Of course," said the woman with a smile. She turned toward the purple mass of flowers and filled her lungs again. "So lovely."

Robin nodded.

"Yes," she said. "Can you excuse me a moment? I need to freshen up."

"Take your time, dear," the woman said without looking away from the azaleas.

Robin went inside and checked the oven, everything browning according to schedule, a crispy curl around the edges. She closed the oven door and hurried to the bathroom. She urinated and then refined her makeup further, polishing what was now bordering on perfection. Then the doorbell rang, and she hurried to answer it.

"Why, hello," said Jimmy as the door swung open.

Robin stood silent, her jaw agape.

"Am I early?" he asked.

He wore a light blue polo shirt and a pair of khaki slacks that made him look very much like a polished, if modest, professional. An accountant, maybe? A tax attorney? It might all be plausible if not for the scruffy jawline and severely crooked nose.

Robin started to say something, but Michael appeared behind her.

"You made it!" he said. "Wonderful."

He glanced down at Robin.

"Aren't you inviting him in?"

Robin swallowed and took a step back.

"Of course," she said. "Please, Jim, won't you join us?"

Jimmy stepped inside and looked around.

"Nice place you have here."

Michael put a hand on Robin's shoulder.

"Thank you," he said. "But Robin deserves the credit. She did all the decorating. I'm barely home enough to hang a picture."

Robin gave a small, closed-lip smile.

"Please, Jim," said Michael. "Join us all outside." He put an arm around Jimmy and led him along. "Do you play golf?"

Robin watched them walk outside, her heart thumping within her chest. She took a deep breath and rubbed her forehead. Then she put on her smile and followed them outside.

As the guests smiled politely, Michael made the rounds with Jimmy, who shook hands and smiled as if he'd been frequenting these sorts of gatherings all his life.

"Melinda," said Michael. "This is Jim."

The woman turned and gasped, her heavily made-up face looking clown-like as her features expanded.

"Good lord," she said. "What happened to your nose?"

Jimmy frowned.

"I'm afraid I used to be a bit of a boxer in my college days," he said.

"My goodness," said Melinda as she sucked from a wine glass, her third already. "You should really get that fixed."

"Melinda!" said Robin, but Jimmy just chuckled.

"No worries," he said. "She's right, but I guess I've just grown used to this face."

Michael nodded.

"Of course," he said. "It suits you."

Jimmy looked at him for a moment, and something passed between them. Something cold and electric. Robin could feel it, but no one else seemed to notice.

It was quiet for a few moments, the birds refusing to fill the silence as they perched mutely in the trees above.

"Jim was a good friend of Robin's father," said Michael at last.

"Oh my," said Melinda as she held her hand out.

Jimmy took her hand and shook it.

"Yep," he said.

Robin swallowed and looked away.

"Yes," said Michael. "Apparently, they were very close, as I understand it."

Jimmy shrugged.

"Well," he said. "I don't know if I'd go that far. We enjoyed each other's company. Let's just say that."

Michael put a hand on Jimmy's shoulder.

"Don't be modest. Apparently, he has some entertaining stories about the man, God rest his soul."

"Oh really?" said Melinda. "I'd love to hear one."

Robin took hold of Jimmy's arm.

"Please," she said. "Let the man get settled before you bombard him with questions. Come, Jim. Let's get some food in you."

Michael watched as she pulled Jimmy to the little table of hors d'oeuvres.

"What are you doing here?" she whispered through a pair of smiling lips.

Jimmy shrugged.

"This is how I work," he said. "I like to get deep into things."

He looked the table over. It was filled with trays of wreaking cheese and strange crackers buttered with dark smears of what looked like potted meat.

"What is this shit?" he asked.

Robin gestured toward a bowl of mixed nuts.

"Just eat those."

Jimmy took up a handful and tossed a few into his mouth.

"Please," said Robin. "Just don't say anything too incriminating. In fact, don't talk at all if you can help it."

Jimmy chewed and shook his head.

"Just relax," he said. "I'm old hat at this sort of thing."

Robin turned toward him, a glint of fear in her eyes.

"No," she said. "This is different. These people, they aren't like you."

Jimmy looked over her shoulder and gave the little crowd a sweeping glance.

"You don't say?"

He brushed past her, and she hurried to catch up. Michael watched him approach as he chatted with Melinda, his eyes sparkling above a relaxed smile.

"Did you find something?" he asked.

Jimmy held up his handful of nuts.

"I did, thanks."

Michael frowned.

"Oh, you really should try the pâté."

Melinda nodded.

Oh, yes," she said as she grinned at Robin. "It's delightful. Very rich. And the texture is flawless."

Robin swallowed and gestured toward her husband.

"Thank Michael," she said.

Jimmy tossed a nut in his mouth and looked at Michael.

"Really?" he asked. "That's a surprise."

Michael cocked his head.

"How so?"

Jimmy shrugged.

"I didn't take you for a cook."

Michael's teeth shone white as he smiled.

"I'm a man of many talents."

Melinda nodded.

"Oh, yes," she said. "Our Michael is extraordinary."

Jimmy crunched on a nut.

"That so?" he said.

Michael's grin widened.

"Well," he said. "I try my best."

They stood for a while without talking, Robin's mind furiously formulating topics of conversation without success. At last, two other partygoers approached, and her misery eased.

"Michael, Robin!"

They all turned to regard a very thin middle-aged man with a sweeping white mustache. He was a proper-looking man who stood with his chin tilted up, and Jimmy thought he looked like the type to wear a monocle if it were still in fashion. At his side stood a heavy-set woman, her big face slathered with far too much makeup.

"Warren, Alice," said Michael. "How are you?"

The couple approached, their faces stretched by great smiles.

"Wonderful!" said Alice. "It's so nice to be out of the house."

Warren looked Jimmy up and down.

"And who do we have here?" he asked.

"Warren, Alice," said Michael. "This is Jim."

They each stuck out a hand, and Jimmy shook them.

"Jimmy is an old friend of Robin's," Michael continued. "And also an old friend of Robin's father."

"Really?" asked Alice. "So, you must be a member of the Guild then."

Jimmy started to speak, but Robin saved him.

"No, Alice," she said. "Jim and my father were only business associates. Their friendship extended from a professional relationship."

Michael frowned.

"Hmm," he said. "Friends with Donald but not a member of the Guild. How fascinating."

Warren rubbed his chin thoughtfully.

"Yes," he said. "That is curious."

"Well," said Jimmy. "I mean, he mentioned it a time or two. But I guess I was never officially invited."

They all stood quietly, Melinda, Warren and Alice all rubbing their chins as they looked Jimmy over once more. Robin flinched as Michael slammed his hands together.

"You know what?" he said. "Why don't we fix that?"

Robin shook her head.

"No, I don't think Jim would—"

She stopped talking as Michael flashed her a look.

"Nonsense," he said as he turned toward Jimmy. "This coming weekend, Viox Genomics is hosting a private party for several local Guild members. You should come. It would be a wonderful opportunity to do some networking. All you have to do is shake the right hands and make a decent impression. I think the board would have to give strong consideration to a close friend of Donald and his daughter. Don't you agree, Alice?"

Alice nodded.

"Oh, yes," she said. "I think you would have a very strong chance. What do you think, Warren?"

Warren frowned thoughtfully.

"Well, I wouldn't dare to guess. But there's no harm in doing a little networking."

They all turned to Jimmy.

"Well?" asked Michael. "What do you say?"

Jimmy tossed a nut in his mouth and shrugged.

"Sure," he said. "Why not?"

They all exchanged smiles while Robin's guts twisted within her polished facade.

Chapter 9

Night fell over the city like a curtain, and the people changed. The sanitizing sun removed from sight, the streets turned rebellious, like unruly children loosed from a mother's gaze. Amid the urban decay, lights popped on here and there, weak bulbs splotching the concrete with hints of light that were much too dim and even more infrequent.

In the darkest places, where they didn't turn on at all, the nocturnals came out to play. The users with their endless, agonizing hunger and the pushers with their transient relief. The homeless with their shuffling and scavenging. The flesh peddlers with their fishnet stockings and cracked scabby lips.

Among them all, Stanley walked the streets, his filthy collar pulled up over his cheeks, a thick stocking cap tugged down low over his stinking hair. Through the alley, he staggered, his cart tugging hard to the left as the bad wheel twittered in its usual wonky way.

The old man cursed it and pushed on, navigating this way and that around the dead legs of heroine sleepers who protested not at all as he rammed hard into their unmoving feet.

"Goddamn zombies," he said to their unlistening ears. "Get up and get out my way!"

He staggered past them and forced his cart toward the backside of the alley, just by 42nd street, where that bakery threw out all that perfectly good bread. The hard kind with all that butter and garlic, the cornmeal muffins and those good sesame seed sticks. He licked his lips and pushed onward, the bad wheel catching correctly for a moment in a way that made him nod.

"Yes, sir," he said to no one but himself.

He reached the big brown dumpster and stood before it, a frown cutting deep into his bearded face.

The great metal box was cinched up tight with a big chain and heavy padlock, which mocked him with a metallic glint beneath the whisper of light that survived the sucking black.

"I'll be a goddamned motherfucker," he muttered.

He reached out and tugged on the chain, the heavy jingle echoing in the night.

"I'll be a goddamned motherfucker," he said louder.

He brought his leg back and drove his foot into the side of the dumpster, a thunderous bong exploding into the hard, uncaring night. Then he collapsed to the ground and held his leg. As tears welled in his eyes, he clutched his boot, the toes inside already swelling within their tattered cage.

"What was that?" said a voice from down the way.

In a panic, Stanley scurried behind the dumpster and held his breath.

"Did you hear that?" said the same voice.

It was quiet for a moment as Stanley's heart tapped within his chest.

"It is nothing," said another voice, a foreigner, Stanley thought, some kind of Asian man.

Over the soiled, stinking pavement, he crawled, one eye peeking around the edge of the dumpster as the two men approached.

"Jesus!" yelled one of the men as he noticed the ragged vagrant. He tore a gun from his belt and leveled it at Stanley.

"Please," the old man wheezed as he scurried backward.

The other man, Japanese to Stanley's wide eyes, put a hand on the man's wrist.

"A beggar," he said with a sharp accent.

The other man shook his head and put his gun away.

"Let's go."

They walked the rest of the alley, stepping over the comatose heroine zombies while Stanley watched through wide, weary eyes.

Out on the open street, the two men pulled up the collars of their coats and stepped out into the dimly lit city, their faces hard and purposeful as they ambled up the block. While they walked, a dangerous hoard eyed them with curiosity from the shadows, but none felt the spur of courage required to confront men such as these.

On they walked, each with his own brand of confident, almost arrogant gait, past the dice-throwers on Lincoln Ave, past the streetwalkers and their siren calls. Past the unmarked basement bar with the illegal poker, past the other basement bar where they sold clean, untraceable guns.

When they finally came to Eisenhower Ave, they stopped and looked around.

"He will be here?" asked Hiroto.

Marcus nodded.

"From what I understand."

They looked across the street at the dive bar, where a grim-looking bouncer stood before a line of drug-addled patrons who literally itched to get in.

"He collects here every month," said Marcus. "Same time, every time. He's a punctual guy, this one."

Hiroto gave a little grunt and they both receded into the mouth of an alleyway, their bodies disappearing into the depthless dark.

About 20 minutes later, sure as shit, Jimmy's car flashed before their eyes.

"That's him," said Marcus.

They watched while he parked in one of the handicap spots. They watched while he hooked a blue placard to his rearview mirror.

"This guy," Marcus muttered as he shook his head.

Hiroto narrowed his eyes as Jimmy struggled out of his car, an audible grunt reaching their ears from across the street.

"Now?" asked the Japanese man through gritted teeth?

Marcus shook his head.

"No," he said. "Let him do his business first."

Hiroto sucked his teeth while they watched Jimmy limp into the bar.

"Old," said Hiroto.

Marcus nodded.

"Yep."

They stood in the alleyway amid the stinking dumpsters and skittering rats, each one watching the bar, no words between them. Minutes gathered into an hour before Marcus finally reached his end.

"Alright," he said. "You go around back. I'll go through the front."

Hiroto gave a nod, and they crossed the street, each looking all around, though the streets were mostly bare.

When they reached the other side, Hiroto made his way to the back of the bar, which emptied into another alley with its own vagrant populace and unique specie of stink. There he waited, his eyes trained on the back door, hand fondling the knife within his jacket pocket as his teeth glinted in the low light.

On the front side of the bar, Marcus gave the bouncer the fright of his life before finally stepping past him and into the bar.

Within the murk of cigarette smoke, his eyes darted about, assessing the drunken faces, which lurked anonymously in the shadows.

The sweet stench of old spilled beer hung heavy in the air, and it violated his nostrils as he surveyed the small crowd.

"Help you with something?" asked a bald man from behind the bar.

Marcus stepped forward.

"I'm looking for someone."

The barman shrugged.

"Alright."

Marcus looked around.

"I saw him come in, but he's not here now."

The barman pushed out his bottom lip.

"Check the bathroom?"

He hooked his thumb over his shoulder toward a little hallway. Without responding, Marcus moved away from the bar and made his way toward the hallway, no one paying much attention as he passed before their spacey gazes. When he reached the men's room, he gave the door a push, and a stomach-churning odor slapped him in the face.

He gave a little cough and forced his way into the foul atmosphere. A small man pissed in a urinal before a single stall, a low tune whistling from between his lips. Marcus hurried forward and bent to look for feet beneath the stall, but there was nothing to see. Just to be sure, he kicked the door open and the man at the urinal started.

"Jesus," he mumbled. "You made me piss on my hand."

Without responding, Marcus hurried out of the wreaking little room. Outside in the hallway, he stood with a deep frown. Then without much thought, he pushed open the women's restroom and stepped inside. There, a scraggly-looking thing stooped over the sink, her nose snorting up a thin line of powder. Marcus moved past her and kicked open the stall. Screams stung his ears as a tattooed woman shielded her crotch with both hands.

"What in the fuck?" she yelled.

Marcus turned away without speaking and hurried back out into the hallway.

"Hey," yelled the barman from across the room. "What the hell you doin?"

Marcus stomped toward him.

"Listen up," he said. "I saw the man come in here, and he didn't come out."

The barman shrugged.

"Maybe he did come out, and you just missed it."

Marcus balled his fist and crunched it into the barman's mouth. Silence claimed the room as all eyes locked on the two men.

"Where the fuck is he?" asked Marcus as he collected the barman by the hair.

"Out back," he wheezed through a pair of bloody lips. "He went out back."

Marcus slung him away and turned around. As people averted their eyes, he stomped back down the hallway toward the backside of the bar. He turned a corner and entered a little kitchen where a Mexican man sat on an overturned plastic 5-gallon bucket. The little man eyed him with mute indifference as he smoked marijuana from a glass pipe. Marcus waved at the stinking fog and eyed the backdoor. He hurried past the man and took hold of the doorknob, pushing the thing open and spilling out into the night.

He blinked and blinked as his eyes struggled to make sense of the low light. Then he heard a little squeak just off to his left. He reached for his gun and turned to see Hiroto gasping, his neck in a headlock, thin legs bicycling against the concrete. He raised his gun and took a step forward.

"Jimmy!" he said. "Let him go. He's with me."

Hiroto's gasps grew fainter, and his legs began to still.

"Jimmy, goddammit!" yelled Marcus.

Without saying a word, Jimmy released Hiroto, his body spilling against the ground like a flopping ocean catch.

Marcus holstered his pistol and knelt. He turned the man over and slapped his back.

"You're alright," he said. "Just relax."

While the Japanese man coughed and wheezed, Marcus looked up at Jimmy.

"Was that really necessary?"

Jimmy stepped from the shadows into the low light.

"If I'd known he was with you, I'd have squeezed harder."

Marcus shook his head and stood up.

"Always the tough guy, huh, Jimmy?"

Jimmy stared at him with that dead-eye glare.

"What are you doing here, Marcus?" he asked. "You following me?"

Marcus glanced down at Hiroto who was just now crawling to his knees.

"I'm here to collect you, Jimmy," he said.

Jimmy frowned.

"Collect for who?"

Marcus shook his head and spat.

"Who the fuck do you think?" he said. "Mario. Your boss. Or did you forget about him?"

Jimmy took in a slow breath.

"What's he want?"

Marcus shrugged.

"You can ask him."

Jimmy pushed his lower lip out and thought a moment.

"When?"

Marcus held his hands out to his side.

"Right fucking now would be my guess. Why else would he send me to collect you?"

Hiroto climbed to his feet and stood next to Marcus, his eyes narrowed, teeth clenched.

"Alright," said Jimmy. He looked at the Japanese man. "You gonna make it?"

Hiroto said something in Japanese, his words spitting forth like flecks of venom.

"Easy now," said Jimmy.

Marcus took Hiroto by the arm.

"You're lucky, Jimmy. You really are. Hiroto ain't somebody you want to be fucking with."

Jimmy raised his eyebrows.

"Oh, I can tell."

Hiroto said something else in Japanese, but Jimmy had already turned away.

"You going there right now?" Marcus yelled down the alley. "It's my ass if you don't, Jimmy."

He took a step toward the darkness.

"Jimmy!" he shouted, but his voice only echoed back at him, and then the night fell silent.

An hour later, Jimmy pulled up to Mario's place and parked in the graveled lot. The throb of music beat his ears even with his windows closed. He shook his head and opened the door. He swung his feet out and took in a breath. With a grimace, he leveraged himself out of the car, a little whine escaping his lips as he planted his feet on the pavement.

Small rocks crunched beneath his boots as he limped his way to the entrance, where a pair of large men stood talking before the doorway. As he approached, they turned and flexed their formidable bodies, the muscle fibers rippling beneath the pale exterior lighting.

"Hey," said one of the men. "Jimmy. Been a while."

Jimmy approached and nodded.

"Yep," he muttered.

The other man gave Jimmy a nod and pulled the door open.

"You here to see the boss?" he asked.

"I ain't here for the music," said Jimmy as he passed through the entryway.

Inside, colored lights strobed through a tobacco haze, where buxom women danced nude before a small crowd of leering men. Small enough to sour Mario's mood, Jimmy thought, but still not bad for a Tuesday.

As a brunette girl ground her crotch against a chrome pole, Jimmy made his way toward the back office, where another pair of equally massive men stood gazing at the stage.

"He in there?" asked Jimmy as he approached.

One of them, a balding man with a hook nose, nodded.

"He's expecting you," he said with a thick Jersey accent.

Jimmy nodded.

"Well, I'm here."

The man turned and banged his gargantuan fist against the door.

"Boss?" he yelled.

"Yeah?" replied a low, gruff voice from the other side of the door.

The man cracked open the door and stuck his bulbous head through the crevice.

"It's Jimmy."

"Send him in."

The big man moved aside, and Jimmy entered the office. He shut the door behind him and turned to see a great mass of a man seated behind a modest metal desk. Beneath his immense jowled face, an oversized plate of chicken wings sat half-eaten next to a big perspiring glass of iced tea.

Jimmy stepped before the little desk and put his hands behind his back.

"Boss," he said.

Mario's eyes stared down at his thick greasy fingers where a chicken wing awaited its slobbering fate.

"Jimmy," he said without looking up. "Where you been?"

Jimmy shrugged.

"I've been around."

Mario brought the wing to his mouth and gnawed off a hunk of flesh. Jimmy waited while the fat man chewed and swallowed.

"You ain't been where I could see you," he said as he tossed the stripped bone into a little basket to his side.

Jimmy shrugged again.

"Just been helping out a friend."

Mario sucked meat juice from his fingers and thought for a moment.

"Helping a friend," he repeated Jimmy's words flatly.

His eyes searched the plate for another wing. When he found the one he liked, he collected it between two fingers and held it in mid-air.

"You got responsibilities here, Jimmy. That's your first order of business."

Jimmy stood as before, hands clasped behind his back, eyelids low.

"I understand that."

Mario's eyes flicked up.

"Is that right?" he said.

He brought the wing to his mouth and tore away the meat, his eyes watching Jimmy as he chewed. After he swallowed, he tossed the bone in the basket and took up the iced tea. Jimmy watched as he pulled down several swallows. Then he set the glass down and ran his bare arm over his soppy mouth.

"Those are words," he said. "I don't care for words. I care for what I can see. And I ain't seen you in a while."

Jimmy shrugged a third time.

"Nothing's changed," he said. "I made all my collections on time. I always do."

Mario sat back in his chair, which strained audibly under the weight of his massive body.

"This thing you're doing," he said. "This for that lawyer friend of yours?"

Jimmy's expression remained unchanged.

"Yes."

Mario nodded.

"You and that guy," he said, "You got too much history. A little bit of history is good. Too much is bad."

He turned his attention toward his plate and picked at the wings.

"You see, you and me, we got a little bit of history. Just the right amount. Enough history to give me some faith in you. To let me know I can trust you to do what you're supposed to do."

He snapped up another wing and bit into the flesh.

"But you and this lawyer," he said through a mouthful of meat. "You got too much history."

Jimmy started to talk, but Mario held up his hand.

"Do not interrupt me now," he said. "Listen instead. This is important."

He swallowed the meat and tossed the spent wing into the basket. Jimmy watched as he pushed the plate away and leaned forward, the chair crying as he propped his forearms against the desk.

"When you got too much history like you got with this lawyer, it makes you do stupid shit. Because you think you owe that person something, maybe."

He shrugged his massive shoulders and clasped his hands together, sausage-like fingers interlocking on the desk beneath his jiggly jaw.

"Or maybe you feel something for that person. See, that's what history does. It bonds you. And in some cases, a good bond makes you stronger, but in most cases, in my experience, it don't. It makes you weak instead. Cause instead of doing things for yourself, the things you know you ought to be doing, instead of those things, you end up doing something else. Something the other person wants. You get what I'm sayin?"

He stared deep into Jimmy's eyes, but if he meant to read the man by what he saw in them, it didn't work. It never did with Jimmy.

"Yeah," said Jimmy. "I get what you're saying."

Mario nodded.

"That's good," he said. "That's real good."

He sat back and pulled his plate closer.

"This thing with the lawyer," he said. "I want you to let it go."

Jimmy opened his mouth, but Mario cut him off.

"And I don't want to hear no more about it," he said with a deepening voice.

He pointed a finger at Jimmy.

"We got too much heat on us already. I don't need you poking your nose into someplace it don't belong. And that's the end of it."

Jimmy closed his mouth and stood quietly while Mario sat back in his chair and sucked some gristle from his teeth.

"I need you focused on what matters right now," he said. "I need you focused on my business and your own. And that is all I need you focused on. Do you understand?"

Jimmy nodded.

"I need to hear it from you, Jimmy."

"Yeah," said Jimmy. "I understand."

Mario nodded.

"Good," he said as he hovered back over his plate of food. "That's it then. I don't want to hear no more about this. You go do what you do best. Leave the lawyering to the lawyer."

Jimmy turned toward the door.

"Jimmy," said Mario.

Jimmy stopped and turned around.

"We good?"

Jimmy nodded.

"Yeah," he said. "We're good."

With that, he turned and opened the door to see Marcus standing outside. They stood before each other, nose to nose, as the door fell closed behind him.

"You all set?" asked Marcus.

Jimmy looked at him the same way he looked at everyone else, the same dull stare, the same dead eyes.

"Yep," he said.

Marcus pinched his eyebrows down and frowned.

"Tell me something, Jimmy. Ain't you getting a little long in the tooth for this sort of work?"

Jimmy shrugged.

"I heard age is just a number."

Marcus chuckled.

"Sure, Jimmy," he said. "Sure."

Marcus watched as Jimmy brushed past him and made his way out of the bar.

"You ought to get that limp checked out, Jimmy," he yelled over the room as Jimmy walked out the door.

Marcus turned and rapped his knuckle on the office door. He waited until Mario beckoned him inside.

"Boss," he said as he entered the room.

Mario stared down at his plate, another wing suspended between his greasy hands.

"Keep an eye on him," he said. "I don't like this. Not none of it."

Marcus scratched his nose.

"Well, me and Hiroto can take care of it for you."

Mario's eyes flashed upward.

"No," he said. "Jimmy's a good earner. He's been with me a long time. I'm gonna give him an opportunity to fall in line."

Marcus gave a nod.

"Sure, boss, whatever you say."

Mario stared at the wing as if pondering whether to eat it. Then he tossed it back with the others and reclined in his seat.

"Keep your distance," he said.

Marcus nodded.

"Sure."

Mario's eyes bored forward from the sagging flesh which hung like curtains over his dark sockets.

"I mean it," he said. "Keep your goddamn distance. I don't want him knowing nothin unless he has to."

Marcus took in a deep breath.

"And what if he don't let off this thing?"

Mario shrugged.

"Then you'll deal with it," he said. "But not until I say so. Understood?"

Marcus nodded.

"Sure," he said, his face closed and expressionless.

Mario shook his head and eyed the basket of bones, his eyes thoughtful within his sagging flesh.

"We're all doomed to outlive our usefulness," he muttered to himself as much as Marcus. "Everything gets used up eventually."

He waved Marcus away with a flip of the hand and then he sat alone, his dish of chicken wings dwindling in size as he piled high his basket of bones.

Chapter 10

The bartender watched the drunk from the corner of his eye, a hand on his hip as he half-listened to a waitress's vociferous complaints. While he gave little nods, she moved her hands all about, her voice seeming, in his mind, fit to shatter two-inch glass.

"Mm-hmm," he said without looking at her.

He frowned as he assessed the drunk anew: a big man, this one, trouble in his eyes. He'd seen it a hundred times, and his internal radar blared as never before.

"This is a big deal," said the waitress, her springy curls bouncing along with her movements as she went on and on about her schedule.

The bartender tried to listen even as he contemplated the drunk. Something about her child and school and the many injustices of the world.

"Mm-hmm," the bartender muttered again, his eyes fixed on the activities taking place at the other side of the bar.

"Are you even listening to me, Todd?" the waitress asked while she smacked her chewing gum.

"Course I'm listening," he said. "You got a thing with your kid."

The woman's face grew sour, and she studied the barman with big accusing eyes.

"Not a thing, Todd, a recital. My daughter's been practicing for months, and I got to be there for it."

The bartender watched as the drunk teetered on his stool, his attention focused on a group of lightly dressed women.

"Uh-huh," he said.

The young waitress put her hands on her hips.

"Well?"

The bartender looked at her.

"Well, what?"

The waitress raised her eyebrows.

"Well, you gonna let me have Thursday off or not?"

The bartender turned toward her and shrugged.

"It ain't up to me, Linda. It's up to Mel. Go ask him. He's the damned owner."

She opened her mouth to say something but stopped when she heard the yelling.

"Goddammit," said the bartender as he turned to see the drunk with his hands on the two women. "Leave me be, Linda. I've got to deal with this."

He fled the bar and approached the drunk, who now had his hand up one of the girl's dresses, a slobbering grin on his face while his other hand gripped her by the wrist.

"Alright, buddy," he said as he gathered the man up by his collar. "Out."

The drunk turned and looked at the bartender's hand where it held his shirt. Then his eyes drifted up, and the bartender felt a chill.

"Who the fuck are you to put your hands on me?" the man slobbered as he got to his feet. "Do you know who the fuck I work for?"

The bartender's head tilted upward as the hulking drunk swelled before him.

"Listen," he said as he took in the man's immense proportions. "I don't want any trouble."

A little grin leaked across the drunk's face, which was ruined by at least a half-dozen scars.

"Too late for that."

While the two girls took their opportunity to flee, the drunk gathered up the bartender's shirt with both hands.

"Let him go!" cried Linda as she rushed to the phone.

"Yeah," said a voice from down the bar. "Let him go."

The drunk teetered as he looked for the source of the words.

"Jimmy," he said as he dropped the barman. "That you?"

Jimmy sat by himself at the far end of the bar, his head pointed down toward a small glass of scotch.

"Yeah," he said. "It's me."

The drunk swallowed.

"I ain't seen you in a while. How you been?"

Jimmy shrugged.

"Same as always," he said without looking up.

Across the bar, the waitress was reaching for the phone.

"Do I need to call the cops?"

Jimmy looked up at her.

"Nah," he said. "That won't be necessary." He glanced over at the drunk, who seemed diminished in size. "Ain't that right?"

The drunk swallowed again.

"No," he said. "That ain't necessary."

He glanced at the bartender and took a step back.

"Sorry, fella," he said, his hand flattening wrinkles on the man's shirt. "Got a little carried away. Hope I didn't hurt you none."

The bartender looked over at Jimmy, but he was staring down into his glass as if lost in the deepest of thoughts.

"No," he said. "No worries."

They gave each other a nod, and the bartender walked away.

"Good to see you, Jimmy," said the drunk.

Jimmy gave a slight nod without looking up, and the big man hurried away and out the door.

"I appreciate it," said the bartender as he resettled behind the bar.

Jimmy started to speak, but a slow clapping erupted behind him.

"Well, well," said a familiar voice.

Jimmy gave a slight turn and glanced over his shoulder. Through the low light walked a balding middle-aged man with a silver goatee. Just behind him, another man followed, his youthful face tight with forced seriousness. Jimmy shook his head a little and turned back toward his drink.

"Great," he muttered to himself.

"That was something alright," said the older man as he stepped up to the bar. "I thought I might find you here. Didn't expect the show."

Jimmy said nothing, but the man didn't seem offended in the least.

"You know who this is?" he asked the younger man. "This right here is Jimmy Hunter."

The young man pushed his bottom lip out and shrugged.

"So?"

"So," he said. "Jimmy's a big man around town. At least in certain circles."

The young man raised his eyebrows.

"That so?"

The older man nodded.

"Oh yeah," he said. "Definitely not someone you want on your bad side. Or, at least, back in his younger days."

He frowned and rubbed his balding scalp.

"Father Time catches up to all of us, unfortunately." He gave the young man an apologetic frown. "You'll see."

Jimmy lifted his drink.

"What do you want, Martin?" he asked as he took a small sip.

Martin frowned.

"Now, is that any way to greet an old friend?"

He leaned close and put his arm around Jimmy, who flexed his jaw as he set his glass down.

"See, Bobby," he told the young man. "Jimmy and I used to be partners back when he was on the force. Way before you were even born, I think. Back in the old days. Back before all this crazy shit when things made sense. Ain't that right, Jimmy?"

Jimmy held his glass with both hands, his eyes staring down into the amber liquor.

"So, what happened?" asked the young man, his eyes looking Jimmy up and down with brazen contempt.

"Oh," said Martin. "It's a long story, but it ends with him working for the bad guys."

Jimmy shrugged.

"There are no good guys anymore, Martin. You should know that."

A wide smile cut across Martin's face.

"Well," he said. "You're assuming there ever were."

The young man looked them both over through a set of narrow eyes.

"I don't see it that way," he said.

Jimmy and Martin exchanged the briefest of glances.

"Well," said Martin. "Give it some time."

Jimmy took another sip of his scotch and set the glass back down.

"Well," he said. "It's been nice catching up and all, but I prefer to drink alone."

Martin looked hurt.

"I'm not here to bust your balls, Jimmy. I'm here to help you out."

Jimmy raised his eyebrows.

"Oh, yeah?"

Martin nodded.

"Yeah, Jimmy," he said. "For old times."

Jimmy shrugged.

"Alright."

Martin glanced back at his young partner and rubbed his jaw.

"Listen, Jimmy, first I gotta tell you some bad news."

Jimmy lifted his drink to his lips.

"Alright," he said as he took a swallow.

Martin sat down on the stool beside him.

"Howard's dead, Jimmy."

Jimmy stopped drinking.

"Yeah," Martin continued. "They found his body by the docks. A single bullet to the head. Looked like whoever it was had been working on him a little bit too."

Jimmy set his drink down.

"Working how?"

Martin shrugged.

"Fingers mostly," he said. "They uprooted some nails."

Jimmy stared down at his drink without speaking while Martin looked back at his partner.

"Hey, Bobby, why don't you give us a second?"

The young man looked from Martin to Jimmy and then back again.

"Sure," he said.

He walked away with obvious reluctance, and then Martin leaned in closer to Jimmy.

"Listen," said Martin. "I know Howard meant a lot to you, but I didn't just come to break bad news."

Jimmy lifted his glass to his lips again.

"No?"

Martin shook his head.

"No, Jimmy. I came to tell you that they're looking at you for this."

Jimmy sipped his drink and set the glass down. Martin waited for a response, but Jimmy only stared into his glass.

"Goddammit, Jimmy. This is serious. They got your prints all over Howard's office, and everyone who's anyone knows you work for Mario now."

Jimmy shrugged.

"My prints were at Howard's because I worked for him too."

Martin nodded.

"That's right, but that ain't gonna stop them from looking closely at you, Jimmy. And whether you had anything to do with this or not, they're gonna dig deep, and they're gonna uncover whatever they can. And you and I both know that won't be good for you."

Martin leaned back and looked over at his partner, who was pretending not to watch from across the bar.

"Listen," he continued. "Howard ain't no ordinary victim, Jimmy. He's a high-profile guy. His face is plastered all over billboards and bus stops. Hell, he's got all those irritating commercials too. It's a big case. And the DA is gonna want someone to pin it on."

He glanced back at his partner again and then leaned closer to Jimmy's ear.

"You know as well as I do how things work," he said. "They won't care who did this thing. They'll just want someone to pin it on. They need someone to pin it on."

Jimmy slowly spun his glass in a circle on the wooden bar top.

"Thanks for the warning."

Martin looked at him and frowned.

"Sure, Jimmy."

He stood up from his stool and gave a sigh.

"You take care of yourself. Watch your back."

Jimmy nodded without ever looking up.

"I'll see you around," said Martin as he walked away.

Jimmy watched him collect his young partner, and the two exited the bar, Bobby eyeing him with unconcealed hostility all the way to the door. Jimmy waited until they were gone and then summoned the bartender. He ordered another scotch and drank until the voices in his head fell silent.

When his glass was finally empty, he held it between two hands, his eyes staring into the bottom as a glaze settled over his sagging face. After a while, he pushed the thing away and reached into his jacket pocket. With a wobbly hand, he took out his phone and entered a number from memory. Then he tapped out a message and clicked send.

"Important things to discuss"

He set the phone down on the bar top and stared at his empty glass, a rage flowering in his gut as he thought about Howard: His friend's bloated corpse bobbing up and down amid the seafoam, fingernails torn away as he begged for merciful death.

The phone buzzed, and he looked at the message.

"When"

He took up the phone and typed his response.

"One hour," Jimmy replied.

He waited for a response, his drunken eyes squinting to read the tiny text.

"Can't"

Jimmy shook his head and took in a great breath. Then he lifted his phone again and typed.

"What time's the big party?"

He set the phone back down on the bar top and looked around. The place was thinning out, except for the most desperate of drunks and least appetizing women.

The phone buzzed again, and he collected it with patient ease.

"Where"

He tapped in the instructions and asked the bartender for his tab. Then he stood up and staggered for the door.

An hour later, he limped through a dimly lit parking lot, his dry mouth sucking down saliva to quench his swelling thirst. Before him, tall weeds and bushy brambles grew wild along the sides of a creek bed, which funneled endless gallons of street filth away from the city. Behind him, an abandoned mall sat like haunted architecture along a dark and barren landscape, its glass doors long shattered by age and human intervention.

He turned and looked back at the disintegrating structure, like the crumbling ruins of a greater time. He thought he saw something moving in one of the ruined doorways where the C on an old JC Penny sign hung loose overhead. He strained his drunken eyes and staggered a little, but whatever it was had retreated back inside.

He turned away and took a few steps, weeds poking up through the decaying blacktop which crumbled beneath his shoes. Amid the dark, rolling quiet, he bent and spat dryly, weak bits of saliva collecting in his chin whiskers as he cleared the mucous from his throat.

Without much resistance, he collapsed backward onto his ass, his body feeling old and ruined as the pavement rushed up to meet him. Without will or warning, tears began welling in his eyes as he considered the choices that had brought him to the moment. The past and the future all at once. All the wasted possibilities. The irreconcilable versions of himself. And then headlights flared to his left as Robin's car pulled before him.

As the car crept to a halt, it bathed Jimmy in a blinding white glow, his skin looking pale and wrinkled in ways that made her feel scared.

Robin watched as he struggled to his feet, his eyes squinting, hand shielding against the bright hot bulbs. He limped up to the car and stood outside her window, his body wavering as he strained to see inside through the glare. She lowered the glass a crack and peered up at him, now a faceless silhouette amid the low surrounding light.

"Are you crazy?" she asked. "Do you know how hard it was for me to get here?"

He said nothing, his body wavering as he swallowed a burp.

"Are you drunk?" she asked.

Jimmy shrugged.

"I don't think so," he said as he frowned thoughtfully. "A little."

She started to say something else, but he was yanking on the handle to the backseat door.

"What are you doing?" she asked. "Stop."

He stopped tugging, and she unlocked it with a tap of a button. The smell of liquor invaded the car as he plopped down inside, the carriage jostling under his unsteady weight.

"Jesus," she said. "You smell like a refinery."

He fumbled with the door handle and tugged it shut, the stink sharpening as he closed himself inside.

"Good Christ," she said as she pinched her nose. "You should be at home in bed, and I should be anywhere else."

Jimmy leaned back and looked around the interior of the car.

"Fancy," he said. "You and your husband certainly aren't hurting for money."

Robin glared at him through the rearview mirror.

"Is that why you messaged me, Jimmy? To discuss our finances?"

Jimmy pushed his lower lip out.

"No," he said, returning her glare. "I wanted to tell you Howard is dead."

Robin's jaw trembled slightly.

"What?"

Jimmy gave a small nod.

"Yep."

He watched her bring a hand to her mouth, his drunken mind assessing her movements. Appraising the twitches in her face.

"How do you know?" she asked.

He shrugged.

"A cop," he said. "An old friend."

She looked down at her lap.

"What did he say?"

Jimmy worked the saliva around his mouth and swallowed.

"He said they found Howard by the docks. Said he'd been shot and tortured."

Her eyes appeared in the mirror.

"Tortured?"

He nodded.

"How?"

Jimmy shook his head.

"It doesn't matter," he said. "Not anymore."

She looked back down at her lap, face disappearing into the black.

"I want to ask you something," said Jimmy.

Robin's face caught the light as she looked up at him in the mirror, her eyes glistening with what seemed like real tears.

"What," she said weakly.

Jimmy leaned forward in his seat.

"You and Howard," he said. "Were you having an affair?"

She bit her lip as she forced back tears, her chin lowering as she bent toward her lap.

"Yes," she whispered.

Jimmy flexed his jaw.

"Is that why he's dead?" he asked. "Did your husband kill him?"

She shook her head.

"No," she said without looking up. "I mean. I don't think so." She looked up at him through the reflective glass. "I don't know."

Jimmy frowned and leaned back in his seat.

"Well, somebody did," he said. "And I'm going to find out who. And then, I'm going to put a bullet in their fucking head."

Robin wiped her eyes and shook her head.

"Jimmy, listen. You shouldn't push this any further. Whoever did this, whatever their reasons, you need to let it go."

"No," said Jimmy with a shake of his head.

Robin turned in her seat and met his eye.

"Listen, Jimmy," she said. "You need to listen to me. Whatever is going on, you have to let it go. You have to stop following my husband, and you have to stop messaging me." She leaned closer. "And you definitely shouldn't come to this party. Above all else. No matter what. You can't come to this party."

Jimmy shook his head.

"I have to."

Robin pinched her eyebrows together.

"Why?"

He looked at her through the mirror.

"For Howard."

Robin swallowed.

"Howard's dead. You can't bring him back. Neither can I."

Jimmy shrugged.

"That doesn't matter."

Robin shook her head.

"Why?"

Jimmy took a deep breath.

"Because I owe him. Or I did anyway."

Robin waited for him to say something else, but nothing came.

"Jimmy, you can't go to this party. You'll stick out like a sore thumb. They'll see you coming a mile away. And that's if they don't already know who you are, which they probably do."

Jimmy shook his head.

"It doesn't matter. I'm going, and that's the end of it. I have to."

Robin turned back around in her seat and gave an exasperated sigh.

"Why?" she asked again. "What could be so important to make you do something this stupid? I cared for Howard too, Jimmy. Deeply. But you can't pay a debt to a dead man."

They sat in the quiet while the wind cut through the darkness all around them.

"I had a son," Jimmy said at last.

Robin's eyes flicked up to the rearview mirror, but Jimmy's face was concealed by shadows.

"He was 17," he said. "Good kid. Ran the straight and narrow. I made sure of it. Didn't want him to turn out like me."

He turned and looked out the window, but there was nothing much to see amid the weak orange parking lot lights.

"Anyway, it ain't really possible in this place," he said. "Too much negative influence. Too many people like me. So, he got into a few things. Nothing major, some petty crimes. I straightened that out, and he went back to being a good kid."

He shook his head, eyes spacey as he stared out into the night, its mysteries absolute, hidden amid sightless obscurity.

"But I couldn't be there all the time," he continued. "And one night, he and some friends got into it with some jokers at a bar. Nobody connected. Just some dumb punks with too much ego. Too much youth. Alcohol and testosterone. That sort of thing.

"Anyway, I don't know if it was over a girl or a fucking game of pool or something equally as stupid, but the thing spilled out into the alley, and they all got into each other pretty good, and my son must have landed a pretty good shot because he turned out one guy's lights and he fell and hit his head against the concrete, and that was it. They couldn't wake him up. He was done. Just like that."

He sighed and rubbed his bald head.

"So, they gave him 15 years for that," he said. "Fifteen years for a drunken mistake. Or they were going to anyway, but Howard arranged for him to get out of town."

He pursed his lips and took a deep breath.

"He ran?" asked Robin.

Jimmy nodded.

"He ran," he said. "Somewhere else. Someplace I don't even know. We agreed it was best that way. For me not to know. That way the cops couldn't work any angles on me. He got a new name, a new social security number, and he left. And I never knew where."

Robin watched him through the mirror.

"But Howard knew?"

Jimmy nodded.

"Howard knew," he said. "Said he'd tell me when enough time passed or whenever I wanted to know. I never asked. I thought about it every day. But I never asked. I don't know why. Fear, I guess. I always thought there'd be time."

He turned and leaned forward in his seat, his eyes lit by a sliver of orange light knifing in through the window.

"But now he's gone, and so is any chance I ever had to see my son again," he said. "A lot of that's my fault. I understand that. But the fact is, the man who saved my son, a good man, a man I loved. He's dead, and someone is responsible. They took him, and they took something from me, and I'm gonna find out why. I'm gonna pay it back."

Robin looked into his eyes.

"I'm sorry, Jimmy," she said. "I'm sorry for your son. I'm sorry for Howard. I loved him too. I truly did. But you can't go to this party. These people, you don't know who they are. You don't understand them. They can't be hurt. They are the ones who hurt. They'll hurt you, and they'll hurt me because of you."

A tear leaked from her eye as she spoke, and for the first time, she seemed human to Jimmy.

"I want to get out of here, Jimmy," she said. "Just like your son. I have to get away and start over."

Jimmy frowned.

"I can help you with that," he said. "I've got connections for that now, even without Howard. You help me get what I want, and I'll help you leave. You can disappear and have your fresh start. They won't ever find you. You have my word on that. But first, you help me. I'm not leaving until I fix whoever killed Howard. I don't care who these people are, and I'm not interested in taking down whatever it is this whole thing is. I don't care about saving the world. I just want to hurt whoever killed Howard. I want to feel my hands around their throat. You help me with that, I'll help you escape. I promise."

Robin wiped her face dry and nodded.

"Ok," she said. "I'll help you. But you have to do things my way. You can't come to this party. I'll help you any way you want. Just promise me you won't come to the party."

They looked at each other for a long time in the mirror, Robin resisting the screaming impulses to look away.

"Alright," said Jimmy at last. "We'll do it your way." He stared harder as if activating some otherworldly power to deepen a depthless stare. "But you'd better come through on your end."

Without another word, he opened the door and stepped back out into the night, the smell of liquor following him like an invisible apparition haunting his every place.

He stood and watched as Robin pulled away, a closed-lip smile on her face as she gave him a nod. Without reciprocation, he watched her drive off, his dull eyes following until she reached the edge of the lot and disappeared around the corner of the crumbling mall.

He took a deep breath, the night air laced with the smell of early autumn. A sourness festered in his belly as his stomach turned, and he raised a fist to his mouth as a burp seeped out between his lips. He staggered backward and vomited onto the pavement, a jolting pain in his hip sobering his tired mind.

And then lights clicked on in the far side of the parking lot.

Jimmy spun around and straightened as a car crept closer over the crumbling blacktop. Out of reflex, he reached behind his back in search of the pistol. But when his fingers found the mark, they touched only air.

"Relax," said a whispering voice, like something from the mouth of a snake.

He turned to see a tall man, his face concealed within a black ski mask. In one hand, he held Jimmy's gun; in the other, he held a gun of his own.

Without thinking, Jimmy lunged toward the figure, a fury within his gut. But as his boot met the pavement, his hip gave, and a startling pain sent him stumbling forward face first onto the blacktop.

Bootsteps swelled around him as men poured from the vehicle. Then unforgiving hands took him from every angle, and he was up in the air, his stomach swimming as they brought him around the car and shoved him into the trunk.

Chapter 11

Jimmy blinked against the darkness, a low hum buzzing in his ears as the car gobbled up highway road. Amid the deep, hopeless black, he opened and shut his eyelids, blinking and blinking for no reason in particular, over and over, his eyes straining against the suffocating black. No difference, no clarity, the stink of the rubber spare tire thick within his sucking nostrils.

While gravity shifted, his loose body jostled within the darkness, elbows catching against metal, cheeks filling with vomit while he struggled to discern up from down. Pain shot through his forearm as it crashed against the walls of the trunk, hard metal banging against sensitive bone. Vomit up and out of his body. In his hair. On his clothes.

At last, the car came to a stop, and the trunk popped open.

"Shit," said a raspy voice. "He puked."

Jimmy felt hands hook beneath his armpits.

"Just get him inside," said another voice, this one whispering, the same from before.

Now he was being dragged, his hip screaming with pain as his heels skated awkwardly upon the rugged blacktop.

Within moments, the floor changed to tile, his boots skidding as they yanked him forward, the nighttime air replaced with indoor odors that made his stomach turn even more.

"Shit," said a voice as he vomited again. "It's on my leg."

They all stopped, and Jimmy's head lolled. He listened while heavy bootsteps pounded the floor beside him. A sharp crack splintered the air as a hand slammed into someone's cheek.

"Shut your mouth," said the whispering man.

The room fell silent.

"Yes, sir," said a small voice. "I'm sorry."

Now, they were off again, Jimmy's heels skidding against the tile as bars of fluorescent lighting whirred by overhead.

Moments later, they hauled him into a room, his body jolting upright as they dumped him into a stiff wooden chair. He swallowed the sourness in his throat and blinked. Before him stood two masked men, each one holding an automatic rifle, their faces concealed behind twin black ski masks.

Jimmy leaned forward and spat onto the floor. He rubbed his head and looked at the men.

"Can I get an aspirin or something?"

One of the men stepped forward and jammed the butt of his rifle into Jimmy's cheek.

"Shut your mouth," he whispered.

Jimmy turned his head and spat a tooth onto the floor.

"Fuck," he said through bloody lips. "You could have just asked."

"We don't ask," said a voice that seemed both silky and sharp.

Jimmy looked up to see a woman step into the room, a slight smile on her face as she studied him from head to toe. She entered the room like she owned it, and the two men cowered backward as if to prove the point.

Jimmy raised his head and looked the woman over. She wore a simple black sweatshirt, and her dark hair was buzzed down to the scalp. The bones in her face were sharp, and her skin was fair and flawless, but none of that stole from the seriousness in her eyes.

Jimmy tried to look into those eyes, but it was like staring into the sun.

"Hello, Jimmy," said the woman. "It's good to meet you finally."

Jimmy blinked at her.

"Thanks," he said.

She approached and stood before him, her hands hanging loosely by her sides.

"Do you know who I am?" she asked.

Jimmy looked her over and frowned.

"Am I supposed to?"

She frowned.

"Not necessarily," she said. "I just thought I'd ask."

She crossed between the two men, and they turned inward to fill the gap, hands gripping their weapons as they watched her approach the vomit-wreaking man.

Jimmy looked her over, his eyes assessing every movement without gleaning a goddamned thing. She watched him watch her, a perfect set of teeth showing through a smug little smile.

"I've been watching you, Jimmy," she said. "Or my people have anyway." She pulled up a hard metal chair and sat in front of him. "I'm much too busy to watch everything."

He raised his arm and wiped a sleeve over his mouth.

"I'm flattered," he said as he looked over her shoulder toward the masked men. "Can I get a water or something? I have this taste in my mouth."

Her smile widened.

"You're an interesting guy, Jimmy. One second, I think you're savvy as they come. The next," she said with a frown, "I think you're a fucking idiot." Her eyes shot forth with a thousand-watt glare. "Which is it?"

Jimmy shrugged.

"Bit of both, I'd say."

She frowned and stood up.

"I'm gonna need better." She put her hands behind her back. "Much, much better if we're going to work together."

Jimmy gave her that dead, hollow stare.

"I'm sorry to disappoint you," he said. "But I work alone."

Her perfect teeth flashed again as she smiled.

"Tell me, Jimmy, what do you know about the thumbscrew?"

Jimmy frowned.

"The thumbscrew?"

The woman stood up and began pacing, her head pointed toward the ground.

"Yes," she said." The thumbscrew. What do you know of it?"

Jimmy shrugged.

"Not much," he said. "Can't say I like the sound of it."

The woman nodded

"As well you shouldn't. You see, the thumbscrew is a primitive torture instrument first utilized in medieval Europe. It's a very simple device. A person's fingers, thumbs or toes were placed in a small vice and slowly crushed. Sometimes the crushing bars were lined with sharp metallic points designed to puncture the nail beds and increase the intensity of pain. In some instances, larger devices based on the same design principle were used to crush the feet."

Jimmy's frown deepened, but his expression remained unchanged.

"It kind of sounds inefficient when you first hear it," she continued. "I mean, if you want to inflict pain on someone for compliance, why waste time with the thumbs when you can go straight for the genitals?"

She continued pacing like a professor in a classroom.

"But surprisingly, the genitals don't really have as many nerve endings as you would think, relatively speaking. Obviously, I'm not saying that the genitals aren't sensitive. It's just that they don't have or require the density of nerve endings you would find within your fingertips. This is because you need more nerves to discriminate between two different inputs on your fingertips that are near each other."

Jimmy watched her walk back and forth, his eyelids low, always low, always relaxed.

"Imagine if you took two sharp pins and poked your fingertip with them at the exact same time," she continued. "If you moved the two pins close to each other, you would still be able to tell there were exactly two pins when the points were very, very close together. The genitals, and most of the body, don't really require that. If you took two pins and poked your forearm with both, you would only feel a single pin even if the points were half an inch apart."

"Hey, listen," said Jimmy. "I can see where this is going, but—"

"Your lips are actually the most sensitive part of your body," the woman interrupted. "I mean, considering how much electrical input comes from them, relative to their small size. This is critical for speech and for interpreting the surrounding environment."

Jimmy started to mumble something, but she cut him off again.

"The feet have a substantial concentration of nerves, mostly because the brain requires a lot of information to make constant, tiny muscular adjustments necessary for balance."

She stopped and turned toward him, her face cold and hard.

"But your fingers," she said as she approached the table, "that's where you need the most tactile input for finely controlled, coordinated movements and sensation. I mean, just think of the sensitivity necessary to read Braille."

She approached the table and sat back down in the chair across from him.

"That's why the tiniest injuries like paper cuts and nail bruises hurt so bad. Your fingertips are densely packed with nerves, and more nerve endings mean more pain signals to the brain."

She reached across the table and took up his hand.

"Hey," he said. "Come on now."

"And speaking of your brain," she continued, "the area that feels pain has an especially large amount of space devoted just to the fingers. So, whenever the nerves send pain signals up from your fingertip, your brain perceives that pain as much stronger than the pain signals it receives from other parts of your body, such as your genitals, for instance."

He tried to yank his hand away, but she was surprisingly, no, shockingly strong. She formed her thumb and index finger into a tiny claw and captured the tip of his thumb.

"Now, Jimmy," she said, her voice flat and emotionless. "I'm going to ask you to do some things for me. And you're going to do them. Or you're going to get a lengthy demonstration of this lecture."

She began to caress his hand, a pleasurable sensation tickling up his flesh that made him sick to his stomach.

"Do you understand?" she asked.

He frowned and thought a moment, a cold and very real fear within his stomach that made him feel ashamed.

"Yeah," he said. "I understand."

She smiled and released his hand.

"Excellent."

Jimmy took a deep breath and pulled his arm back.

"What do you want?"

The woman turned her palms upward and shrugged.

"I want you to go to that party," she said. "Let's start there."

He pinched his eyes together.

"What?"

She stood up and smiled.

"Go to the party," she said. "Have a good time."

"Hey," said Jimmy as he rubbed his hand, but she was walking toward the door.

"That's it?" he asked.

The woman stopped and turned around.

"For now."

The two men turned, and they all moved toward the door.

"Hey," said Jimmy.

The woman stopped and turned around once more.

"Why?" he asked.

The woman raised her eyebrows.

"Because I said so."

She turned back around and followed the two men out the door.

"I'll be in touch," her voice called from the hallway. "Don't let me down."

Chapter 12

Robin stared into the mirror, her unembellished face looking back without aura, pale and bleak and older than her years. With a slight shudder, she opened her makeup bag and went to work, the warmth of her youth returning with every subtle stroke of her hand.

"Where is my green tie?" yelled Michael from the other room.

Robin frowned into the mirror.

"In the closet," she shouted.

She leaned forward and dragged the pencil over the edge of her eyelid, the white orb seeming paler in contrast with the blackening skin.

"I don't see it," said Michael with a caustic hiss.

The line ran funny as her hand slipped its mark.

"God damn it," she muttered. "I don't know, Michael; it's wherever you left it."

She soaked a cotton ball with solvent and scrubbed against the flaw.

"I know you put it somewhere," he shouted. "You had it dry cleaned, remember?"

She shook her head and stared at her unpainted reflection, a plain and foreign face, another person entirely, someone to escape.

"Just wear your blue one," she yelled back as she started again.

As the minutes passed, her face took on color and form, the cheeks bulging with false prominence, eyes more piercing, a hint of mischief somewhere within. When she was satisfied with the falsity, she put her makeup away and turned toward the bathroom door, where Michael stood wearing his finest frown.

"It's not there either," he said with the same voice he might use to accuse her of fucking the neighbor.

She shook her head and pushed past him.

"Did you look?" she asked as she moved down the hallway.

"Of course, I looked," he said. "I've been looking for an hour."

She threw a look over her shoulder.

"An hour?" she said. "It's been ten minutes, maybe."

He followed her into the bedroom.

"It's been longer than that," he said as he folded his arms. "Go ahead. It's not in there."

She opened the closet and rifled through his wardrobe. Within seconds she removed both the green and blue ties.

"They're right here," she said as she pushed them toward him.

He took one in each hand and frowned.

"Well, you hid them in there," he said. "I don't know why you always do that."

She put her hands on her hips.

"We really don't have time for this," she said. "I'll take a thanks in place of an apology."

He clenched the ties within two fists and started to speak, but his voice was interrupted by the chime of the doorbell. Confusion wiped the sternness from Robin's face, but her husband only smiled.

"Ah," he said. "That must be our plus-one."

He turned and hurried down the hallway, Robin hot on his heels as he approached the door. With a swift pull, he yanked the thing open, his face taking on its most amiable form as he flashed his bright, polished teeth.

"Jim," he said with exaggerated pleasure. "So glad you could make it."

Robin peered around Michael's shoulder and felt her heart drop. Jimmy looked back with an apologetic half-smile.

"Wouldn't have missed it," he said. "Hope I'm not too early."

Robin stepped backward as Michael turned sideways.

"Nonsense," he said. "You're right on time."

They led Jimmy into the house and set him at the dining table, Robin eyeing him the entire way with unconcealed hate.

"I'd offer you some coffee," said Michael. "But it's better to keep a sharp appetite at this sort of gathering."

He smiled down at Jimmy, his teeth looking whiter than Jimmy remembered.

"Sure," said Jimmy. "No problem."

Michael gave a nod.

"Well, if you'll excuse me, I'll put on a tie, and we'll be off."

Robin watched him leave with an affectionate grin. Then she turned and swelled before Jimmy.

"What are you doing?" she whispered. "I thought we agreed on this."

Jimmy frowned.

"Well," he said. "I guess I had second thoughts."

Robin held her hands out to her sides.

"Second thoughts?" she whispered. "You have to get out of here. Make an excuse. I don't care what it is. You're sick. You shit your pants. Whatever. Get yourself out of here now."

Jimmy opened his mouth, but Michael was already entering the room.

"Shall we?" he asked as he straightened his tie. He looked down at Robin and smiled. "I went with the blue."

She gave it a look and nodded.

"It looks nice."

Jimmy struggled to his feet.

"Yeah," he said. "Real sharp."

Michael gave an affable smile.

"You just follow us in your car, Jim. In case you want to leave early. These things can go all night."

Jimmy raised his eyebrows.

"Wow," he said. "That crazy?"

Michael shrugged.

"Well, it's not always easy to predict. Sometimes they're quite ordinary. Sometimes there are stories to tell. My best advice is to keep an open mind."

Jimmy glanced at Robin, but she was looking at the floor.

"Sure," said Jimmy. "I'm up for anything."

Michael flashed a mouthful of teeth.

"Wonderful. Well, let's get going."

They walked outside into the failing day, the suburban scent of freshly cut grass in the air. Michael stopped on the porch and filled his lungs.

"A slice of heaven," he said as he scanned the block. "This is America as it should be."

Jimmy looked around.

"I always had an affinity for concrete," he said.

Michael glanced over his shoulder.

"Well," he said. "To each his own. That's American too."

They stepped off the porch and parted, Michael and Robin approaching their luxury sedan while Jimmy limped toward his car at the curb.

"Wow," shouted Michael with a smile. "That's got some character. Is it a classic?"

Jimmy looked at his car and shrugged.

"No," he said. "But when you get to be my age, you develop an affinity for stamina."

Michael flashed his teeth again.

"Well said." He looked over at Robin, but she was already halfway into the passenger seat. "Just follow us."

Jimmy gave a nod and sat down in his car.

"This fucking shithead," he muttered to himself as Michael backed out of his driveway.

With a sudden turn, the man squealed forward, his high-performing sedan gobbling up the road as it left Jimmy in the dust.

"Shit," Jimmy muttered as he jammed his foot against the gas pedal.

The car trembled as it lurched forward, a stinking black fog belching backward as he rumbled up to the road. Soon, he was out of the neighborhood and onto the streets, Michael and Robin weaving in and out of traffic as they claimed their superiority among the everyday motorists in their ordinary cars.

As the blinding sun burned red before him, Jimmy raised a hand before his face, his car weaving left and right as he struggled to keep pace.

"This fucking shithead," he muttered again as he gripped the steering wheel, his knuckles whitening under the squeeze of his forearm flesh.

After a time, they cleared the mob of cars and raced onto a stretch of clear road, Jimmy's car trembling in its pursuit, like a space capsule plummeting against the rake of atmospheric pressure on its way back to the Earth.

After a terrifying stretch of driving, Michael and Robin exited the highway, Michael's vehicle slowing at last as they drove into the parking lot of a luxury hotel. While Robin and Michael pulled before the valet, Jimmy stowed his car in the parking lot, the engine clattering as he brought it to a merciful still.

With a great sigh, he pulled his key from the ignition and watched from afar as Michael handed his keys to the valet.

"Fucking shithead," he muttered as he struggled out of the car.

He stood and looked around at the parking lot, half filled with cars that put even Michael's to shame. His eyes flicked up to the hotel, where impeccably dressed people flowed into the event center like low-key actors at a posh Hollywood event. He looked down at his suit and frowned. Nothing for it now, he thought as he slammed shut the car door.

With an obvious limp, he made his way across the parking lot.

"You should have used the valet," said Michael as Jimmy approached.

Jimmy limped up the stairs and caught his breath.

"Didn't see it," he said.

Michael frowned at him.

"Problem with the leg?" he asked.

Jimmy straightened and looked around.

"Should we go inside?"

Michael grinned at him.

"Sure," he said. "Follow me."

He turned and started toward the door while Robin looked at Jimmy with a sad set of eyes.

"You shouldn't have come," she said.

Jimmy shrugged.

"Too late for that now."

She looked over her shoulder where Michael was chatting up someone at the door.

"Try to keep your head down. That's the best you can do at this point."

Jimmy looked at her.

"I can take care of myself."

She gave him another sad smile.

"Sure," she said. "Come on then."

He followed her up the steps and into the event center, where a light flow of well-dressed guests streamed into the building. As they stepped inside, a pair of large men stood in immense tuxedos, their eyes watching everything with passive interest.

Jimmy glanced over his shoulder at Robin.

"Is that security?"

She took him by the arm and led him toward the ballroom.

"Just try to relax and don't do anything stupid tonight, please?"

He shrugged.

"I'll do my best."

Just ahead near the ballroom entrance, Michael was waving them forward, his face alight with a wicked grin.

"Jim, Robin," he called. "Over here."

They made their way through the gathering crowd of guests, Robin offering smiles and nods as she went.

"Well," said Michael as they approached the ballroom door. "What do you think?"

Jimmy looked into the great room, where a growing hoard of elites conversed amid an elegant setting with gilded ceilings, priceless fresco paintings and sparkling crystal chandeliers. Amid the striking baroque décor, the guests gathered like kings and gods, their smug faces glowing with self-satisfied smiles.

"Nice," said Jimmy with his usual flat tone. "Very posh."

Michael's grin faltered for a moment as Robin threw Jimmy a glare.

"I mean," said Jimmy. "It's really something. Uh, very nice, like, uh, a fairy tale. Or something like that, I guess."

This restored Michael's smile, which he now shared with the room.

"Marvelous," he said. "Let's join the party, shall we?"

He led them into the sprawling room, where they were engulfed by a noxious atmosphere of varied colognes and perfumes, which mingled in the air like invisible apparitions at war.

While the ballroom buzzed with chatter, gentle music swelled from the stage, where three men in tuxedos played light classical music that seemed almost eerie to Jimmy's untrained ears.

A waiter passed by with a trayful of champagne glasses, and Jimmy snagged one with a sweep of his hand. The server's head snapped backward, and he smiled.

"Anyone else," he said politely.

Michael took two glasses and handed one to Robin. The waiter gave a nod and pushed his way into the crowd.

Jimmy turned the glass up and sucked down its contents while Michael watched him with delight.

"What?" asked Jimmy as he lowered the glass from his mouth.

"Nothing," said Michael. "How was it?"

Jimmy shrugged.

"Fine," he said. "I'm more of a beer man, though."

Michael brought his hands together and laughed.

"Michael," snapped Robin.

Michael collected himself and frowned.

"I'm sorry," he said. "It's just, that was a $100 glass of champagne."

Jimmy looked at the empty glass.

"Well," he said. "It'll do, I guess. Unless you have a $100 glass of beer."

Michael's smile faltered again.

"Why don't we join the party?" asked Robin.

Michael and Jimmy eyed each other for an uncomfortable moment, neither taking several reasonable opportunities to look away from the other's glare.

"Michael," said Robin.

As if broken from a trance, he looked down at her and revived his smile.

"Of course," he said.

There was a small commotion in the middle of the grand room, and Michael raised up on his toes to get a better look.

"Ah," he said. "Jim, let us introduce you to a handful of acquaintances. I think you'll find that some of these people are worth much in the way of amusement."

Robin followed Michael's eyes and snapped her head back.

"No, Michael," she said.

Michael turned and looked down into her eyes.

"Whyever not?" he asked. "He's a friend of Donald's, after all." He raised his eyebrows. "Right?"

Robin swallowed and smiled.

"Yes," she said. "Of course." She held her arm out. "Lead the way."

Michael grinned.

"Come on, Jim," he said.

He pushed his way into the crowd while Robin took a step toward Jimmy.

"Don't say anything," she said. "Not unless you have to."

Jimmy shrugged.

"Alright."

"No," said Robin, her forehead glinting with perspiration. "I mean it."

He looked into her eyes and saw the truth of her words.

"Alright," he said.

They turned and followed Michael, who was once again peering over the crowd from atop his toes.

"Jean Paul!" he shouted to someone across the room.

He turned back toward Robin and Jimmy.

"This way," he said as they followed behind him.

They pressed through all the people and approached an old fat man in a motorized wheelchair. He had a deep purple scar on the side of his neck, and a sparse layer of thin gray hair strung horizontally across his freckled head. One of his eyes was cloudy, and a yellow chunk of crust had developed in the corner near the nose. But none of this seemed to concern the gorgeous young blonde woman at his side.

Jimmy looked the creature over with disgust, but everyone else seemed to regard him with awe.

"Robin, Michael," wheezed the old man in some sort of Eastern European accent. "So good to see you both."

He held up a trembling hand, and Jimmy watched with revulsion and wonder as Michael and Robin took turns kissing it.

"And who is this?" asked Jean Paul, his few remaining teeth showing brown between his wet, purple lips."

"This is Jim," said Michael with a smile. "He's a guest of ours. An old friend of Robin, apparently."

Jean Paul raised the back of his trembling hand toward Jimmy, who eyed the split yellow fingernails with a frown.

"Um," he muttered. "Nice to meet you."

He reached out and gave the hand a quick shake. As if someone had broken a priceless vase, the people all around them fell silent for several heartbeats. Then Jean Paul chuckled, and everyone continued as before.

"Marvelous," he wheezed. "We are so fortunate to have friends. They are the flowers in the garden of life."

A small crowd had formed around the old man, and everyone nodded solemnly as if he'd spoken some sort of prophecy.

"Well," said Jimmy. "Can't argue there, I guess."

Jean Paul watched him through his one good eye.

"No," he said.

It was quiet for several seconds, Jean Paul staring up at Jimmy, who looked back with his same dead-eye stare.

"And you, my dear," he said as he flicked his eye toward Robin. "Is all well?"

Robin swallowed.

"Of course, Jean Paul."

The fat man grinned.

"Oh, I'm so happy to hear it. You are such an important part of our family."

Robin gave a polite smile.

"Thank you."

Jean Paul moistened his lips with a flick of his tongue.

"Well," he said as his fingers drifted down to the control panel on his wheelchair. "If you will excuse me."

Everyone gave a slight bow, and the crowd split apart. Jimmy watched as the old man motored through, the impossibly beautiful woman hurrying to keep pace at his side.

"Quite a character," Jimmy said.

The other guests turned toward him all at once as if he'd muttered the greasiest of racial epitaphs.

"Yes," said Michael with a smirk. "Jean Paul is one of a kind."

The other guests looked Jimmy up and down and then dispersed while he stood watching with a deep frown.

"Did I say something offensive?" he asked.

Robin said nothing as Michael slapped Jimmy on the back.

"No, no," he said. "It's just that Jean Paul is quite revered among this group. Among a great many people really, all throughout the world."

Jimmy shrugged.

"Wow," he said.

Michael turned toward the ballroom of people, all conversing with lively, interested faces. He raised up on his toes and narrowed his eyes.

"Ah," he said. "There's Juan Carlos."

He turned toward Robin and Jimmy.

"If you'll excuse me, I need to do a bit of networking." He winked at Jimmy. "I'm sure you know how it is." Without waiting for a response, he bent down and pecked Robin on the cheek before rushing away to join the party crowd.

Jimmy watched Robin, who was rubbing her cheek as if it had been burned by a cigarette.

"Everything all right between you two?" he asked.

Robin dropped her hand and glanced up at him.

"You tell me," she asked. "Isn't that the reason you got involved in this?"

Jimmy looked out at the people, a throng of elites glittering in their tailored clothing and oversized jewelry.

"I'm not sure," he said. "But I'll figure it out."

Robin took in a deep breath and shook her head.

"You'd better figure it out soon," she said. "Dinner will be served within the next hour."

He looked at her and bunched his forehead up.

"So?"

Robin looked up at him with an almost pitying expression.

"You really shouldn't have come, Jimmy."

With that, she turned and walked away, stopping for just a moment to throw a look over her shoulder.

"Please stay out of trouble. For both our sake."

He watched her move forward and blend into the crowd, her face alight with big smiles for every person crossing her way.

While the ballroom stirred with shifting circles of people, the band continued their light music, while Jimmy looked around without seeing much to interest him.

"Are you Jim?" asked an elderly woman with a crooked posture.

Jimmy looked down at her.

"Yes," he said.

"Oh, good," said the woman. "I'm Iris."

She looked up at him with an expectant grin, her weathered face powdered with far too much makeup.

"Nice to meet you," he said as he stuck out a hand.

Iris looked at his hand and frowned, her face flesh wrinkling as she clenched her dentures together. She leaned in closer as if speaking to the deaf.

"I'm Iris," she said louder.

Jimmy furrowed his eyebrows and looked from left to right.

"Nice to meet you," he said louder, his hand still hanging in the air before her.

She looked at him over her glasses, large and red-rimmed.

"I'm Donald's sister," she said. "Robin's aunt?"

Jimmy dropped his hand and straightened.

"Oh," he said. "I, uh…"

He started to look around again, but she was on him like a tick.

"Donald never mentioned me?" she asked.

Jimmy licked his lips.

"I'm not sure," he said. "My memory isn't what it once was, if I'm being honest."

She pursed her lips and nodded.

"Yes," she said. "I understand."

He tugged at his collar and looked around.

"Well," she said. "Donald and I were twins, of course. We were very close. Inseparable really. We entered the Guild together. We shared a ceremony, if you can believe it. That's exceedingly rare."

She blinked at him over her oversized glasses.

"Yes," said Jimmy, his eyes narrowing some. "Tell me about that, if you don't mind. Honestly, I'm sure Donald mentioned it before, but like I said, my memory and all."

Iris nodded.

"Of course," she said.

She looked down at the floor and pinched her face together, unseen gears turning within her elderly head.

"What were we talking about?" she asked at last.

Jimmy opened his mouth to speak, but a young man was closing in behind the old woman.

"Grandmother," he said as he arrived behind her.

Iris turned and smiled.

"Oh," she said. "This is my grandson, Lucas."

Jimmy stuck out a hand, and Lucas shook it.

"Grandmother," he said with the sweetest of smiles. "Father is asking for you."

Iris lifted her eyebrows.

"Oh, alright," she said.

He took hold of her hand and began leading her away.

"We'll talk later, Jim," she said.

The young man glanced up at Jimmy for a moment.

"Alright," said Jimmy as he looked into the young man's eyes. "I look forward to it."

The young man watched him a moment longer, and then the two were lost in the crowd.

Minutes later, a tall, stern-looking man in a white jacket entered the room and announced the start of dinner. As if burned in the rump by cattle prods, everyone hurried into the banquet room, Jimmy following the current, head whipping all around as he searched for Robin.

When he stepped into the great ornate room, he saw her waving at him from the far side of an enormous dining table, Michael at her side grinning like a madman.

Jimmy pushed his way through the other guests to join them.

"So, what's on the menu?" he asked as he approached.

Michael gave a little chuckle, and Robin threw him a glare.

"There will be several courses," she whispered. "Just keep your voice down."

They all took their places around the massive table, everyone standing behind their chairs in anticipation as Jean Paul motored up to the very head place, his fleshy torso jostling as his wheelchair came to a sudden halt. A sterling silver bell sat upside down before him, and he lifted it in his hand like a conductor orchestrating a symphony.

"Please," he said with one shake of the bell. "Be seated."

Like foot soldiers drilled in the art of conformity, every guest slipped into his or her seat, Jimmy struggling to match the striking synchronicity as he grappled with his bad hip. While everyone settled in place, Jean Paul surveyed each one, his wet mouth hanging open somewhat as he breathed in air.

"Thank you all for coming," he said in his odd accent. "It is my honor to play host to such a diversity of talented people, both Guild members and guests."

He coughed a little and cleared his throat.

"To the gentlemen of Viox Genomic, I express my gratitude."

He nodded to a pair of pale men sitting to his right, each one strikingly similar to the other in dress, stature and, to Jimmy's eye, shiftiness. Indeed, each one smiled back at Jean Paul with snake-like grins, their bony rat faces tilting downward as they replied with the slightest of nods.

Jean Paul coughed again, this time loosing something slippery and vile from deep within his lungs. This he swallowed while everyone pretended not to notice, their eyes captivated, mouths bent upward into fawning smiles.

"We all have much to discuss this evening," he said. "And later," he continued with a grin. "Much to share."

Everyone chuckled a little while Jimmy watched with suppressed confusion, his face the same as always, never a tell, never a slip.

"But first," he said. "We dine!"

The table erupted with applause as he shook the lustrous bell, tings and pings cutting through the clapping like a blade through a ripe melon. In an instant, a hoard of well-dressed servers entered the room, each one hoisting a tray filled with plates of steaming meats. Almost all at once, they slid a plate beneath the chin of every guest, faces lighting up as they inhaled the savory aromas which traveled the invisible air up and into their snorting nostrils.

Jimmy looked down at his plate, large and white and empty except for a log of dark-colored sausage.

"Hmm," he thought as he rolled the thing around with his knife and fork.

With a shrug, he sliced a piece off and forked it into his mouth. He chewed a couple of times and then stopped.

"What the hell is this?" he muttered.

"Blood pudding," whispered Robin.

Jimmy grimaced.

"What?"

He chewed again and swallowed it down, chasing the flavor with a few gulps of water.

"I thought blood pudding was pudding," he said.

Robin carved a thin slice and speared it with her fork.

"No," she said. "It's a sausage made of blood, kidney fat, grain, raisins and spices." She slipped it between her lips and chewed slowly. "It's quite good once you get used to it. It's very popular in Britain. Or it used to be, I suppose."

Jimmy stared down at the tube of meat on his porcelain plate.

"Yeah, that's not my idea of food."

Robin shrugged.

"I'm afraid this will likely be the most ordinary thing you will eat tonight."

Jimmy frowned as the server staff brought more serving trays.

"Shit," he whispered.

Robin dabbed her mouth with a napkin.

"You'll have to eat, or you will stand out," she said. "You really shouldn't have come."

Jimmy took a deep breath.

"I'm starting to think you're right."

True to Robin's word, blood pudding was the most ordinary thing of the night. First came balut, which Jimmy quickly discovered to be a fertilized developing duck egg embryo boiled and eaten from the shell. There was a crunch and a juicy squirt, but the flavor wasn't all bad.

Then came jellied moose nose, held together in a jiggly loaf of gelatinized broth. With a trembling hand, Jimmy forked off a sliver and raised it to his lips, some eyes sneaking subtle glances at him, others watching with audacious glares. He held his breath and pushed the wiggly mass between his lips, a hidden shudder chilling his body beneath his itchy clothes.

Robin watched him chew from the corner of her eye, his face taking on a deathlike pallor as he forced a swallow.

"Good Christ," he said as he reached for his water. "How do you eat this stuff?"

Robin raised a forkful to her lips.

"It's quite good, actually," she said softly. "Once you develop a taste for it."

Jimmy gave a grunt and sampled his water.

"Don't drink too much," said Robin. "You'll want to save room for the next course. It will be easier that way."

Jimmy pulled at his collar, his forehead breaking out in a flu-like sweat.

"You've got to be kidding me?" he muttered. "Worse than this?"

"Not worse," said Robin. "Just different."

Her ominous forecast proved accurate as servers brought tray after tray of delicacies, each slick, gritty or wreaking in its own repulsive way. Jimmy watched all the others consume each bizarre offering with glee while he chewed and chewed amid a waking nightmare.

He ate insects and their wriggling larvae, their innards bursting outward as he crunched their abdomens between his teeth. He sampled haggis and casu marzu, which he later learned to be a sheep milk cheese flavored by the digestive juices of live maggots. And he finished with Hasma, which Robin defined as a Central Asian dessert made from the dried fatty tissue near the fallopian tubes of frogs.

All the while, the other guests watched him with curious eyes even as they chatted noisily among themselves.

"Ugh," said Jimmy as he dabbed his mouth with a napkin. "Where's the bathroom?"

Robin gestured with her head.

"Near the entrance," she said.

Jimmy burped as he stood.

"I'll be a minute," he said.

She grabbed his arm and leaned closer.

"Try to vomit quietly."

He swallowed the foul taste in his mouth and walked past her, but Michael pushed his chair back from the table to block his way.

"Taking a break?" he asked as he took Jimmy by the arm.

Jimmy burped up stomach acid and swallowed.

"Bathroom," he muttered.

"Ah," said Michael as his face assumed a look of deep concern. "Yes, you don't look well."

Jimmy tried to pull his arm away.

"I'll be fine," he said.

Michael wiped his mouth with a napkin and tossed it on the table.

"Perhaps I'll join you," he said.

Robin turned toward them.

"Leave him alone, Michael," she said.

Michael's eyes moved from Jimmy to Robin.

"I don't think I was talking to you, was I?"

Robin flexed her jaw.

"Let him go," she said. "He's not feeling well."

Michael looked up at Jimmy.

"No?" he asked. "Something you ate?"

He grinned up at Jimmy, who regarded him with his usual bored expression.

"Is everything all right?" asked a heavily accented voice.

The room fell silent, and everyone turned toward the head of the great table.

"Yes, Jean Paul," said Michael as he released Jimmy's arm.

Robin swallowed and nodded.

"Yes, Jean Paul," she said.

The old man watched them through his one good eye, his knife suspended over a thin cut of wet meat. Every eye in the room locked on Jimmy, Michael and Robin and then drifted with care over to Jean Paul. No one ate. Some barely breathed.

"Good," said the old man at last.

He bent back over his plate and started slicing into the meat, which spurted juices as he cleaved it with the blade.

As if nothing had happened, everyone returned to their conversations. Clinking dishes and laughter, servers refilling glasses while food disappeared from plates. Robin turned toward Jimmy, but he was already gone. Michael flashed his teeth at her and then turned back toward his plate.

An hour later, Robin sat sipping coffee with Stacia and the other wives, some of them 60, one 17. While they prattled on about their senior-citizen husbands, she glanced around for signs of Jimmy without success, her thumb running back and forth along the underside of the pearls around her neck.

"Well, he's just so busy with work," said the youngest wife, a precious little thing with blinking Bambi eyes.

One of the elders put a hand on her wrist.

"Be glad for it, dear," she said. "All you need is their plastic."

The others stifled laughter with their silken gloved hands. Robin took it all in with a half-present smile, her eyes still scanning for any sign of Jimmy.

"What about you, dear?" asked one of the wives. "How are things in paradise?"

Robin turned her eyes on the woman, once kind and beautiful, now bitter and well past her prime.

"Lovely," said Robin.

The woman sucked her cheek as Robin gave her a simple closed-lip smile. They glared at each other for several seconds, and then she and the others were onto something else.

"I need to talk to you," whispered Stacia.

Robin glanced at her.

"Now?"

"Yes," said Stacia. "Please."

Robin nodded.

"Will you excuse us, ladies?" asked Robin as she stood up.

The other wives gave polite nods and returned to their chatter.

The rest of the party had now broken up into their typical factions, the important men encircling Jean Paul while the lesser watched from afar with jealous curiosity. Robin and Stacia navigated the landscape with inconspicuous footsteps, artfully practiced over several years.

When they were safely alone in one of the little meeting rooms, Stacia began to cry.

"I just can't do it anymore," she said. "It's too much."

Robin sighed and rolled her eyes.

"Shh," she said as she rubbed the girl's arm. "This is not the place for this, Stacia."

Stacia looked into Robin's eyes, but something different shone forward this time.

"No," she said. "I mean it. I'm done."

Robin glanced over her shoulder at the closed door and then turned back toward the girl.

"What are you saying, Stacia?"

She wiped her eyes and shook her head.

"I'm saying I'm done. It's over. I'm getting divorced and getting away from him. From all of this."

Robin smirked.

"What?"

Stacia shook her head.

"I don't want any part of this," she said. "I'm going to divorce Donald and move back to Oregon."

Robin tightened her lips and nodded.

"Just like that, huh?"

Stacia nodded.

"Yes," she said. "It'll be hard, but I can live with my mom for a little while until I get a job."

Robin chuckled without making a sound.

"What?" asked Stacia. "What's so funny?"

Robin looked at the floor and shook her head.

"You poor idiot."

Stacia swallowed.

"What do you mean?"

Robin looked up at Stacia and collected her hand.

"Listen," she said as she stared deep into her eyes. "You aren't going back to Oregon, and you're certainly not getting a divorce."

Stacia tried to wrench her hand away, but Robin held it tight.

"Stop," she said. "Let go."

Robin flashed her teeth.

"Shut up," she said, her voice calm, eyelids relaxed. "Jean Paul is not going to let you divorce your husband. How fucking stupid are you? Your husband is a part of the Guild. And he is also an immense liability." She squeezed Stacia's hand tighter. "As are you."

Stacia grimaced as Robin squeezed her fingers.

"Let go," she whimpered. "You're hurting me."

"Shh," said Robin, her purring voice soft, like that of a nanny comforting an addled child. "Shut up now and listen to me. You can't leave Donald. Not ever. If you even contact a divorce lawyer. If you even suggest dissatisfaction in the marriage, to a friend, to a coworker, to the neighbor across the street, the Guild will intervene."

Robin started crying.

"What do you mean, intervene?"

Robin frowned.

"What do you think I mean?" She took a deep breath as if summoning the patience to cope with the smallest of minds. "All the things you can think of. All of your worries. All of your fears."

Stacia burst into tears.

"Shh," said Robin.

Stacia jerked her arm.

"Let go of my hand!"

Robin released her grip, and Stacia rubbed her fingers, a tingle in the flesh as the blood rushed back.

"I can't do it, Robin," she said as she stood up from her chair. "I have to get out."

She tried to rush toward the door, but Robin snared her arm.

"Stacia," she said. "Don't be a fool. You know how it is. This isn't the way."

Stacia tore her arm away.

"You've given up," she said. "But I haven't. I'm going to Oregon. Don't try to stop me again."

She turned toward the door, but there was a man standing there.

"Oh," she said. "Excuse me."

Jimmy turned sideways and let the girl rush past. He watched her scamper down the hallway and around a corner. Then he turned his attention back to Robin.

"What was all that?" he asked as he entered the room.

Robin stood up and dusted her hands together.

"Nothing."

Jimmy stepped forward and took hold of her.

"Don't feed me that shit," he said. "I heard every word you said to that girl."

Robin's eyes drifted to his hand around her arm and then up to his face.

"You should go, Jimmy," she said calmly. "You really shouldn't be here."

He squeezed her arm.

"And what about you?" he asked. "You said you wanted out. And then I just heard you tell that girl there was no way out."

Robin said nothing as Jimmy leaned in closer.

"What the hell is going on here?" he whispered.

Robin said nothing, Jimmy's eyes staring into hers, pretty and pale blue. An emptiness within.

"That's what I'd like to know," said Michael as he entered the room.

Jimmy released Robin and turned to face him. Michael frowned and looked at Robin.

"Everything alright?" he asked as he took a step closer.

Robin gave a weak smile.

"Yes," she said. "Everything's fine."

Jimmy said nothing, his eyes fixed on Michael.

"Is that right?" asked Michael as he turned toward Jimmy.

"Yeah," Jimmy said flatly.

"Really?" asked Michael. "Because what it looked like to me, and please correct me if I'm wrong, is that you had your fucking hands on my wife."

Jimmy said nothing, his eyes boring forth from behind his low eyelids.

"It's fine, Michael," said Robin as she stepped in between them. "Let's go back to the party."

Michael stared at Jimmy, his jaw flexing beneath the skin.

"You've got some nerve," he said. "We invite you to a very exclusive party, and you repay us with such disrespect."

Jimmy said nothing as Robin took Michael by the arm.

"Come on, Michael, don't do this."

Michael shook her loose and stepped toward Jimmy.

"Do what?" he said. "Defend my wife?"

Jimmy stood as before, his breathing slow, eyes nearly lifeless within their sockets. Michael stared forward, his sleek, muscular body swelling beneath what was at least a $4,000 suit. Robin pulled at his arm again, but it was like trying to uproot a tree.

"Well?" said Jimmy.

They stared at each other a moment longer, a cold silence filling the room.

"Please," whispered Robin.

Michael kept his eyes on Jimmy a moment longer, and then his face softened as he let slip a little smile.

"Sure, dear," he said as he flashed his teeth. "Whatever you say."

He started to turn his body away from Jimmy, Robin leading him away toward the door. But just as her heart began to slow its rapid pace, he broke loose from her again and spun with a shocking suddenty, his fist leveled and swinging at Jimmy's jaw.

With an effortless motion, Jimmy dodged the blow and levered his arm under Michael's jaw, spinning him around and securing him in a headlock.

"No!" hissed Robin as Michael choked and gagged. "Let him go."

Jimmy lowered his eyebrows.

"He swung at me first."

Robin put her hands to her head and glanced back at the door.

"That doesn't matter," she said. "You have to let him go now!"

Jimmy chewed his teeth and squeezed harder. Then he dropped Michael to the floor and watched the man choke and cough. Robin collapsed to the carpet next to her husband and cradled his head like a newborn child. Jimmy stood above them both with his arms to his side, both fists clenched. As Michael vomited up some of his dinner, Robin looked up at Jimmy with panicked eyes.

"Go," she said. "Leave quickly."

Jimmy took in a deep breath and exhaled. Then without saying a word, he walked toward the door. As Michael continued his coughing, Jimmy made his way down the hallway and back into the ballroom, where the crowd had grown lighter by at least a third. Even still, he had to push his way through, people throwing him indignant glances as he banged a shoulder or two.

When he finally pushed through the mass of people, he popped out near the front entrance, where a half-dozen large men stood with stony expressions and folded arms. Like granite statues, these men watched over everything and nothing, their faces expressionless, muscled bodies rigid and still.

Jimmy collected himself and approached with an easy expression.

"Fellas," he said with an amiable voice.

One of the men put a hand up.

"I'm sorry, sir," he said. "You'll have to wait until the event's conclusion."

Jimmy looked at the man's hand.

"I think I've had my fill for the night."

A second man turned his head toward Jimmy.

"No one leaves until the end of the event," he said. "It's Guild policy."

Jimmy swept his eyes over the men.

"Sure," he said.

While they watched, Jimmy took a step back and turned around, his eyes searching the place for a second way out. As he looked all around, his eyes fell on the far side of the room, where Michael was limping around the corner, his hand rubbing the flesh beneath his jaw. Behind him, Robin trailed quietly, her head pointed toward the floor.

As several guests turned to look at them, Jimmy rushed toward another hallway on the opposite side of the ballroom.

"Jim, is it?" asked an old man in a red suit vest, his long mustache waxed into curled tips on both sides.

Without responding, Jimmy pushed past him and continued toward the hallway.

"Well," said the man as he looked down at his wife, who protested the umbrage with a roll of her eyes.

While Michael relayed his experience to other guests, Jimmy slipped around the corner and hurried down the hallway, which ran a length of about 100 feet before ending at a pair of great polished oak doors. He limped his way over a plush red carpet, shoes hammering silently with every hurried step. When he reached the doors, he wrapped a hand around the polished brass handles. He gave a hard tug, but they were hopelessly locked.

As a commotion swelled in the ballroom, he spun around and looked up and down the hallway where a scattered collection of doors lined the walls, likely only meeting rooms, almost certainly dead ends. Without hesitating, he approached one of the doors and ripped it open.

Inside, a mob of nude men and women were busily at work with an astounding array of fleshly acts.

He froze in the doorway and watched as women engaged in oral obligations while men took them from behind, faces red, skin bleeding sweat. Only inches from them, men wrestled together, their bodies entangled in a twitching diversity of lurid homosexual acts. In one far corner, a pair of old men had their way with a woman who appeared to be drugged. A few feet from them, a very young girl lay unconscious, her makeup smeared, arms covered with human bite marks.

Jimmy watched with mute horror as he stumbled backward, brain trying to make sense of what his eyes gave it. He started to turn, started to run, but there were arms around him now. Big, muscled arms wrapping around his waist and neck, squeezing and pulling like steel vices, ripping at his clothing and dragging him back out into the hall.

Soon he was down on the ground, and then he was lifted up in the air, his legs kicking as they carried him back out into the ballroom.

"Throw him out!" yelled a woman.

"Kill him!" said an old man.

Faces flashed by as Jimmy was hauled across the room. Some wore looks of shock and horror. Others flashed teeth and hateful glares while obscenities spat from their hollering mouths. Then he felt himself being carried up steps and through the front doors, where the nighttime air gushed around him, and the stars twinkled in the heavens above his face.

And then he felt himself being hurled out into the air and felt the crunch of the hard concrete as it smashed into his body.

"Don't come back!" yelled one of the enormous men as he went inside the building.

Jimmy struggled to his hands and knees, a taste of iron in his mouth as blood leaked from between his lips. He coughed a red splatter onto the pavement and felt a searing pain in his ribs. He turned to look at the entryway, where the giant doormen were trying to disperse the small crowd of partygoers who had gathered to watch.

With great effort, Jimmy struggled to his feet, his head numbed by shock and worry. With every limp toward his car, he waited for a bullet in the head or an ambush from behind. But nothing came, and soon he was driving, the building growing smaller in his rearview mirror as the streetlights rushed by in an incandescent blur.

Chapter 13

Jimmy paced back and forth within a little gas station, his ribs screaming with pain at every subtle turn. Outside, sheets of cold rain beat the pavement, while tiny rivers formed in the street gutters, their currents glutted with cigarette butts and other paper filth that swirled and flowed into rusty drainage grates where they were swallowed down into a labyrinth of ancient filth within the city sewers.

"Come on," he muttered as he checked his phone, a handful of customers glancing as he voiced his feelings aloud. "Come on."

While he shuffled before the soda taps, the cashier watched him, eyes alert, face tense with concern. At last, the young East Indian man conjured the wherewithal to speak.

"Please, sir," he said. "If you do not plan to make a purchase, I must ask that you wait outside."

Jimmy raised his head, and the man flinched a little.

"Out there?" he said as he gestured toward the big glass window.

The cashier glanced at the heavy downpour and frowned as lightning cut electric stitches in the night sky. He swallowed and looked at Jimmy.

"I'm sorry," said the young man. "It is store policy. You could perhaps wait in your vehicle."

His words came out more like a question than a demand, and the young man flinched when the thunder shook the sky.

Jimmy looked around and plucked a bag of sunflower seeds from a shelf.

"Here," he said as he approached the cashier.

He tossed the bag onto the glass counter.

"Will that be all?" the man asked.

Jimmy nodded.

"Yes."

The man tapped buttons on the register.

"$2.06," he said with a weak voice.

Jimmy handed him a five-dollar bill.

"Keep it," he said as he walked back to his previous spot.

The cashier took the money.

"Please, sir," he said. "You require change."

Jimmy looked at his phone and cursed.

"Keep it, goddammit," he said.

The cashier looked at the five-dollar bill in his hand.

"But—"

"Keep it!" Jimmy hissed.

The young man swallowed.

"Yes, sir."

As startled customers gave him a wide berth, Jimmy gripped his phone, mind willing forth a message. Something to ease his anxiety. To make everything ok.

The phone buzzed, and he turned it upward, holding it away from his bad eyes to sharpen the blurry text.

"The boss wants to see you"

"NOW"

He moved his lips silently as he read the messages.

"Fuck," he whispered as he dropped the phone to his waist.

"Please, sir," said the cashier. "You must go outside."

Jimmy looked out the windows at the rain-soaked concrete.

"Are you kidding?" he asked.

The cashier shrugged.

"I'm sorry," he muttered. "It is the store's policy."

Jimmy stuffed his phone into his jacket pocket and shook his head.

"Fine."

The cashier cowered behind his register as he watched Jimmy stomp through the doors, the rain enveloping his figure as he disappeared into the night.

Outside, the cold rain stung his hot skin, his clothing gathering water weight as he limped across the parking lot. When he reached his car, he yanked the door open and hurled his body into the front seat, the fog of his breath gathering on the windshield as he shut himself inside.

While raindrops popped against the roof of the car, he reached into his pocket and retrieved his phone. No new messages, save for Mario's summons and the reckoning to come.

He dropped the phone to his lap and shook his head. Then without thinking, he lifted the phone and started tapping, letters forming words, against his screaming intuition, too many words, too much information, too many questions, all for Robin.

When he finished, he stilled his finger over the send icon, his tongue running between his lips as he contemplated the consequences of his actions. Amid the gentle thrumming of rain, he ran the possibilities. The pros and the cons, all the reasons to put his phone down and simply drive away.

Then he felt something press against the back of his head.

A cold chill ran up his spine as his mind grappled with the harsh reality of the moment. Countless times he'd hobbled into his car and not once had he failed to check the backseat. Until tonight when it finally mattered. Was it fate or folly? He almost laughed at his carelessness.

Without speaking, he placed both hands on the steering wheel and took a deep breath, his mind waiting for the bullet, a long time coming and probably well deserved.

It was quiet except for the rain, which pecked the top of the car like the beaks of a thousand tiny birds.

He felt the pressure increase, the gun pushing him forward until his head tilted down toward his lap.

Seconds seemed like minutes, but his heart remained even as ever.

"Well," he said at last. "Get on with it."

He breathed in and out, the lids low over his eyes as he waited for life to wink away.

"Why would I do that?" said a whispering woman's voice.

Jimmy relaxed and shook his head.

"Jesus Christ," he said as he felt the gun pull away from his head. "Is that absolutely necessary?"

The woman leaned back in her seat and chuckled.

"Very few things are absolutely necessary," she said as she put the gun away.

Jimmy adjusted the rearview mirror and peered into the backseat. The woman sat alone, her face nearly invisible in the shadows, save for her mouth which held an amused little smirk amid the tiny streak of light flashing in through the window.

"Not many people can say they got the jump on me," he said.

"Really?" said the woman as she watched him through the mirrored glass. "I was barely trying."

Her smirk turned into a disappointed frown.

"You really should check your backseat. I expected better."

Jimmy shook his head a little.

"Yeah, well, it's been a long night."

"I can imagine," she said with a smile. "So, how was the party?"

He looked at her through the reflective glass.

"Let's see," he said. "I thought the people were a bit strange until I ate the food. And then that seemed very strange up until I saw the orgy. But things really took off when they picked me up and threw me out into the parking lot."

The woman raised her eyebrows and nodded.

"Sounds about right."

Jimmy turned around in his seat.

"I want to know what's going on with that place, this Guild or whatever."

The woman shrugged.

"What would you like to know?"

Jimmy scratched his whiskered jaw.

"Well, for starters, why the hell did you send me there?"

The woman sat back in her seat.

"Reasons."

Jimmy shook his head.

"Fine, then, what the hell are they up to? I mean, I know it's something illegal."

The woman cocked her head a little.

"Does that bother you?"

Jimmy frowned.

"What do you mean?"

The woman turned her palms upward.

"You work for one of the biggest criminals in the city," she said. "Why should it matter if this Guild is on the up and up?"

Jimmy shook his head and turned back around in his seat.

"Maybe it matters, maybe it doesn't," he said as he stared forward. "But they killed my friend."

The woman eyed the back of his head.

"Maybe they didn't kill him."

Jimmy looked at her reflection in the mirror.

"What do you mean?"

The woman shrugged.

"Maybe I killed him," she said. "Maybe Mario killed him."

Jimmy shook his head.

"No," he said. "That wouldn't make any sense. They killed him. Or they had something to do with it, at least. I'll find out either way."

The woman pursed her lips.

"Can I ask you a question?"

Jimmy nodded.

"What?"

She lowered her eyebrows and looked at him, her eyes like two black holes in the low light.

"Why do you work for Mario?" she asked.

Jimmy frowned.

"I don't know," he said. "It's work. Why?"

The woman shrugged.

"You seem like a decent guy," she said. "I mean, from what I can tell anyway. Compared to the other trash in this city. The other trash in your line of work."

Jimmy frowned.

"Thanks, I guess."

The woman smirked a little.

"So?"

"So what?" asked Jimmy.

"So, why work for Mario?"

Jimmy took a deep breath and looked at her through the mirror.

"There's a limitation to how he works," he said. "A restraint."

The woman's smirk grew.

"You mean he doesn't deal in narcotics?"

Jimmy watched her through the mirror.

"Yeah."

The woman shrugged and looked off to the side out the window.

"Interesting that he wouldn't," she said.

Jimmy lowered his eyebrows a little.

"Why?"

The woman shrugged.

"I know a little about him," she said. "I know he likes money. And from an economic perspective, illicit drugs are just another commodity. And a particularly lucrative one at that."

Jimmy shook his head.

"No," he said. "With drugs, there are addicts. There are innocents that get ground up in the whole thing. There are kids."

The woman kept staring out the car window.

"But not with Mario's dealings?" she asked, her eyes flaring slightly as she spoke.

Jimmy scratched his whiskered jaw.

"Well," he said. "Most the people who get hurt in this business, the one I deal in, they have it coming. Not all, but most."

The woman gave a little nod.

"So, drugs are your dealbreaker. How interesting," she said. "But what about other commodities?"

Jimmy shook his head.

"What like grain and livestock?"

The woman laughed a little.

"Sort of," she said. "But more the illegal kind."

Jimmy let out an impatient sigh.

"I wish you'd say what you mean."

The woman turned toward the mirror, and there was fire in her eyes.

"I mean people."

Jimmy returned her glare through the reflective glass, his jaw flexing beneath the skin.

"Is that what this is all about?" he asked. "Some kind of human trafficking? Is that what this Guild does?"

The woman leaned back in her seat and put her hands behind her head as if she were taking her ease on the most relaxing of days.

"Kind of."

Jimmy turned around, so they were face to face.

"What the hell do you mean, kind of?" he asked. "It is, or it isn't."

The woman licked her lips.

"You a meat-eater, Jimmy?" she asked.

Jimmy narrowed his eyes.

"What?"

The woman shrugged.

"You don't strike me as a vegan, but I've been surprised before."

Jimmy shook his head.

"Yeah, I eat meat. What of it?"

The woman nodded.

"What do you like?" she asked. "A big steak?"

She gave a little smile as she looked him up and down.

"Yeah," she said in a low, almost sexual voice. "I'll bet you like a nice juicy ribeye. Hardly cooked. Just a little flash in the pan. Very red and awfully bloody."

Jimmy felt his hands turning into claws, and he thought he might reach out to strangle the woman.

"Goddamn it," he said. "Stop with this bullshit and tell me what the fuck is going on."

The woman sucked her cheek and stared at him a moment longer as if pondering whether he would even understand.

"What's the purpose of human trafficking, Jimmy?"

Jimmy shook his head.

"Goddammit—"

"Just humor me," she said.

Jimmy stared into her eyes.

"To make money."

The woman chuckled.

"Oh, Jimmy, you reveal yourself in so many ways." She shook her head. "No, I mean, where's the demand?"

Jimmy sighed.

"Sex."

The woman nodded.

"That's right," she said. "But not always. I mean, that's what it is these days, at least for the most part. In the past, not very long ago at all, unfortunately, the primary purpose of human trafficking was slave labor. I'm not just talking about American history and the Transatlantic Slave Trade. I'm talking about the Romans, the ancient Greeks and Persians, the Hittites and Babylonians. The history of slavery spans many cultures, nationalities, and religions from ancient times to the present day. Likewise, its victims have come from many different ethnicities and religious groups. As far back as 3500 BC, as long as humans have been around in actuality, slavery has existed, and thus, so has human trafficking."

Jimmy rubbed his jaw.

"What is the point?"

The woman shrugged.

"The point is that people have always been a commodity. Like sugar and cotton. Like corn or wheat."

Jimmy pursed his lips.

"So, you're saying this Guild is trafficking people, for what, slaves?"

The woman shrugged.

"Humans are one of the most versatile commodities," she said. "Throughout history, they've been used for sex and labor. They've been used as sacrifices to appease the gods. Hell, many ancient cultures routinely incorporated them as part of their diets."

She sat back in her seat and folded her arms, her eyes locked on Jimmy's, the rain thrumming the car above them.

"What are you saying?" he asked.

The woman raised her eyebrows.

"I think you know what I'm saying."

Sour bile rose up in Jimmy's throat, and he struggled to force it back down.

"Are you saying I ate a person at that party?" he asked.

The woman chuckled and shook her head.

"No," she said. "They don't invite outsiders to that kind of feast. They save that sort of thing for special kinds of parties."

Jimmy swallowed.

"Like a cult," he muttered.

The woman thought for a moment.

"Sure," she said. "If that helps."

Jimmy turned around in his seat and shook his head.

"No way," he said. "This is too weird. I don't buy it."

The woman leaned forward and cocked her head.

"No?" she asked with a slightly confused expression. "With all you've seen on the news? With what you've seen yourself? All the deviant lusts and urges of the human race. The murders, abductions and rape? Millionaire pedophiles buying islands so they can traffic pre-teen girls? But this? This is a bridge too far?"

She chuckled and sat back in her seat.

"You really need to get out more."

Jimmy sniffed and rubbed his forehead, his mind spinning as it struggled to cope with this fresh collection of morbid thoughts.

"So, what?" he asked. "This Guild kidnaps people and eats them?"

The woman shrugged.

"Some of them," she said. "The juiciest cuts, maybe."

She chuckled a little as if she'd made the wittiest of jokes.

Jimmy swallowed another rising sickness in his throat.

"And the rest?"

The woman shrugged.

"Sold."

Jimmy turned his head toward the window, the puddles glittering beneath the light as they gathered rain.

"Why here?" he asked. "I mean, when you take someone here, it's gonna get noticed. It's going to get news."

The woman frowned.

"Well," she said. "It might be easier to take some people off the streets of a third-world country, but who wants to eat that? You can't charge a premium for it. But an accountant in New York City? An 18-year-old student from Ithaca College? Soft, supple skin, pretty blue eyes. They'll pay big for that. It's part of the kink."

Jimmy looked down at his lap and rubbed his forehead. Then he pulled his hand away and froze.

"Before," he said. "When you mentioned Mario and commodities."

He looked into the rearview mirror and saw the woman nodding.

"He's part of this?"

The woman pursed her lips and raised her eyebrows.

"He's their main supplier, Jimmy," she said. "At least locally."

Incandescent rage surged through Jimmy's body and then receded under the weight of his shame.

"Jesus," he whispered. "I'm part of this."

The woman shook her head and leaned forward.

"No," she said. "But you can be."

He looked at her through the mirror, his eyes wide open. Anything but dead. Alive.

"What do you want me to do?"

She sat back in her seat, piercing eyes locked with his.

"The Robin girl," she said. "We need her."

Jimmy sniffed and rubbed his jaw.

"What for?"

The woman raised her eyebrows.

"It's complicated," she said. "But it's the best way for you and me to get what we both want."

Jimmy looked at her.

"And what do you want?" he asked.

She shrugged again.

"It's complicated."

Jimmy shook his head and looked out the window, his mind working over all the potential outcomes of every possible action.

"And she'll be safe?" he asked. "I mean, if I help you, will you promise not to hurt her?"

The woman looked a little surprised.

"Really, Jimmy," she asked. "Is this love? I must say I'm surprised. I mean, you're old enough to be her father."

Jimmy showed his teeth a little.

"It's decency," he said. "I said I'd help her."

The woman raised her eyebrows and smiled.

"Ah, decency," she said. "How noble of you." She shook her head. "And after she lied to you. After she put you in harm's way."

He pushed his lower lip out.

"People have their reasons for things," he said. "I try not to judge. Just tell me you're not going to ambush her. If you tell me that, I'll help you as best I can."

The woman shrugged.

"If you'd accept a promise from me, you're not the man I pegged you for."

He flexed his jaw again, but her smile remained.

"I'll tell you what," she said. "I won't hurt either of you unless I have to. That I'll promise."

Chapter 14

Robin stood before the bathroom sink, her eyes staring down at the running water while she gripped the toothbrush in her hand. A sickness swam within her stomach as she watched the water splash against the porcelain, where it swirled together in a little vortex and vanished down the sucking drain.

With a trembling hand, she smeared a dab of light-blue toothpaste onto the bristles and brought them to her mouth. In a robotic, automated sort of way, she inserted the thing between her lips and scrubbed her teeth while a pale, sickly-looking thing looked back in the mirror with red, wired eyes.

"Hurry up," said Michael's harsh voice from the other room. "We leave in 20 minutes."

These were the first words he'd said to her in two days, and she celebrated the moment with a shiver and frown. Despite her ragged state, she polished every tooth in turn before vigorously scrubbing her tongue and rinsing her mouth clean. Then she spread a thin layer of deodorant over her armpits and carefully applied a generous amount of makeup in a way that made it look like she wore very little makeup at all.

As time ticked away, she dressed her body in professional attire that was modest enough for the moment without being too plain. When she was finished, she slipped on her shoes and snapped up her purse, the same one that Michael had emptied out on the floor the day before.

When she stepped out into the living room, he had already exited their home. She approached the window and looked outside, where he sat behind the wheel of his running car. With a tremendous sigh, she approached the front door and stepped out into the morning light, the birds welcoming her with thin little chirps, freshly cut grass perfuming the warm air.

As she walked to the car, Michael watched her, his eyes boiling with hate as he flexed the muscles in his jaw.

"Hurry up," he shouted out the open passenger seat window.

Without speaking, she opened the door and sat down, the car moving backward before she had her second foot off the ground. The tires squealed as she shut the door tight, and then they were out on the road, and he was swerving through traffic, the fibers of his thick forearm muscles dancing beneath his tanned skin.

"I can't believe you've done this to us, Robin," he said.

She stared out the window, her eyes glazed with fear.

"You may have ruined us both," he said. "You've certainly ruined yourself."

She swallowed.

"You'll be fine, Michael."

He shook his head.

"You don't know that."

She turned to look at him.

"I do," she said.

He glanced at her, a genuine look of concern on his face.

"What do you think they'll do?"

She shrugged.

"I have no idea," she said. "Kill me?"

He swallowed.

"That won't happen," he said.

She turned and stared out the window, trees flashing past as they sped down the road.

"What do you think they'll do to me?" he asked.

She said nothing, her head shaking slightly as she watched the world whir by.

Minutes later, they pulled up to the gate, where an armed security man stood outside a little brick shed.

"ID?" he asked as they pulled up.

Michael passed over his driver's license.

"We're expected," he said.

The security man held the license up to Michael's face.

"Yes," he said. "Go ahead."

The gate inched open, and they drove up the winding path which led through the woods to the soaring mansion on the hill. As they drove closer, the thing seemed to grow in size, reaching upward into the heavens like something from another time.

"I've never been in this place before," said Michael. "Have you?"

They pulled before a valet who stood with his hands behind his back.

"Yes," she said as she opened the car door. "Many times."

As they both stepped out of the car, the valet approached, his face expressionless, eyes kind.

"Hello," he said. "May I please take your keys?"

Michael held them out, and the man snatched them away with a metallic jingle.

"Thank you," he said as he brushed by and walked to the driver's side door.

Michael and Robin watched as he sat down inside and drove the car away. They exchanged glances and turned toward the mansion where a group of armed men was pouring from the front door. At their point, a blonde man stepped forward, his hand pressed to his ear as he listened to instructions.

Without thinking, he gave an affirmative nod to the voice on the other end. Then he straightened before the two of them and smiled.

"Hello," he said. "Please follow me."

He turned and walked away from the front door around the side of the great structure. Michael looked at the front door and frowned, but Robin was already following the blonde man, her head pointed down, face resigned.

"Please, sir," said one of the armed men.

He gestured with a nod, and Michael hurried to catch up to his wife.

Around the great structure, they walked, the group passing through manicured gardens with lush greenery and brightly colored flowers, past exquisite water features and striking Greek-style statues that seemed like things on loan from museums.

All the while, Michael looked on with awe, while Robin moved past with little awareness as if she walked through a neighbor's landscape of tomato plants and garden gnomes.

"Right here," said the blonde man as he stopped before what looked like a cellar door.

Michael stopped before the metallic passage.

"Here?" he asked with a trembling voice.

The blonde man gestured to his men, who arranged themselves on either side of the doors and pulled them apart. As the doors swept open, a musty smell rushed out, overwhelming their noses and the fresh summer air.

"Go ahead," said the man as he gripped his machine gun.

Michael swallowed, his eyes darting about as he contemplated his predicament. He turned to say something to Robin, but she was already halfway down the creaking wooden steps.

"Please, sir," said one of the gunmen.

With a hard swallow, Michael hurried to catch his wife, the light winking out behind them as the men shut the cellar doors.

Now came a poorly lit hallway with a wet stone path that squeaked beneath their shoes. Through what seemed like an ancient underground concourse, they crept, roots snaking out from between the stone walls, a bitter mildew in their nostrils as modern LED lights illuminated their way.

As they walked, insects crunched beneath Robin's feet, their exoskeletons squelching beneath every other step. Without regard, she walked onward, Michael yipping as a rat hurried past their shuffling shoes.

After a while, they reached a rusted metal door, all of them stopping while the blonde man rapped a series of code-like knocks. With a nauseating squeal, the door pushed open, revealing a young woman with a large pointy nose.

Robin and Michael looked her over, and she returned the favor, a polite smile spreading over her unattractive face.

"Hello," she asked, her voice as off-putting as her appearance. "I'm Christine. Are we all present?"

The blonde man nodded.

"Michael and Robin Patterson," he said.

Christine nodded.

"This way," she said.

The blonde man stood aside and gestured them forward with his machine gun. They passed through the door, and the woman closed it behind them, shutting away the gunmen and all the skittering vermin, along with the festering stench and wet, stinking walls.

"I'm so very sorry," said Christine with a believable smile. "Jean Paul insists that all Guild members enter through the traditional corridors. It's one of his ... wonderful quirks."

She smiled again and held out a hand.

"Please," she said. "This way."

Without waiting for a response, she turned and hurried forward, the floor beneath their feet changing from stone to tile, lighting growing brighter with every step.

"If you'll forgive the odor," she said as they moved through the hallway, "it will improve as we get closer to the holding compartments."

As promised, the odor turned agreeable as they pressed on, the musty scent growing faint and then evolving into something quite pleasing. Strawberries in the air?

"They pump scents through these," said Christine as she gestured toward little vents above their heads. "I hope it pleases you. I can't really smell it anymore. Something to do with acclimation." She shrugged. "I've gone smell blind."

She chuckled as they walked, her footsteps surprisingly quick for a woman of her considerable size.

Soon the hallway grew wider, big windows appearing on both sides, their clear membranes exposing large rooms, some empty, some occupied. All soundproof against the horrors inside.

As they walked, Robin looked into one of the rooms with a subtle glance. Inside, a great fat man lay on a puff of green silk blankets, his arms and legs ceasing abruptly in toeless, fingerless nubs that were neatly bandaged in clean, fresh gauze. In that briefest of glances, she saw him, his bulging eyes rolling within a sedated existence, an IV feeding him sedatives, face looking sick as a cloaked man shoved spoonfuls of milky, white gruel between his slobbering lips.

She moved onward, more windows appearing on either side, no one looking to assess the contents within. After several minutes, Christine slowed and put her hands on her hips.

"Finally," she said. "This place really is a maze."

Along one side of the hallway, there was a metal door, its hinges colored by flakes of orange rust.

Christine approached the door and gave it a sharp knock. A metallic bong echoed up and down the hallway, and Michael gave a noticeable flinch. Almost immediately, the door flew open, and a large man stepped out. He looked at all three of them in turn. Then gave the woman a nod.

"Well," said Christine. "This is where we part." Her face grew somber as she looked the two of them over. "Good luck."

She gave a closed-lip smile and pushed past them while the large man gestured them toward the open door.

"Please," he said.

Michael followed Robin through the door, and they looked around. Before them, two metal chairs sat side by side in the middle of an empty room, the walls and floor consisting entirely of cold concrete. They both flinched as the man slammed the door, leaving them alone together amid the blaze of a bright fluorescent overhead light.

Michael looked at Robin, but she was already walking toward one of the chairs.

"What's going on?" he asked. "What do we do now?"

Robin sat down in one of the chairs.

"Be quiet, Michael," she said.

He looked all around the room and swallowed hard. Then he approached the other chair and sat. He tapped his foot and looked at the door.

"What happens now?" he whispered.

Robin said nothing, her skin perspiring even in the cool, dry air. Seconds later, the door swung open, and they heard the low whir of a motor. They both perked up in their seats as Jean Paul's wheelchair crept into the room. He gave them both a sour look while the large man stepped inside and closed the door behind him.

"How disappointing to see you both here," he said, his quiet words bent by his Eastern European tongue. "So very disappointing."

His one good eye studied them as his wheelchair encroached closer, the motor squealing as it struggled with his weight.

"Each of you with such potential," he said. "Such pure lineage." He shook his head. "To find yourselves here. Such a disgrace."

Michael opened his mouth to speak but fell mute under the gaze of Jean Paul's milky dead eye.

"So, what to do with you?" he said as he tapped a split yellow fingernail against the control panel on his chair.

Robin said nothing, her eyes trained on the inch of floor in front of her shoes.

"Listen," said Michael. "We can—"

"Silence," hissed Jean Paul as he stared at Robin's face.

Michael swallowed and looked into his lap.

"You know, Robin," said Jean Paul. "Your father was a very important man." He shrugged his flabby shoulders. "I never liked him much, but I would never deny his significance. His father, your grandfather, was one of the founders of our order. His legacy will always be part of everything we do. Everything we touch."

He took in a long breath.

"Your father, himself, well, I'm not sure he did very much. Not directly anyway. He was mostly a gluttonous drunk. But his connections, well, they always served to further our interests. None could argue against that."

His tongue darted out to moisten his lips.

"It was a shame when he died," he said. "But now he has become part of us." He gave a wet smile. "Quite literally, in fact."

Michael glanced upward, but Robin continued staring at the floor.

"The same will be true of you," he continued. "And of young Michael here, our skilled butcher. Our gifted artist. When the time comes, all of us will live on within future Guild members. Even me, though I do not imagine there will be a happy face at that dinner table."

He chuckled until something broke loose from inside his lungs. This he swallowed before speaking again.

"Nonetheless, so it shall be. It is tradition, after all."

He moved closer, the motor in his wheelchair whirring as it crept forward.

"It is not a matter of if, but only of when," he said.

He reached out and collected Robin's arm, and she did not resist.

"When?" he asked as he ran a finger up and down the underside of her forearm, the nail bed looking yellow against her pale skin.

"I must confess," he said with another lick of his lips. "I have long coveted this flesh."

He smiled as he stared at her eyes, but she did not return his gaze. Michael said nothing, his eyes pointed down at his lap, bladder struggling to hold in its contents.

"I would much prefer it now, while it is supple," Jean Paul whispered. "While it is ripe."

He took in a deep breath and seemed to shudder with the agony of a subtle orgasm.

"Now would be best," he said, his head nodding as if to agree with himself. "Before the withering."

He held her arm a little longer, his one good eye fixated on her skin. At last, he drew her hand closer to his mouth, a big purple tongue sweeping out to moisten his lips.

Despite Herculean efforts, her composed face shattered into a grimace as she felt his hot breath against her skin. As if tickled somewhere deep inside, he grinned at this, pausing a moment longer before finally smearing his puckered lips against her hand and stamping it with a wet kiss.

In a sudden gesture, he released her and backed his wheelchair away.

"You have betrayed your oath," he said without looking at them. "And now you must face the consequences."

Michael stared at his lap while Robin wiped her hand against her dress, a gelatinous glaze reflecting beneath the low light.

"I didn't do any—" Michael started.

"Silence, butcher," said Jean Paul flatly. "Yours is an esteemed position in our Guild. But do not think yourself irreplaceable." He turned his wheelchair and eyed each of them. "You have brought shame to yourselves and to all of us, in turn."

He shook his head and showed his rotten teeth with a rat-like sneer.

"Affairs are forbidden," he yelled with a thunderous shriek. "Adultery is forbidden!"

They both dropped their heads as his wheelchair raced up to them.

"You have strayed outside your marriage," he said with the same shrieking roar. "You have brought unwanted attention to our order!"

Spit flecks rained down on the backs of their necks as he bellowed his charges, his fat face reddened by fury, eyes bulging like overcooked hardboiled eggs.

"I'm sorry," whispered Robin. "Please forgive me, Jean Paul."

"Yes," said Michael, his trembling voice betraying him with obvious signs of terror. "Please forgive us."

Jean Paul leaned back in his wheelchair and rubbed a fat thumb against his chin.

"This man you brought to the party, what do you know of him?"

"Nothing," said Michael. "He said he was—"

"Not you!" Jean Paul shouted.

Robin looked up at him and swallowed.

"He worked for Howard," she said. "The man I was seeing."

She glanced over at her husband, but he was staring at his lap.

"Yes, yes," said Jean Paul. "We know all this. But what else did you know?"

Robin tried to look into the old man's face, but his milky eye made her cringe.

"He said he was going to find out what happened to Howard," she said. "He knew the two of us were involved, and he threatened to expose the affair if I didn't help him."

Jean Paul watched her thoughtfully.

"And why didn't you come to us for help?"

Robin swallowed.

"I should have," she said. "I was scared. And I was ashamed. I didn't want Michael to know. I didn't want the Guild to know." She shook her head and wept into her hands. "I'm unworthy."

Jean Paul watched her with contempt.

"Yes," he said.

He looked them over once more and turned away.

"We will handle this man," he said. "And then you will each face the Board. They will determine your guilt." He looked at them. "And your punishments."

He turned his wheelchair toward the door and looked at them one last time.

"It will not be pleasant," he said. "I would be on my best behavior over the next few days."

He powered his chair forward and stopped before one of the men.

"Drive our young Michael home," he said. "He looks to have soiled his pants."

He glanced back at the two of them once more, but they were still fixated on their laps. He turned back toward the man and summoned him downward. Jean Paul whispered into his ear, and the man gave a sharp nod. Then, he stood straight with his hands neatly clasped behind his broad back.

"Very well," said Jean Paul. "Good day."

With that, he motored through the door and disappeared down the hallway. While Robin stared down at her lap, two more men entered the room and approached Michael.

"Let's go," said one.

Snot had collected at the rim of Michael's nose, and he wiped it away with a quick pull of his sleeve. He stood up on baby deer legs, his knees trembling, a wet spot on the inner thigh of his slacks. Without acknowledging Robin, he crossed the room and followed the two men out the door.

Silence stormed the room as the door shut behind them. Robin remained seated alone in the middle of the floor, one broad-shouldered guard standing stoically against the wall. Seconds turned to minutes before she finally cleared her throat and lifted her head to look around.

"Is there something else?" she asked, her voice faltering as the words tumbled out of her mouth.

The large man said nothing, his square jaw flexing as he continued staring into the space above her head. Another ten minutes passed before the door finally opened again. Another man entered, this one half the size of the guard but equal in height. He had a thin, manicured mustache and a dark tailored suit. His black hair was slicked back over his head, and he consumed the world with a rat-like glare.

He approached and looked her over. He bent his mouth into a sharp slit of a smile.

"Hello, Robin," he said.

Robbin swallowed hard.

"Hello, Benjamin," she said with a tiny voice.

He looked down at her and shook his head, a twinkle in his bright green eyes as his smile cut wider across his pale, gaunt face.

"I must say, I am very surprised to see you here," he said.

Robin said nothing, her eyes falling back down to her lap.

"Well," said Benjamin as he clapped the heels of his shoes together. "Let's be on our way. I have a busy schedule."

Almost robotically, she forced herself onto her feet, a slight dizziness in her head as she tried to collect herself. Benjamin looked her over from head to toe, his jewel-colored eyes glittering as he appraised her figure.

"Lovely as ever," he said as he turned his body and held a handout. "Shall we?"

The large guard opened the door, and they followed him out into the hallway. This time, they went a different way, and her heart picked up as she realized they were pushing deeper beneath the mansion and not back toward the entrance.

They moved quickly as if they'd wandered these halls countless times, and her shoes clicked against the tile while she hurried to keep up.

Soon, the scent of strawberries returned, the smell now seeming sickening and artificial, the odor harsh and biting, more chemical than fruit.

Onward they walked, the overhead lights growing more infrequent with every step, dark stretches between each one, Benjamin whistling as they probed deeper beneath the over-structure. At last, they stopped in the middle of a hallway, another set of expansive windows on both sides.

"Here we are," said Benjamin.

Robin looked through one of the windows and saw that the chamber was empty, save for a foul medley of blood spatters and white gruel on the concrete floor. She looked the space over and swallowed.

"This isn't necessary," she whispered. "I heard what Jean Paul said."

Benjamin looked confused.

"No," he said. "We're not here for that."

She looked at him and saw that he was smiling.

"We're here for this."

He flipped a switch, and a light popped on behind her. She turned and looked through the other large window, her hand covering her mouth as she gave a little cry.

Inside, Stacia lay upon her own puff of green silk blankets, hands and feet stripped away, limbs neatly bandaged at the wrists and ankles. As Robin stumbled backward, the young woman stared back through glazed, uninhabited eyes, although her jaw continued to work somehow as a cloaked man shoved spoonfuls of milky gruel between her drooling lips.

Robin turned away from the glass while Benjamin watched her with a frown.

"It is tragic anytime the Guild is forced to take action against its own," he said. "But especially with someone so young." He shrugged. "And yet, it is the young who are most drawn to folly. Like a moth to a flame. I was young once too, as hard as that may be for you to imagine."

Robin held a hand over her mouth and choked back tears.

"Anyway," he said. "Jean Paul insisted that you see, and now you have seen."

He snapped his fingers at the big man, and they both turned back the other way.

"Are you coming, my dear?" said Benjamin.

Robin swallowed hard and turned, her feet falling mindlessly as Stacia disappeared from her view.

Minutes later, she exited the subterranean passages and stepped up through the cellar door.

"Goodbye, Ms. Patterson," said Benjamin as he looked up at her from the bottom of the stairs. "I really do wish you the best."

Without speaking, she turned away from him and faced the group of armed guards, one of them holding a hand over his ear and straining to listen.

"This way," he said at last.

As she studied the grass before her shoes, the gunmen led her back through the manicured gardens, all the vivid flowers perfuming the air while the Greek-style statues stared down with their vacant eyes.

When she reached the front of the mansion, the valet brought around her car. She took the keys and sat down behind the wheel. She started the engine and pulled away down the winding path toward the steel security gate. And though she drove away from the mansion, in her rearview mirror, it seemed to take on greater size, its Victorian-style construction looking ancient and ominous in the reflecting glass.

When she finally pulled up to the security gate, the guard allowed her passage with a stony glare. And then she was driving, fast and free, back into her world. A world of luxury, fashion and fine dining. Of power and privilege, emptiness and despair.

She wept.

Sometime later, she pushed out of the countryside and back into the city streets, which greeted her with an assault on all five senses. There was the scent of belching car exhaust wriggling up into her nostrils. The vibrations of the steering wheel as her tires rattled over bad road. There was the sound of construction clatter as she pushed further down aging streets. And the taste of sour bile as she contemplated her fate.

Soon, there would be a reckoning. But first, she would have to go home and face Michael. Her stomach turned at the thought, and for a moment, she considered veering into the oncoming lane, only to amend her thinking when she considered the formidable safety features in her high-end automobile.

She approached an intersection with an expiring green light and slowed her pace as it went from yellow to red. She eased to a stop and idled while an old woman struggled over the crosswalk with a cane in one hand. She tapped her fingers, mind lost in dark thoughts. And then she felt the heat of a stare from someone in the other lane.

She turned and saw a woman sitting in a small black car, her hands at ten and two, eyes watching her through oversized sunglasses that gave her an insect-like appearance. Robin lowered her eyebrows and swallowed as the woman scanned the length of her car, face young and fair, cold and unsmiling.

After surveying the entirety of the car, the woman gave Robin one last look and then turned her head to the road. Robin watched her a bit longer and then finally returned her attention to the crosswalk.

The light remained red for quite a while, but little traffic built up behind her. Robin began tapping her fingers again, this time to bear the hardship of delay. At last, the light turned green, and she began to press her foot against the gas.

But just as the car began creeping forward, the passenger door swung open. Robin turned to see a large man forcing his way inside. She crushed the accelerator, but he was already seated beside her, a pistol against her ribcage, the barrel stabbing against her like a fresh bruise.

"Slow down," the man whispered through a baggy ski mask, his voice raspy and low, like a gentle stream dribbling over coarse stone.

She swallowed hard and nodded.

"Please don't hurt me," she said as she brought the car to a reasonable pace. "I don't have any cash."

The man silenced her with a purring shush.

"We don't want your money."

Robin's heart throbbed within her chest.

"Who is 'we?'" she said with a stutter.

"Shh," whispered the man as he dug his gun in deeper. "Turn right up here."

Robin looked into the rearview mirror and saw that the woman in the black car was following them.

"Please," she said. "I can get you money."

"Save your offers for later," hissed the man. "Now turn right up here."

She turned right and then left and then right again, the woman close behind the entire way.

She glanced at the man, his body large and imposing and entirely unfettered by a seatbelt. She considered slamming into the car before her, imagined his body bursting outward through the windshield, his gun flipping from his hand and clattering onto the street. The airbag would deploy. The police would arrive. She would be safe. She almost chuckled at the notion.

"Slow down and take the second left," said the whispering man.

Robin slowed the car and turned into a small parking garage.

"Park right there," said the man as he gestured to a long row of empty spaces.

She slotted the car between two painted lines.

"Turn off the ignition," said the man.

Robin killed the engine and looked at the man.

"Please," she said. "I'm sorry. I'm loyal to the Guild. Always. I can make things right."

Before the man could answer, the driver-side door flung open, and Robin was jerked from the car like a passenger being sucked through a hole in a punctured airplane. She began to scream, but a hand sealed shut her slobbering mouth.

Robin's feet skidded against the concrete as the sunglassed woman dragged her to the black car. With a bewildering strength, she lifted Robin up and tossed her into the backseat. Then she slipped in alongside and shut the door.

"Drive," said the woman as the whispering man climbed behind the wheel.

Robin looked at the woman with the eyes of a frightened child.

"What," she said. "Who?"

"Shut up," said the woman.

She snatched up Robin's right wrist and pinned it to her knee. She removed a device that gave off little intermittent beeps. Robin watched with confused terror as the woman moved it all around the top of her hand.

"What is that?" Robin asked. "What are you going to do?"

"Shut up," said the woman as she strained to interpret the slow, intermittent pulses.

As the car turned out of the parking garage, the woman flung Robin's hand away and collected her other wrist. She pinned it to her knee and scanned that hand with the device, which began pulsing much faster.

"Got it," said the woman as she removed the scanner and placed it inside a cloth bag.

Robin watched as she withdrew a knife, the chrome blade glinting in the sunlight bleeding through the window.

"Try to keep it steady," the woman told the driver as she leveled the blade over Robin's supple flesh.

"What are you doing?" cried Robin. "Please, stop!"

Robin grabbed the woman's wrist with her other hand, but it was like trying to stop a machine.

"Please!" she cried as the woman cut into her flesh. "No!"

As she struggled with an impossible game of tug-of-war, the woman cut a one-inch slit that freed only a modest amount of blood.

"Calm down," the woman spat. "This will be over in a second."

With a considerate suddenty, the woman jammed her fingers inside the wound, blood boiling up and onto her lap. Robin cried out as she watched the mutilation, her consciousness threatening to wink out as her heart rate climbed and climbed.

As she began to hyperventilate, the woman's fingers continued to probe within, her eyes darting around, teeth biting her tongue.

"Got it," she said at last.

The whispering man watched in the rearview mirror as the woman extracted a tiny RFID transponder and held it up to Robin. She lowered the window and flicked the tiny tablet away. She turned back toward Robin, who clutched her bleeding wound, her face a medley of fear and awe.

"There," said the woman. "Now, we can take our time."

Chapter 15

The young brunette stomped around the chrome pole, her high heels punching the stage with every exaggerated step. As red lights strobed around her, she glowered at the crowd of leering men, her sleek, sensual body moving with the beat of the music, which throbbed from the great tremoring speakers hidden all about the club.

They cheered as she ripped away a lace bra and exposed a pair of large jiggly breasts. And then they brawled over the perfumed garment when she tossed it among them with a flick of her wrist.

The base beat on and on as she teased and taunted them with acrobatic sexuality. And then she turned away, slender back diving downward from her shoulders into her firm round buttocks, a palm held to her ovular, red-rimmed mouth as she looked back with innocent surprise.

And this stirred within them animal cravings constrained only by the armed thugs pacing about, their eyes sweeping the room for trouble, big hands clenching into hairy fists as they wove through the wild-eyed, slobbering crowd.

All the while, Marcus eyed the door to Mario's office, a toothpick jutting out from one corner of his mouth.

"How long have they been in there?" he asked.

Hiroto shrugged.

"Hour maybe."

Marcus tongued the toothpick from one side of his mouth to the other, his foot tapping a furious and chaotic tune on the floor.

"You think this has something to do with us?"

Hiroto said nothing, his eyes transfixed on the dancer as she gripped the chrome pole with vice-like thighs.

"Hey," said Marcus. "As he turned toward the tall Asian. "This is fucking serious."

Hiroto shrugged.

"Relax."

The girl arched her back and thrust her bare buttocks in Hiroto's direction. As she waved it back and forth hypnotically, she peered back at him over her shoulder with a coquettish blink of her heavily lashed eyes. He flashed her a narrow grin, his gold tooth glinting beneath the strobing red lights.

Marcus looked at him and then turned toward the girl.

"Hey," he yelled. "That's it. You're done."

The girl stopped dancing, and the crowd groaned while Hiroto glared at Marcus as if he meant to set him afire. Marcus responded with a heated stare of his own, the girl watching them both through terrified sea-blue eyes, her hands reflexively placed over her bare genitals.

"Here," said Marcus as he jammed his hand into his pocket. "He withdrew a money clip and tore off a few bills. "Take a break," he said as he tossed the cash onto the stage.

The girl swallowed once and then collapsed to her hands and knees. With a practiced sweep of the hand, she gathered up the money and hurried off the stage.

Hiroto said something in Japanese and stormed away, while Marcus turned his attention back toward Mario's office.

At last, the door swung open, and a pair of large men stepped out, followed by a thinner man with a manicured mustache and dark, slicked-back hair. Marcus folded his arms and watched them with false disinterest, his heart rate picking up as they approached.

"You are the one we see at the docks?" asked the man. He had bright green eyes and a nasal voice that matched his rat-like appearance.

Marcus looked at the man's associates, each dressed in finely tailored suits that did little to mask their formidable physiques.

"Yep," he said. "One of them anyway."

The man looked him up and down as if appraising an animal at a stock show.

"You do well," he said. "For the most part."

Marcus raised his eyebrows and pushed his lower lip out.

"Alright."

The man looked at him and frowned.

"We'd prefer to see some youth next time, however."

Marcus gave a little nod.

"Alright."

The rat-like man punctuated the exchange with a thin-lipped smile, and the three men pushed past and headed for the door.

"Mario wants you," said a voice from behind.

Marcus gave a nod and turned without acknowledging the big man who was already lost in the movements of a curly-headed young woman strutting onto the stage.

While the big man followed with a reluctant gait, Marcus approached Mario's office and waited outside while the place erupted with the dancer's music, something digital with a heavy, thumping beat.

"He out there?" yelled Mario from within his office.

"Yeah, boss," said the big man.

"Send him in."

The big man held out a hand.

"It's all you," he said with his thick Jersey accent.

Marcus walked into the room and stood with his hands behind his back.

"Everything good, boss?" he asked as the door fell shut behind him.

Mario sat at his desk, his eyes angled down toward his hands, which strangled each other in a fleshy entanglement of sausage-sized fingers, each one patterned with amateur prison tattoos that held hints toward his violent youthful days.

"You got your wish," he said with a soft growl.

Marcus raised his chin and lowered his eyebrows.

"What's that?"

Mario's bulbous eyes flicked upward.

"Jimmy's gone off the rails," he said. "It's time to rein him in."

Marcus took a step forward.

"Just say the word."

Mario sat back in his chair, and it squealed against the throes of his weight.

"You sure you're up for this?" he asked, his depthless eyes boring forth from within their sunken sockets, old but alive, like swirling pools of boiling ink.

Marcus looked into those eyes without faltering.

"Cut me loose," he said. "I only need 24 hours."

Mario held him in his gaze, his jaw working, eyes curious like a jeweler appraising the resilience of a stone.

"You know who you're dealing with?" he asked. "Do you understand?"

Marcus gave a quick nod.

"Yes."

Mario firmed his mouth.

"No bullshit," he said. "Do you really understand?"

Marcus nodded.

"I can handle it."

Mario tapped his finger on the desktop, mysterious thoughts running around within his oversized head. He watched the man before him a while longer, fingertips tapping faster and faster against the top of the desk.

"Alright," he said at last. "Do it."

Marcus nodded and turned.

"Marcus," said Mario, his voice like a lasso ensnaring the younger man's neck.

Marcus swallowed and looked back over his shoulder.

"Don't give him a chance," Mario said, something sad in his formidable stare. "That's all he needs. Just one chance. Test it, and you'll see."

Marcus gave a nod.

"He won't have a chance."

Mario gave a little nod.

"Get to it then."

He watched as Marcus rushed outside with all the vigor of youth. The same vigor Mario had known when he still had something to prove. When his body rippled with muscle and his plans were big enough to cow the world. Before he learned the world of his mind was not the world of the real. Not a world for the taking, where god-like men claimed their portion. But a world of rats and vermin, where people lie and kill to build their mountain of crumbs.

The door fell shut, and the old man sat in the lonely silence, his mind playing out possibilities, the things to come and the things best left in the past. Then he reached into his desk and withdrew a bottle of liquor which he steadily emptied as the night filled his thoughts with dread.

Chapter 16

Robin sat before a small wooden table, her buttocks aching against the unforgiving sternness of a stiff metal chair. She blinked around at the large, windowless room, which sat empty save for a small table and her chair and a floor lamp in the far corner, which gave off weak light and frightening shadows that stretched like giant fingers over the bare, unfinished walls.

A foul odor moved upon the air, a formidable scent of old sweat that hinted at the misfortunes of previous occupants. She clutched her bandaged arm and groaned as the musty fragrance wriggled its way up her nose and into her body with every shallow breath.

She swallowed dryly, her tongue swollen with thirst. Then she gave away what little moisture remained in her dehydrated body when she bowed her head to cry.

Almost as if cued by her weeping, the door shot open, and light poured into the room. Robin looked up to see a woman step inside, her eyes afire with flagrant satisfaction.

She had an ordinary build, and her hair was buzzed down to the scalp, but her eyes stared back like live wires, and her face seemed to be carved from marble stone.

Just behind the woman, others followed, heads pointed down in deference to their obvious leader. Just behind them came Jimmy, his face a mask of emotionless curiosity.

Robin raised her head and started to look them all over but quickly abandoned the enterprise under the weight of the woman's glare.

"Hello, Robin," said the woman. "It's nice to meet you at last."

Robin's lips quivered as the woman's words poured over her.

"Do you know me?" asked the woman, her head slightly acrook.

Robin swallowed.

"Yes."

The woman gave a closed-lip smile.

"How much do you know about me?"

Robin firmed her mouth.

"Enough."

The woman nodded.

"Good," she said. "That will make things easier."

She snapped her fingers, and one of her men brought a second chair which he placed on the opposite side of the table from Robin. The woman sat down and settled in her chair while the men leaned back against the far wall behind her.

"Sorry about the arm," said the woman. "You know how it is."

Robin swallowed and took several short breaths.

"What do you want from me?"

The woman sat back in her chair, her eyes running over Robin's bloody bandages.

"You know, I knew your father," she said. "A long time ago."

Robin said nothing, and the woman's eyes flicked over to her face.

"Nothing to say to that?"

Robin shrugged.

"What do you want me to say?"

The woman raised her eyebrows.

"Say whatever you want."

Robin looked past the woman.

"Why is he here?" She pointed toward Jimmy, who was standing between a pair of masked men on the other side of the room. "Does he work for you?"

The woman turned and looked back at Jimmy, who watched Robin with uninterpretable eyes.

"No," she said as she turned back. "He's your mistake" She shrugged. "A happy accident from my point of view."

Robin looked down at the table, her face looking pale and featureless where the tears had torn a path through her makeup.

"Am I here to die?" she asked.

The woman leaned back and laughed.

"No," she said.

Robin's eyes flicked upward.

"Then why am I here?"

The woman's smile disappeared.

"You're here to make things right. Or start on it anyway." She shrugged. "It's a long road toward making everything right. All the things you and your family have done. A long, long road. Probably longer than you've got to be honest."

Robin's face trembled as she tried to look at the woman, tears welling at the corners of both eyes.

"Not me," she said. "I never had a choice."

The woman gave a little smirk.

"No?" she asked as she looked Robin up and down. "Little miss put-upon, so innocent, so misunderstood." Her lip curled as she looked into Robin's face. "You don't think you have anything to apologize for? What about your man, here?"

She stuck a thumb over her shoulder without looking back while Robin glanced at Jimmy with a confused expression.

"What?"

The woman shrugged.

"He's been looking out for you, hasn't he?" she asked. "Taking up where poor Howard left off. I'm not sure he's on your side anymore, though. Not after you lied and put him in such danger." She clicked her tongue against the roof of her mouth. "Such terrible, terrible danger."

Robin glanced up at Jimmy, but his face was stony as ever.

"That's not true," she said. "I tried to keep him out of trouble. I warned him every step of the way. I told him to give it all up. To go on his own fucking way. I told him not to come to my home. I told him not to come to that party. I told him over and over, but he didn't listen."

The woman frowned.

"But you did lie."

Robin glanced up at Jimmy again, and then her gaze drifted down to the table.

"Yes."

The woman gave a closed-lip smile and tilted her eyebrows low.

"And what about his friend, Howard?" she asked. "You lied to him. You put him in danger."

Robin's eyes flicked up at Jimmy again, but he wore that same infuriating Jimmy mask.

"Yes," she said.

"Why?" asked the woman. "Why invite Howard to investigate your husband when you already knew everything there was to know? Why would you invite him into your little horror show? I mean, I like a good fuck as much as anyone, but I leave them alive so they can tell the story."

A tear broke loose from Robin's eye, and she reached to wipe it away.

"I didn't mean for Howard to get hurt."

The woman turned her palms upward.

"Jesus Christ," she said with a chuckle. "You know the Guild. You know what they're about better than anyone. Better than me, even. What did you think was going to happen?"

Robin looked up, unconcealed rage in her wet, red eyes.

"I didn't know," she said. "I didn't think. I just wanted out."

She swallowed and looked up at Jimmy, who stood with his arms folded, a sharp glint in his emotionless stare.

"Jimmy, I'm sorry," she said. "I really, truly am. I didn't want this. Not any of it. I asked Howard to help me get away, but he didn't understand. I wanted to start over somewhere else. Just like your son. I wanted a new life. I wanted a new name. But Howard wouldn't listen. He kept telling me to calm down. That I was being irrational. I thought if he saw, if he really saw, he would understand and help me get away."

Jimmy looked back at her with that selfsame stare, but his jaw was working overtime beneath his whiskered chin.

The woman eyed Robin for a moment, her eyes dancing over her skin, her hair, her bleeding wound and, finally, her bold, wet eyes.

"Alright," she said at last. "I can work with that."

Robin looked at Jimmy and then back at the woman.

"What?"

The woman leaned back in her seat and smiled.

"You know, Robin," she said. "You and I aren't really that different."

Robin looked at her as if she'd spoken French.

"What?"

The woman put a hand up.

"Don't get me wrong; we're very different. Just not in the ways you think."

The woman leaned forward, and Robin jerked back.

"Believe it or not, I really was once like you. Helpless and wanting, unsure of my every step.

The woman's face took on a look of unchallengeable compassion.

"I know," she said, her voice like satin. "I really do." She leaned ever closer and clasped Robin's hands." You're not a bad person for what you've done. You didn't have any choice. I get that. That's what they do, Robin. They make you an accomplice in their game. They don't give you a say." She leaned back in her chair and shrugged. "You have my sympathy. All that I have left anyway, which I have to be honest, isn't much at this point."

Robin's eyes dipped back down toward the table, her chin dimpling as she forced back more tears.

"Robin," said the woman, a sharp crack knifing the quiet air as she snapped her fingers.

Robin looked up, her eyes advertising hopelessness and fear.

"I'm going to stop them," said the woman with a broad, terrifying grin. "I'm going to make them pay for what they've done. They'll pay. They'll pay in ways you can't imagine. Oh, yes, they'll pay and pay."

Robin shook her head, eyes gleaming with moisture.

"You can't," she said. "No one can."

The woman leaned forward and looked her in the eye.

"I can," she said. "With your help."

Robin rubbed her forehead and let out a bumpy sigh.

"How?"

"Your husband," said the woman.

Robin shrugged.

"Michael?" she asked.

The woman frowned.

"Do you have any other husbands we don't know about?"

Robin looked up at Jimmy, but he stared back like someone who'd already heard this speech.

"How can Michael help?" she asked.

The woman eyed her with genuine disappointment.

"Are you kidding? He works at Viox Genomics, for Christ's sake."

Robin shook her head.

"So?"

The woman chuckled and shook her head.

"Viox is everything, Robin. What, did you think they just made cold medicine and vaginal cream?"

Robin pinched her eyebrows together.

"I don't understand."

The woman scratched her jaw and took a deep breath as if summoning the patience for the smallest of minds.

"You don't have to understand," she said. "You just need to get him on board."

Now it was Robin who choked back a laugh.

"Get Michael on board?" She gestured toward Jimmy and the masked gunmen. "With this?" She shook her head. "Why would he risk his life for this? Why would anyone go along with any of this?"

She waited for a response, but the woman said nothing.

"Why not just force him," said Robin at last. "Why not just take him like you did me?"

The woman shook her head.

"No," she said. "He has to be willing. This is no small feat. Viox is not a company. It's a fortress with its own version of the CIA. It will take weeks. Months, maybe. I'll need Michael deep on the inside, blending in like always. Fully compliant. Not with a knife to his throat but with a purpose. A deep, meaningful purpose fueling his every move."

Robin looked away and sighed.

"This is insane," she said.

The woman raised her eyebrows.

"It's your one way out. Your only way out."

Robin frowned up at her face and met her electric gaze.

"Why are you doing this?" she asked. "Why does any of this matter to you?"

The woman shook her head, her face relaxed, but her eyes seemed to light up from the inside.

"Why does it matter?" she asked. "Would the answer change anything?"

Robin sniffled and wiped her eyes.

"Why should I help you?" she asked. "What can you offer me?"

The woman smiled.

"I can help you get away, A new life, a brand-new name. You said before that you knew who I was. If you really do know me, then you know I can do this for you."

Robin looked over the woman's shoulder, but Jimmy's face gave her nothing to work with.

"I can save you from them," said the woman. "I can save you from this life. From the terrible things coming your way. But most of all, I can save you from yourself."

Robin wiped a tear from her cheek and stared down at the table.

"What do I have to do?"

The woman raised her eyebrows.

"Just convince Michael to get on board," she said. "I'll do the rest after that. You can leave and live your new life. You help me, and I help you. It's that simple."

Robin's eyes flicked up.

"What about Jean Paul?" she asked. "Aren't you scared of him? Isn't he dangerous?"

The woman's eyes widened.

"Oh, yes," she said. "More dangerous than you can possibly imagine. You'd be shocked by the things he's done. Whatever you can think of, however terrible, however brutal, he's done them all. And those things he's done, they don't even scratch the surface of what he's willing to do. What he would do if given the power."

The woman leaned forward and interlaced her fingers atop the table.

"But he's not the one you should be worried about."

Robin gave a half-exhausted chuckle and wiped more tears from her eyes.

"Really?" she said. "There's someone worse than him?"

The woman nodded slowly.

"Oh, yes. There's always someone worse."

Chapter 17

The woman watched as Jimmy and Robin climbed into his car, their faces stony as they digested the change in their worlds. Jimmy stuck the key in the ignition and brought the thing to life. Then, without the slightest hesitation, he backed the car out of the lot and sped away.

In the rearview mirror, he could see the woman watching them, her arms folded, eyes cold and hard even as she diminished in the distance. At last, they turned a corner and escaped her piercing stare, the car joining highway traffic which moved in drone-like masses amid the darkness of night. Jimmy's cheeks puffed up as he blew out a great sigh.

"There's an intensity to that woman," he said.

Robin rubbed the bandage on her arm.

"I'm sorry, Jimmy," she said.

He looked at her and frowned.

"For what?"

She glanced at him for a moment and then looked away.

"For deceiving you."

He shrugged.

"Forget it," he said. "I understand."

She started to say something else, but he cut her off.

"Just save it," he said. "I'm not interested in apologies. What I am interested in is that woman. You seem to know her. Who is she really?"

Robin stared out the window, the streetlights flickering across her face in the darkness.

"Someone dangerous."

Jimmy gripped the steering wheel.

"No shit," he said. "That's not good enough. I need to know more. I need to know a lot more. I need to know everything you know. With what we're into, I have to know everything."

Robin looked over at him.

"We?" she said. "I'm the one who's in trouble, Jimmy. Not you."

Jimmy flexed his jaw.

"No," he said. "We're both in trouble now."

Robin said nothing, her eyes watching his face, which seemed vulnerable now and older than ever.

"I was told to let this whole thing go," he continued. "And I didn't. So, now I have to face the consequences."

Robin pinched her eyebrows together.

"What do you mean?" she asked. "Told by whom?"

Jimmy shook his head.

"It doesn't matter. The point is I don't have a lot of time to work this out, and I need to know everything you know."

Robin shook her head.

"No," she said. "If you want to know what I know, tell me what you're talking about."

Jimmy stared forward, his jaw working beneath his whiskered flesh.

"I'm not what you think," he said. "I mean, I am in some ways." He rubbed his chin as cars rushed past in the night. "But I work for some bad people."

Robin watched him, her face paled by fear and exhaustion.

"I thought you were a private investigator."

He shrugged.

"I am," he said. "I mean, I am part-time."

She swallowed.

"And the rest of the time?"

He scratched his jaw.

"Look, it's not important," he said. "What's important is I made mistakes, and now they've come back to bite me."

Robin watched him, her eyes assessing him anew.

"Howard said you used to be a cop."

Jimmy's jaw flexed.

"Yeah, well. I used to be a lot of things. A cop. A husband. A dad. I used to be worth a shit. Someone you could count on. Someone who always knew the right way. Someone who always took the right way no matter what." He cleared his throat and swallowed. "I used to be better, but now I'm this. That's what I am now, and there's nothing for it."

Robin breathed in the silence.

"What are you saying, Jimmy?"

He bit at his lip.

"I'm saying I've done a lot of bad things to get me to this exact point in my life. Made all kinds of bad choices. Sometimes for the right reasons. Mostly for my own. But whatever the case, there's a whole crew of connected people looking for me right now. You can bet your life on that. And if they find me before we do this thing, I'll be dead, and so will you if you're with me when they catch up, which they will eventually. No way around it."

Robin turned away and looked out her window, the world seeming distant in the darkness beyond the window glass.

"I used to be something too," she said. "Or at least I thought so. Now, I don't know. Now, I think I might be the villain in this story. It makes me want to laugh. Me, this scared, pathetic person. The villain. How is that possible? How can someone this weak be a villain?"

She shook her head and snorted as tears streamed down her cheeks.

"Maybe I was always like this. Maybe it's all been a story I told myself."

Jimmy frowned into the distant taillights.

"No," he said. "You're just caught up in some shit. If you were a villain, you wouldn't want out. Trust me. A true villain can tell."

She whipped her head around.

"You're not a villain, Jimmy," she said.

He frowned.

"Ok," he said. "That's enough."

She swallowed.

"No, I mean it."

He squeezed the steering wheel.

"Alright," he said. "I appreciate it, but stop."

She watched him in the darkness, his scruffy face looking tired from the night and all the long years.

"Ok," she said. "If that's what you want, I won't say how I feel. But what I will say is this. I want you to go. If what you say is true, if there are people coming for you, then go. Don't wait around for them. Just go. Don't let me be the cause of your death. I can't handle that."

He stared forward into the night, his jaw twitching as he chewed his teeth.

"I hate to leave you high and dry."

She shook her head.

"You're not. There's nothing you can do anymore. It's all up to me now."

He took a deep breath and frowned.

"What about Howard?" he asked. "Someone needs to pay for that."

She shook her head.

"That's out of our hands, now, Jimmy. There's nothing we can do."

He stared at the road, his eyes taking in the world, mind considering her words.

"Well," he said. "I wish you luck."

She nodded and looked away, her eyes leaking fresh tears as she watched the city lights twinkle in the gloomy night. They rode in silence the rest of the way, and when he dropped her off at her car, there seemed to be a growing distance between them.

He watched her open the door and step out of the car, his head bending low to get a view of her face.

"Robin," he said.

She turned and looked at him, her body hunched in a way that made her seem weak and small.

"You're not pathetic," he said. "There's strength in you. I can see it."

She snorted the air and gave a closed-lip smile.

"Thanks for your help, Jimmy."

He nodded.

"Good luck."

She turned away and got in her car.

Chapter 18

10:30 P.M.

Jimmy's car crept over the empty parking lot, his tires crunching the cracked asphalt as he looked all around. High above, wisps of clouds sailed the air, blotting out the moonlight as they drifted across a starless sky. While the engine gurgled in the quiet night, he peered into the blackness, his eyes straining to see movement of any kind. But amid the inky pitch, he couldn't make out anything at all, save for the abandoned self-storage facility with the rusted metal gate.

He finally stowed his car next to the crumbling structure and stepped out into the night, pain knifing up and down his leg as he struggled to his feet. He slipped his pistol into his waistband and looked around once more, his nose testing the air for, what? He wasn't sure. After a couple of minutes, he limped away from the vehicle, his shins lashed by the tall weeds jutting up from great cracks in the broken blacktop.

After about a hundred yards, he reached the chain link fence, which cut a lonely path across a sprawling undeveloped grass lot. He put his hands on his hips and looked up at the shaky structure, orange with rust and twelve-feet high. He bent his head and spat. Then he dug his fingers into the wire mesh and pulled himself upward hand over hand until he arrived at the top.

There he paused, his teeth clenching hard as he took several quick breaths, like a shivering diver summoning the will to plunge into an icy lake. With a little yelp, he threw his bad leg over and straddled the fence top, the pain instant and white-hot. As sweat bled from his forehead, he brought across his other leg and carefully descended to the ground.

With a final burst of pain, he dropped to his feet, his breathing rapid as he gathered his composure. Above in the heavens, the clouds pushed past the moon for a moment, and the space grew visible around him. He looked over the barren land, the tall yellow grasses spoiled by beer cans and other garbage as it flitted in the warm wind.

A putrid scent stung his nostrils, and he followed the odor down to the creek, its gushing waters thick with toxic pollutants and septic waste. With a sigh, Jimmy plopped down onto the ground and removed his shoes and socks. Then he rolled up his pant legs and climbed back to his feet.

In a rare gesture of mercy, the heavens closed up again with cloud cover, and the stinking creek disappeared into the sightless night. Blindly, Jimmy stepped down into the rushing slurry, his toes pushing deep into a greasy sludge. As oils and feces gathered around his bare knees, he slogged across the foul stream, his leg plunging into sucking holes that threatened to take him down into the suffocating filth. At last, he arrived at the other bank and climbed up onto dry ground, where he bent and heaved dryly over a pile of broken glass.

When he finally collected himself, he gathered up a fistful of dried grass and scrubbed his legs and feet half-clean. Then he rolled down his pants and put on his shoes.

Now, he was hurrying across the other half of the field, the faint hint of another fence growing larger amid the blackness. When he finally reached the flimsy sheet metal wall, he walked a familiar path until he reached a warped stretch that ended in a flapping fold.

He took the edge of the metal and bent it upward until he'd created enough space to squeeze through. With some effort, he knelt and pushed himself into the gape and onto the other side.

He stood and looked around at his little neighborhood, no suspicious vehicles, everything ordinary as ever, at least to the naked eye. He reached back and touched his pistol as if to make sure it was still there. Somewhere in the distance, a dog barked.

Still reeking of putrid creek water, Jimmy trotted through the darkness, his footsteps quiet even hindered by injury and age. With all possible caution, he made his way to the backside of his little house, where he peered through windows, gun up and ready, heart steady as ever. Inside, he could see little, the weak light above the stovetop, slices of streetlight on the floor as it bled in through the front window shades.

After a few more minutes, he crept up to his backdoor and pushed a key into the deadbolt lock. With a quick twist, he unlocked the door and slipped inside, his gun up and sweeping left to right as he crept across the linoleum tile.

As he approached the kitchen entryway, he stopped and waited for his dog to growl. To come shuffling into the room. To do anything at all. But his straining ears were greeted by silence, and this made him choke his fingers around the pistol grip.

With a gentle hand, he pushed the door shut behind him and flipped the lock to cover his backside. Then he moved across the kitchen floor, his pistol leveled at the passage leading into the living area.

When he neared the opening, he flattened his back against the wall and eased himself closer to the edge, his gun in both hands close to his chest. With a practiced movement, he spun his body around and filled the opening, his gun up and ready as he sank to one knee.

A low whimper broke the quiet, and Jimmy sucked in a breath.

"C'mon, Barney," he said as he lowered his pistol.

He heard a slow shuffling as the yellow retriever limped into the room, his happy face weakly lit by the streetlight filtering through the window.

"Hey," whispered Jimmy as he reached out a hand. "Come here."

The dog came closer, and Jimmy rubbed his ear.

"You hungry?"

He stood up and crossed the floor, the dog following behind with little wheezing breaths. Jimmy opened the pantry and took out a large can of dog food. He worked it open with an old-school handheld can opener and shook the stubborn contents out with a wet shloomp into an empty metal bowl. The dog sniffed the food and ate.

Jimmy scratched the dog's ear and frowned.

"That's right," he whispered. "Eat up, buddy."

He stood up and explored the rest of the house for the sake of caution, knowing all the while every closet would be empty if the dog was this calm. When he finished, he lowered the gun and slipped it back into his waistband. He rushed across the floor and peered through the window shades, his eyes assessing the sleepy street without finding reasons for concern.

Then, as if muted by stress, his senses regained consciousness and alerted him to the smell. With a quick hand, he tested the front locks to make sure they were secure and then hurried into the kitchen, where Barney slowly gummed his food. While the dog ate, Jimmy stripped away his clothing and stuffed it into a large plastic trash bag. Then, against his better judgment, he hurried to the bathroom and twisted on the shower.

He shut the bathroom door and set the lock. He set his pistol on the toilet and stepped beneath the rushing water, the soothing warmth raining down on his flesh and washing him clean.

Amid the darkness, he scrubbed away the creek filth, other people's body waste coming loose and swirling brown around the slurping drain.

Something creaked outside the bathroom door.

As the shower sprayed down on his skin, Jimmy cocked his head and listened.

Another creek.

While the water ran, he pulled back the vinyl curtain and stepped out onto the floor, water puddling on the tile beneath his naked body.

Amid the steaming blackness, he fumbled for his gun, wet hands knocking it off the toilet and onto the indiscernible floor. With a silent curse, he knelt and searched all around, his eyes trained on the strip of weak light at the bottom of the door.

As his fingers probed all around, a shadow interrupted the light. Someone outside.

Without looking away, he continued searching all around until his hand finally found the cold metal pressed up against the porcelain tub. With a sudden motion, he collected the gun by the barrel end and flipped it around like some sort of street performer doing uncommon tricks.

Now the strip of light reformed as the shadow disappeared. Jimmy waited and watched, steam fogging the air as the shower pounded the tub.

After a couple of moments, he stood up and raised a hand to the doorknob, the metal slick and wet like everything else in the room.

With a slippery twist, he turned it and pulled open the door, gun leveled and ready, face covered in water and new sweat.

Barney looked up at him and whined.

"Jesus," he said as he lowered his weapon. "You scared me half to death, boy."

The dog looked up at him and whimpered.

"Alright," said Jimmy as he reached for a towel.

He dried his body and dressed. Then he went into his bedroom and opened the closet door. He struggled down onto his knees and pulled the carpet back, exposing a flat piece of plywood. He placed his palm against it and worked it free with a wobble. He lifted it and set it aside. Within the hollowed space, there was a big black bag. He collected the bag and zipped it open. Inside, there was a passport, a change of clothes and $50,000 in cash. He zipped it shut and set it aside. Then he replaced the wood and the carpet and struggled up onto his feet.

He turned his head and saw the dog standing in the doorway, its face limp, eyes neither curious nor accusing. Jimmy looked at him and frowned.

"Alright, buddy," he said. "Let's go."

11:13 P.M.

On the good side of town, Robin pulled into the driveway and killed the engine. She looked at the house and swallowed, her hands turning white as she strangled the steering wheel.

The inside of the house was completely dark, save for a weak bulb leaking light from a pair of cloth curtains in the kitchen window. She looked at it and took a deep breath, her pulse picking up as she opened the car door and stepped outside.

The smell of cut grass wafted through the evening air as the moonlight bathed her pale skin in a luminous glow. She looked at her hands and tried to stay the trembling. Then, she took another deep breath and made her way to the front door.

With a reticent hand, she jammed her key into the doorknob and twisted, but the door was already unlocked. She pushed it open, and the hinges gave a little cry which split the quiet and sent a chill up her spine.

She looked around, her eyes peering into the darkness, one foot in, one foot still outside, as if part of her still held out hopes for some improbable alternative reality.

"Michael?" she called, her voice weak and faltering in the hollowness of the dark home.

One by one, she flipped on the lamps and overhead lights, each one providing a pop of warmth that made her feel stronger and more secure. Then, one by one, she searched the rooms, her hands curled into little fleshy hammers. For what purpose? She did not know.

"Michael?" she called as she moved from room to room, her shoes creaking on the wood floor with every tiny step, heart tapping against her chest with rapid little beats.

But every room sat empty, save for the painstaking order and overpriced décor. She walked into the living room, where their wedding photo stared down from the center of the wall.

"Bonded for eternity," it said on the frame, lustrous silver and polished every day. Her lip curled as she looked it over, her younger self staring back with youthful beauty and hopeless naivety that filled her with rage and pity and depthless shame. She shook her head and put her hands on her hips.

"Michael?" she called one last time.

She waited for an answer, her heart rate slowing amid the comfort of apparent solitude.

And then she saw him through the sliding glass door.

With a start, she flinched as if laying eyes on the masked killer from some third-rate horror movie, the teenage star's head dangling from his bloody hand. But Michael wore no mask and held no head. Instead, he sat on the back porch with his back to the house, shoulders slouched, head bowed in what seemed like authentic grief.

She watched him through the glass door, his broad body silhouetted in the low light. Above his slumping head, summer insects swarmed the weak bulb in a cloud of flickering wings. Near his foot, their dog lay still and quiet, tail flipping from one side to the other, big eyes watching its master with a longing — no, loving — stare.

Robin approached the dining table and put her hands on the back of a chair. As she looked upon her husband, slouched and defeated and small despite his size, she probed the depths of her inner workings for feelings, something to make her care. If not love, then compassion. Whatever had been there in their early, dream-filled days. But if there was any fondness left in the dregs of her wilting heart, it turned to hate when she watched him draw back his boot and drive it into the dog.

"Michael!" she shouted reflexively as the animal's cries filled the backyard.

With a chilling slowness, Michael turned his dark, featureless body and looked into the house. Without thinking, she took an involuntary step back and swallowed the void in her throat. Then, while the dog limped off to the far corner of the yard, she shook her head and stormed away.

Michael watched her disappear around the corner. Then he reached down and collected his glass of red wine. With a tip over his chin, he emptied the glass with three big swallows. He stood and stretched his back while the dog watched him from afar with mute terror. Michael glared at the animal until it looked away. As the evening breeze bent the hairs on his arm, he inhaled the night. Then he turned away and dragged open the sliding glass door.

Inside, he found Robin seated upon the small sofa in their bedroom, her legs crossed, toe bouncing as she watched him enter the room. He staggered in with a drunken gait and sat down on the edge of the bed.

"Where have you been? he asked, voice flat as if he didn't really even care.

She shrugged.

"I wasn't as lucky as you."

He looked at the big bandage on her arm.

"Did Jean Paul do that?"

She said nothing, her eyes boring into his. He bit his lip and shook his head.

"What have you done to us, Robin?"

She swallowed and firmed her mouth.

"I'm sorry, Michael."

The eyebrows lowered over his heavily pupiled eyes.

"Sorry?" he said. "You're fucking sorry?" He leaned forward and showed his perfect teeth. "You may have gotten us killed, Robin. We have to stand in front of the board now, and who knows what the fuck they're going to say. We could end up in one of those rooms, Robin. No matter what, we'll end up with demotions. And you know what that means? It means relocation, Robin. Somewhere cold and isolated. It means no freedoms and no privileges. It means being watched all the fucking time." He raised his hands and gestured toward the walls. "It means no more of this. No more money. It means building back up from the bottom."

Robin said nothing, her eyes struggling to hold his gaze.

"And you fucked that guy," he said with disgust. "That fucking lawyer from TV. You let that guy stick his filthy dick in you."

Robin showed her teeth.

"And how many women have you stuck your filthy dick in, Michael? Not just since we've been married. Let's just start with the last couple months."

He turned his head and sniffed.

"That's different."

She leaned forward.

"Why?"

He turned back toward her and sneered.

"Because it didn't get us in trouble with the Guild."

She watched him stand and storm out of the room, her heart racing, foot bobbing as she calmed her nerves. After a couple of minutes, she stood and made her way to the kitchen, where Michael was busy filling another glass of wine.

"Michael," she said. "Stop drinking."

He chuckled as he continued to pour, the dark liquid sloshing over the rim and onto the granite countertop. Out of habit, she felt herself starting to admonish him, starting to explain how the little splash would leave a permanent stain in the porous natural stone. Then she almost burst into laughter at the ridiculousness of her thoughts.

"Michael, I'm serious. We have something important to talk about."

He finished pouring and set the bottle aside.

"Do we?" he asked as he raised the glass to his lips.

Robin watched as he took two big swallows.

"Michael," she said. "I need you with a clear head right now."

He chuckled again and shook his head, eyes pointed toward the cabinetry, hair uncharacteristically mussed.

"You need me," he asked. "Well, what do you know?"

Robin rubbed her forehead.

"Come outside with me, Michael," she said. "Let's talk."

He watched her slide open the glass door and step out beneath the halo of porch light.

11:35 P.M.

The detective had interviewed all the relevant witnesses, and he still didn't have a suspect. The pretty college student had an alibi, and she gave it with a flick of her long, lovely lashes. She said she was asleep in her dorm room, and her roommate could corroborate the story because she was just a few feet away studying for the big exam.

The accountant's story was just as strong. He was in Omaha at a conference, and there were 50 other attendees that could confirm his presence.

The ex-husband's story seemed just as ironclad. He was on a date with a girl he met online, and there were plenty of digital records to back up his claim.

Patty Jenkins knew better. And not just because she'd seen this episode before. She had a knack for this kind of thing, and she never missed a chance to advertise it.

"You still don't know?" she asked her husband.

"Quiet, Patty," he said. "I haven't seen this one."

Patty tapped her foot and frowned.

"Come on, Robert," she said. "It's just so obvious."

"Damn it, Patty. Let me watch it."

The detective slammed his hand down on the interrogation table, and the accountant flinched.

"Is it him?" asked Robert.

Patty shook her head and shrugged.

"I'm not telling."

"It's the college girl," said a little voice from down the hall.

"Allie!" Patty yelled as she turned in her chair. "You're supposed to be in bed!"

Robert shook his head and reached for the remote.

"That's it," he said as he leveled it at the television. "I'm watching the late show."

There were three sharp bangs at the door.

"What in the world?" asked Patty as she stood up.

Robert watched her cross the room, his mouth tugged down into a frown.

"Look in the peephole," he said.

Patty looked back at him and rolled her eyes.

"I mean it, Patty," he said as he struggled out of his recliner.

Patty approached the door and pulled it open.

"Who is it?" asked Robert as he rushed up behind her.

Jimmy stood beneath the porch light, his face looking tired as ever.

"Hey, Jimmy," she said. "What's up?"

"Hello, Patty," said Jimmy with a closed-lip smile. "Robert."

Robert sidled up behind his wife and frowned.

"Kind of late, ain't it, Jimmy?"

Jimmy gave an apologetic nod.

"Yes, and I'm very sorry," he said. "I wouldn't bother you unless it was important."

"Barney!" yelled a little girl's voice.

Patty and Robert parted as Allie rushed between them. They all watched as she knelt to embrace the dog.

"I need someone to watch him," said Jimmy. "I have to leave town for a while."

Patty smiled.

"Of course, Jimmy," she said.

The little girl shrieked with delight while Robert scratched his chin.

"How long will you be away?" he asked.

Jimmy shrugged.

"Oh, not too long. Just a few days, hopefully."

Robert started to say something, but Patty silenced him with a glare.

"It's fine, Jimmy," she said. "Whatever you need."

Jimmy reached into his pocket and withdrew a handful of cash.

"This should cover his food," he said. "And help with the inconvenience."

Patty started to object, but now Robert wielded the glare.

"That's just fine," he said as he collected the money. "We'll take good care of him." He looked down at the girl and smiled. "Ain't that right, hon?"

Allie looked up and grinned.

"Yes!"

Jimmy looked down and nodded.

"That's what I figured," he said. "I appreciate it."

Patty smiled.

"Of course."

Jimmy knelt down and rubbed Barney's ear.

"Alright," he said to the whining dog.

Barney looked at him, and somewhere in the depths of those old wet eyes, it seemed like he knew.

"I'll see you, boy," said Jimmy as he leaned in closer.

The old dog whined again and licked his nose.

"Alright," Jimmy said again, a catch in his throat that no one could miss.

"Everything alright, Jimmy?" asked Patty as she eyed him with evident concern.

"Oh, yeah," said Jimmy. "I'm good."

He stood up and swallowed while the little family watched from the other side of the threshold.

"Thanks again."

With that, he turned and walked away with his head pointed down, the dog watching as he disappeared into the night.

12:17 A.M.

Robin sat in a little lawn chair, her hands folded neatly atop her lap, eyes slightly wet and glistening in the moonlight as she gazed up with unconcealed desperation.

Before her, Michael paced across their back porch, shaking his head in disbelief as he tried to make sense of what she had told him, his reality irrevocably altered as her words shattered all his grand ambitions and dismantled his carefully crafted plans.

"You cannot be serious," he asked. "This has to be a joke."

Robin unclasped her hands and leaned forward.

"Listen, Michael," she said slowly. "This is our only way out."

Michael shook his head in disbelief.

"No, Robin, this is fucking suicide."

Robin firmed her mouth.

"Suicide is doing nothing, Michael. Suicide is lying still and waiting for the guillotine to slide down and chop off your head."

Michael turned his back and looked out into the yard, where the dog watched him, its body nearly invisible within the darkness.

"That's easy for you to say," he said. "I'm the one who will have to do all this. I'm the one who will be putting everything at risk. You don't know Viox. They're not what you think."

She said nothing while he rubbed his forehead and thought. At last, he turned around.

"Who is this woman?" he asked. "Do you even know her?"

Robin nodded.

"I know of her," she said. "From my father."

Michael rubbed his jaw thoughtfully.

"Can we trust her?"

Robin swallowed.

"Yes," she said. "I think so."

Michael dropped his hand to his side.

"You think so."

Robin shrugged.

"What other choice do we have, Michael? We're out of options at this point. We're in too deep."

Michael shook his head.

"No, you're out of options," he said as he withdrew his cellphone from his pocket. "I can call Benjamin or Jean Paul right now and tell them what you're up to."

Robin's eyes flicked to the phone for a moment and then settled back on Michael's face.

"And what do you think they'll do, Michael?" she asked. "I'll take all the blame, and you'll get off with a warning? Perhaps you'll get a new wife, someone younger maybe, a bit fitter, silicone tits that never go flat. Then they'll set you both up in a nice upscale property in Malibu. You can work on your golf game while you butcher the locals."

She crossed her arms and sat back in her chair.

"Get real. You're in this as deep as me."

His face turned pale as her words flowed over him. Then the color came rushing back, and his face lit up with rage.

"You put me in this bind," he said, his voice starting to slur now, slobber at the corners of his mouth. "We had everything, and you fucked it all up."

Robin stood up and pointed a slender finger at him.

"No, Michael, you have everything." She took a step forward. "You got to go out and live your life. I had to turn into Suzy Homemaker while you got to become someone."

Michael narrowed his eyes.

"Oh yeah, you had it so bad," he hissed. "Shopping all the time, spending money on clothes, living a life of luxury, while I worked my ass off, plunged my hands into filth, every fucking day, to give it to you."

They stood before each other, fists clenched, eyes throwing out hate. The evening breeze washed between them. An owl hooted up in the trees.

"Fine," said Robin in a low, flat voice. "I'll be the villain, and you can be the martyr. I don't care anymore. If that's what it takes, I accept it. But we have to work together to get out of this mess. It doesn't have to be forever. It just has to be right now. For however long it takes. Then we can both start over and go our separate ways."

He looked her up and down with disgust, his drunken body wavering in the moonlight. Then, without speaking, he pushed past her and went back inside.

"Michael," called Robin as she turned to follow him.

He had the wine bottle again, its thin neck strangled amid his clenched hand.

"Stop drinking, Michael," she said. "You need a clear head."

With a sudden movement, he spun around and hurled the bottle at her, his flashing face a blur of rage and gritted white teeth. Robin raised her hands, but the bottle clanged off the top of her shoulder and spun end over end toward the sliding glass door, which shattered to pieces in an explosion of big geometric shards.

Robin turned and looked at the broken door, a shaky hand clutching her shoulder, evening air washing through the great jagged gape. Out in the yard, she could see the dog watching, its eyes set afire by the moonlight, like two glowing orbs amid the black night.

She turned toward Michael, but he had already left the room.

"Jesus Christ," she whispered to herself with a quivering voice.

She crept out of the kitchen and into the living room, where she confronted more shattered glass. This time, from their wedding photo, which Michael had torn from the wall.

There it lay on the floor at her feet, the image warped by the impact, frame bent all wrong. She looked around the empty living room and listened to what sounded like Michael sobbing in the master bedroom. She swallowed hard and looked at her purse, a deep internal gravity pulling her toward the front door. She glanced toward the hallway, toward the muffled whimpers and snorts. And then she collected her purse and hurried out of the house.

Seconds later, she sat behind the wheel of her car, the engine idling as she stared ahead toward the garage door. She had a hand on the gear stick, ready to put it in reverse. Ready to flee this house and this man. Ready to drive forever without looking back. Drive and drive and drive until ...

Until what? Until she ran out of gas? Until her money was all gone? Until she was homeless and hunted and hopelessly alone?

A deep despair chilled her aching body, and she bent her head to cry. As the steering wheel pressed against her forehead, she considered every option, every possibility. But her predicament was certain, so she brought a trembling hand to the ignition and turned the key. As the engine fell silent, she lifted her chin and breathed the air, her lungs filling with several jittery breaths. Then she stepped out of the car and forced her legs to carry her back into the house.

She opened the door and crept inside, her mind willing her body and face into something wooden, a sturdy facade that advertised confidence. Then she stepped over the mangled wedding photo and made her way to the master bedroom.

Inside, Michael sat at the foot of the bed, his broad back turned, blood dripping from a cut on his right hand.

"Michael," Robin said softly as she held the door jamb for support. "Are you alright?"

He didn't answer, his body heaving with rapid breathing as he stared at the bottom of the wall.

"Michael," said Robin. "I'm sorry I upset you. I'm sorry for everything. I truly am."

He said nothing, the silence like a splinter in her ears.

"Michael— "

"It's too late," he said with a low flat tone.

Robin took a step into the room.

"I know it feels that way," she said. "But it's not true. It's not too late. There is still time to make things right. There is still time to make a good life."

He turned and showed her his bloodshot eyes.

"No," he said. "It's too late."

She looked at his hand, and her face went white.

"What did you do, Michael?"

He followed her eyes to his hand and shrugged.

"What I had to," he said. "You didn't leave me a choice."

In his hand, damp with blood from his small wound, he held his cellphone. He looked at it for a moment, and then his eyes shot up to hers.

"They're coming," he said. "Tonight. Right now."

Without another word, she turned and ran, her shoes clacking the wood floor as she entered the living room. But before she could make it halfway to the door, he was upon her, his big, muscled body pulling her to the ground.

With a thin cry, she fell, her body crunching under his weight against the floor, sharp pains knifing through her ribs and collarbone. Without much effort, he raised up and straddled her waist, his hands pinning her wrists up over her head.

"You're not leaving," he said.

Spit flecks dropped from his mouth and stuck against her face.

"Stop it, Michael," she shrieked. "Let me go!"

He hovered over her, his lips curled up over his teeth.

"I'm not taking the fall for you," he said. "You're going to pay for this. Not me."

She looked up at him, her eyes wild with terror.

"You're crazy, Michael. They're not going to let you go. They're going to kill you. They're going to kill us both. Or worse. You know it's true."

He shook his head.

"No," he said. "You're wrong. They already told me on the phone."

Robin licked her lips and raised her eyebrows.

"Listen to me," she said slowly, her chest heaving as she struggled to breathe beneath his weight. "They will say anything to get their way. But they will kill you, Michael. They don't forgive. Not for things like this."

She thought she saw uncertainty take root within his bulging eyes, some tiny ember of doubt, so she steadied her voice and tried to fan it into a flame.

"You have to let me go," she said. "Now, before it's too late. You can come with me. We can help each other. I have help lined up. We can get away."

He looked off for a moment, the gears turning in his head as he worked it out in his mind.

"No," he said as he shook his head. "It's too late."

"It's not, Michael," she said.

He squeezed her wrists as if trying to pinch her hands off her arms. She screamed as he leaned down closer.

"Shut up," he yelled.

He let loose of her wrists and took hold of her neck.

"Shut up! Shut up! Shut up!"

She wheezed and gasped as she wrapped her newly freed hands around his wrists, her face purpling as he choked the air from her brain.

And then he stopped and turned his head toward the low growl to his side.

As if held at gunpoint, he released Robin's neck and raised his palms into the air.

"Easy, boy," he said with his silkiest voice. "Shh."

The dog was there watching his movements with wide, dark eyes, its lips curled up from its gleaming white teeth, hackles raised down the length of its spine.

Michael reached toward it with a slow hand, his face a mask of kindness and serenity, eyebrows up, lips stretched into a soft, gentle smile.

As if jolted by something electric, Robin jerked conscious, her body bucking upward as she struggled against Michael's weight. With a sudden reflex, he slapped her with the back of his other hand, and the dog lunged forward, its mouth open in a whir of snapping teeth.

Michael shrieked as the dog ensnared his hand, blood spurting over its nose as it pulled and shook.

He yelled and cursed, his other hand hammering down on the animal as it anchored its body low and pulled him toward the ground.

While Michael struggled with the dog, Robin wormed her way free and spun over onto her hands and knees.

Soon she was up on her feet, stumbling toward the kitchen while Michael pounded his fist against the beast's brow, blood puddling on the floor beneath its pink-stained jaws.

At last, one of the blows stunned the beast, which released its hold and yelped as it retreated against the wall. Michael climbed to his feet and drew his leg back to drive a kick into the cowering animal, but it had seen this movement before and responded by fleeing around the corner and back out into the yard.

Drunk, wild-eyed and leaking blood, Michael stomped toward the kitchen, his shoes pounding the floor like hammers on an anvil.

He rounded the corner and stood watching as Robin backed against the wall, skin pale, mascara smeared across her sweaty face.

"Get back, Michael," she said, her voice weak and raspy.

In her hand, she held a large, serrated knife, which glinted its warning beneath the artificial light. Michael looked her up and down with disgust.

"What are you going to do with that?" he asked.

She gripped the knife and swallowed.

"I'm leaving Michael."

He shook his head and showed his perfect white teeth.

"No."

She squeezed the knife as he started toward her.

12:45 A.M.

Marcus gripped the steering wheel and flexed his jaw, the highway traffic gushing around them as people blared their horns. He chewed his teeth and shook his head.

"Why is he driving so fucking slow?" he asked as he focused on the sedan.

Hiroto squinted toward the taillights burning small and red in the distance.

"He old," he said. "All drive slow."

Marcus shook his head.

"He sees us. He's testing to see if we're following him."

Hiroto shrugged.

"Let him test," he said, his gold tooth showing through the crack between his sneering lips. "It make no difference anymore."

Marcus snorted the air and relaxed in his seat.

"This one's personal. I've been waiting a long time."

He gripped the steering wheel harder, a hungry look in his eyes. Hiroto glanced at him.

"Feelings no good," he said. "You make mistakes."

Marcus shook his head.

"Don't worry about me. I'm not the one who got choked out."

Hiroto looked at him and narrowed his eyes.

"Don't follow too close," he said.

Marcus looked down at the speedometer and let his foot off the gas. Hiroto shook his head and lengthened his sneer.

"Feelings no good," he said again as he turned his face back toward the road.

More cars rushed past as they followed Jimmy's sedan, which cruised the center lane at about 15 ticks below the speed limit.

"Fuck," said Marcus as a trucker whooshed by, his hand hanging out the window, middle finger erect in the low light.

He frowned and gripped the steering wheel.

"I'm gonna kill this fucker slow," he said.

About thirty minutes later, the sedan exited. Marcus watched the big green road signs and considered the implications.

"He's headed for the goddamn airport," he said.

Hiroto frowned.

"No airport," said the Japanese man. "Bus station."

Marcus shook his head.

"He's taking the bus to the airport."

Hiroto looked confused while Marcus eased the car into the exit lane.

"Trust me," said Marcus. "This is an old-school play. I grew up around this shit. I know all the stories. All the old tricks. He's taking a bus to the airport. That's his play."

Hiroto still looked confused, his face pinched together like he caught the scent of something rotten.

"How you know?" he asked.

Marcus narrowed his eyes at the red taillights in the distance.

"He knows we can kill him in the airport parking garage," he said. "He thinks we won't do it on a bus full of people."

Hiroto shrugged.

"We won't?"

Marcus watched the road.

"I'd kill a busload of babies if it meant putting a bullet in that fucker's brain."

1:07 A.M.

They came with the van, a nice plain white model with no windows on the backside. They had stickers for everything: pizza and catering, cable TV, plumbing and landscaping, even a dog grooming service. None of those would work tonight. Nothing really would. What kind of company visits a home after 2 a.m.? Security?

Paramedics? They didn't have stickers for those, so they left the van blank and chose to lean heavily on haste.

The house was mostly dark when they pulled into the driveway, the van creeping slowly over the concrete as they eyed the front door. No porch light, Benjamin thought as he looked the property over. That might be a problem.

"The porch light should be on," he said as much to himself as the big bald driver.

The burly man shrugged.

"Maybe he forgot."

Benjamin rubbed his finger and thumb over his thin, manicured mustache.

"Perhaps."

He ran a hand over his oily slicked-back hair and turned to the driver.

"Well, let's go see, shall we?"

The driver nodded, and they both stepped out into the night. While Benjamin waited, the big bald man hurried to the back of the van and swung the doors open. Inside, an enormous, refrigerated cooler took up most the space, its motor humming like a great mechanical insect. Just next to it, there sat a large black leather bag. The bald man gathered it up and softly shut the doors. Then he hurried around the vehicle, the knives and saws jingling audibly inside their oversized container.

Benjamin watched him approach, his sharp green eyes cutting through the night.

"Shh," he said with a hiss. "We mustn't scare the rabbit."

The bald man swallowed and nodded. They turned toward the dark house and approached the front porch. As they neared the door, Benjamin ducked beneath a hanging pot of purple flowers, their fragrant scent tickling his nose as he moved past. He waited for the bald man, who crept along with a careful gait, the bag clenched over his chest with both arms.

Benjamin watched him with disdain, his bright eyes seeming iridescent in the white moonlight.

"Hurry up," he whispered.

He watched the man approach with an unmistakable sneer. Then he reached into his tailored sport coat and removed a long, curved filet knife that gave off brief flickers of fire in the limited light.

"Mr. Grant," said Benjamin as he ran a thumb over the blade.

The hulking bald man looked at him and swallowed again.

"Yes, sir?" he whispered.

"Please produce your pistol," he said with a hard voice. "Just in case."

The bald man hooked the bag's strap over his shoulder and reached into his jacket. Benjamin looked at the .45 caliber pistol and frowned.

"Only in an emergency," he said.

The bald man nodded.

"I understand," he whispered.

Benjamin's eyes bored forth, his slight frame seeming larger than life behind that gaze.

"Good," he said. "After you."

He stood aside and let the big man move past.

"Now?" asked the man.

Benjamin frowned.

"Yes," he said. "Of course, now."

The bald man nodded and wrapped his big hand around the doorknob.

"It's unlocked," he said without looking back.

Benjamin shook his head.

"Please proceed then, Mr. Grant."

The bald man gave a little nod.

"Yeah," he said. "Alright."

He twisted the knob and opened the door, a thin squeak breaking the silence as a long slice of moonlight cut across the dark interior floor.

"Hello?" said the bald man as he stepped into the house.

Benjamin slapped his head.

"Shut up, you moron," he said as he pushed past him.

He flipped on a light and looked at all the glass and blood on the wood floor. He shook his head and looked back at Mr. Grant.

"Keep your gun ready," he said.

The big bald man tossed the bag onto the floor and raised his pistol.

"Good man," said Benjamin as he turned back toward the wreckage. He dropped the filet knife to his side and took a deep breath. "Mr. Patterson?"

His deep voice carried through the house. They waited and listened. They strained their ears to hear.

"Mr. Patterson?" called Benjamin, this time louder.

There was a shuffling from the other room, the dining area, Benjamin guessed, though its contents were cloaked in darkness. He took a step back and looked over at Mr. Grant.

"Take a look," he said.

The big bald man nodded and moved forward, his gun leveled at the dark space before him. With every step, he strained to see into the blackness, broken glass crunching beneath his boots which slid on blood spatters atop the slick wood floor.

"Mr. Patterson?" said Benjamin. "Please identify yourself, or we will be forced to fire."

The bald man paused and waited.

"Listen," he said.

Benjamin squinted his eyes and strained to hear what sounded like faint rustling.

"The light," he said.

The bald man swallowed.

"What?" he asked.

"Get the goddamned light," yelled Benjamin.

Mr. Grant took another step forward, his gun pointed at the darkness as he approached the entryway. With a trembling hand, he reached around and fumbled for the light switch, his other hand gripping the pistol, finger fondling the trigger, ready to open fire.

The shuffling grew louder, and he took a step back.

"Fuck," he said, his voice inflecting as he spoke. "Mr. Patterson?"

"Good Christ," said Benjamin as he stormed past. "Give me that."

With a quick movement, he snatched the gun away and reached around the corner. Then, he fondled the wall until he found the switch plate. With a flick of a finger, he bent the switch up and bathed the dining room with light.

Both men froze as their eyes adjusted to the scene before them.

"Shit," said the bald man as he raised both hands.

Benjamin swallowed as he looked upon the dog, which eyed both men with an electric gaze.

"Easy, boy," Benjamin whispered, his face relaxed, voice like velvet. "Take it easy."

Throaty growls gurgled from the animal's mouth, its lips curled back over a jagged set of bloody teeth.

"Shoot it," said Mr. Grant, his eyes wide, broad chest heaving with rapid breaths.

Benjamin bit down on his teeth.

"Shh," he whispered. "We don't want to wake the neighbors."

The dog eyed Benjamin's hands and deepened its growl, its ears laying low as it widened its yellow eyes.

The bald man took a step backward, and Benjamin ticked his tongue against the roof of his mouth.

"Please stay still, Mr. Grant."

The dog glanced over at the bald man, and Benjamin took the opportunity to slip the knife behind his back.

"Shh," he said as he lowered the pistol. "It's alright."

The dog's eyes returned to Benjamin, its tail curled up under its back legs, which shivered in a way that made Benjamin smile.

"Come here," he whispered as he knelt down on the floor. "It's alright."

He set the gun down on the tile and raised an empty palm, his other hand gripping the narrow blade behind his back. The bald man watched, his eyes wide, heart pounding within his chest. And then, as if satisfied with the display, the dog perked up its ears and whimpered.

"That's it," said Benjamin as the dog wagged its tail. "You're a good boy, aren't you?"

He held out his palm, and the dog lowered its head, its nose sniffing the air as if to assess the human by scent.

"Come on," Benjamin cooed.

The dog took a step forward, and Benjamin's smile broadened, his fingers squeezing the knife as the animal approached.

"That's right," he said, his voice soft and coaxing as if he were manipulating forward an infant child. "Come on."

Now the dog was within two inches, its blood-stained snout sniffing the tips of Benjamin's fingers.

"Yes," whispered Benjamin. "Almost there."

A loud scuffling erupted from the kitchen.

"What the fuck?" yelled the bald man.

As if barbed by a cattle prod, the dog flinched, its feet skittering as it tried to move backward, tongue lolling as its eyes went wide.

With a sudden jolt, Benjamin lunged forward, his knife revealed and stabbing down at the beast as it struggled to find traction on the slick tile floor.

The dog yelped as the knife sunk into the webbing between one of its front feet, the toes splitting apart in a tiny fountain of blood.

Unfazed by the flesh wound, the animal caught the floor with its claws and scampered past Benjamin, scooting between the bald man's legs on its way out the front door.

Benjamin shook his head and collected his pistol from the floor.

"Come on," he said to the bald man.

Mr. Grant hurried up behind him, and they followed the scuffling sounds into the kitchen.

"Shit," said the bald man as he looked at the floor.

Amid a growing pool of blood, Michael lay sprawled, his heels kicking the tile as he held a hand to a gushing wound on his throat.

Benjamin sighed.

"Well, this certainly complicates things."

They both watched while Michael held up a hand, his eyes wide with panic as he struggled to staunch the bleeding from his slick red throat.

"What now?" asked Mr. Grant.

Benjamin took in a deep breath and shook his head.

"We find the girl."

Michael looked up at the two men, his body twitching less and less as his color ran pale.

"And what about him?" asked Mr. Grant.

Benjamin frowned.

"He's meat now. Close the front door and get your tools."

1:34 A.M.

Jimmy stowed his car about a block from the bus station and looked around. The other vehicle had vanished, but he knew it was somewhere nearby. And probably not alone. One of many, maybe. Was he really that important anymore? Maybe not, he thought.

Without more rumination, he grabbed his bag and stepped outside the car. Again, he surveyed the area, his eyes taking note of the vagrants and street people, an ordinary collection for this time of night.

The scent of car exhaust and wet garbage danced in the air. In the distance, a train announced its presence with a lonely blast of its horn.

Jimmy bent over and spat. Then he trotted across the street with a noticeable hitch in his gait. He arrived at the other side of the street and stepped up onto the sidewalk. As he reached for the door to the station, a sleepy beggar looked up at him and blinked.

"I can sleep here if I want to," he said through a set of brown teeth.

Jimmy looked down at him.

"Alright," he said.

Jimmy started to pull the door and paused as his phone buzzed within his pocket. He waited until it stopped buzzing. Then he gave the street another quick appraisal and stepped into the bus station.

Inside, the floor was strewn with more homeless, some asleep, some watching him through lifeless eyes buried deep within twisted locks of unwashed hair.

Jimmy stepped around them as he made his way to the ticket booth. Behind the bullet-proof barrier, an old black man stood, his face looking tired and entirely sapped of emotion.

"Help you?" he asked in a dead, monotone voice.

"One ticket to the airport," said Jimmy.

"When?" asked the man.

"Right now is fine," said Jimmy.

The old man sighed and tapped on his keyboard.

"Next one's in 15 minutes."

Jimmy nodded.

"I'll take it."

He settled up with the man and turned away from the booth, ticket in one hand, bag in the other.

Vibrations tickled his flesh as his phone buzzed again. Out of habit, he felt his hand drifting into his pocket. And then he stopped himself and let it go to voicemail.

The door to the bus station opened, and Jimmy set his bag on the floor.

The ticket man looked up and frowned. Some of the homeless sat up and scurried back up against the walls.

Jimmy watched the two men enter, his eyes darting from one to the other as they moved away from each other until they were spaced about 15 feet apart.

"Well, well," said Jimmy. "You fellas taking a trip?"

Marcus raised his eyebrows.

"Boss needs to see you, Jimmy."

Jimmy looked at him thoughtfully.

"That so?"

Marcus nodded.

"Yeah," he said. "It is so."

Jimmy glanced at Hiroto, who looked back at him through narrow, furious eyes.

"I'll have to catch up with him later," Jimmy said. "I'm a little busy right now."

Marcus shook his head and grinned.

"Arrogant to the end," he said.

Jimmy raised his eyebrows.

"This is the end?"

Marcus let his smile vanish to nothing.

"If you don't come with us right now, then, yeah, it's the end."

The vagrants watched the exchange with mute fascination, their eyes alert, as if they'd acquired a contact high from the invisible electricity in the air.

"You boys take this shit outside," said the ticket man. "I don't want no trouble in my station."

Jimmy's hand moved toward his gun, and Marcus smiled.

"Now, now," he said as he pulled back his jacket to reveal his own pistol. "I know you're a quick hand, Jimmy. But there's two of us, and there's only one of you."

Hiroto flashed a thin smile, and his gold tooth flickered beneath the overhead light. Jimmy kept his eyes on Marcus, but even still, he could see the Asian man's hand drifting toward the inside of his long leather coat.

"That's enough," said the ticket man, as he stuck the barrel of a shotgun out the service hole in his bullet-proof casing. "Take this shit outside."

He punctuated his sentence by leveraging a shell into the chamber of the gun. Then he picked up the phone in his other hand and started dialing.

Marcus looked past Jimmy at the old black man and frowned.

"What are you doing with that phone, old-timer?"

Without responding, the man put the phone to his ear.

"Yes, sir, we got armed troublemakers down here at the bus station, and I need the police here five minutes ago."

Marcus looked at Jimmy and took in a deep breath.

"How long do you think you can run, Jimmy? Where are you gonna go? There ain't no place we can't find you. But first, we'll start with your boy."

Jimmy watched him with his dead eyes, his slack face advertising neither fear nor anger. Marcus smiled.

"That's right, Jimmy," he said. "We know where your boy is. We squeezed it out of your friend Howard." He held up his hand and made a tight fist. "Like taking juice from a spent lemon. Not easy. Lots and lots of pressure."

He shrugged.

"But if you squeeze long and hard enough, you get the juice. Every single time."

Hiroto's narrow face stretched as his grin widened. The ticket man hung up the phone and looked from one man to the other while the homeless shifted atop the floor.

"The cops is comin," said the old black man. "You best get gone."

Marcus looked at the old man and sighed. Then he turned his eyes to Jimmy and shrugged.

"Another time, then," he said.

He nodded at Hiroto, and they turned toward the door. Jimmy watched them, his face hard and completely devoid of emotion.

As he reached the door, Marcus stopped and looked back over his shoulder.

"We don't want your boy, Jimmy," he said. "We just want you. Do the right thing. Don't make other people pay for your sins."

He pursed his lips and gave a little nod. Then he and the Asian stepped outside. Every eye in the room watched them until they were gone, and then they all looked at Jimmy.

"You best get gone too," said the old man. "Police will be here in a minute."

Jimmy started to say something but stopped when he felt the buzzing in his pocket. With a trembling hand, he reached inside and took out the phone. He looked at the messages, a dozen at least, all from Robin. He frowned and looked up at the ticket agent.

"There a back way out of here?"

The old man gripped his shotgun while he looked Jimmy up and down.

"That way," he said. "You best hurry."

Jimmy gave a quick nod, and then he walked away, his jaw flexing as he limped past all the gawking eyes.

Chapter 19

They sat together in Jimmy's car, the smell of sweat and blood thick within the interior. Without words, each one stared straight ahead through the windshield, where the first hints of dawn paled the rim of the sky above a bleak and hopeless urban horizon.

Still, the darkness surrounded them, and they sat there together in silence amid the thinning residue of a sleepless night, each empty of answers, both wrapped in a blanket of morbid thoughts.

At last, Jimmy turned and looked at the ragged woman next to him, flesh raked by fingernail scratches, hair all knotted in dried blood. Her lower lip was torn at the corner, and a penny-sized hunk of skin had been taken from her left cheek. The white of one eye had turned red from trauma, and now she looked somewhat demonic in the sparse light.

He shook his head and turned back toward the windshield, his eyes staring forward into the eroding night.

"So, he's dead then," he said with a parched, raspy voice.

Robin rubbed tears from her eyes and nodded.

"Yes."

Jimmy shook his head.

"Then our goose is cooked."

Robin started weeping again.

"There's got to be another way," she said. "There has to be something we can do."

Jimmy scratched his jaw and realized for the first time that he hadn't shaved in days.

"What other way?" he asked. "This isn't charity, Robin. It's a deal. A deal with a very dangerous person. We give her your husband, and she helps you disappear. We don't have your husband now. We have nothing. We got shit. In fact, if anything, we've made things worse for her. For all we know, she's planning to put us down. Her and that fucking whispering maniac. We'd be fools to even approach her again."

Robin's chin firmed, and she looked up at him, her face seeming old in the scattered light.

"What do I do, Jimmy?" she asked. "I don't know what to do."

Jimmy watched as she bent over and wept, her hands wrapping around the back of her head, gathering up fistfuls of hair.

"I'm scared," she whimpered through choking sobs. "I'm so fucking scared."

Jimmy reached out to pat her back and then thought better of it.

"Ok," he said. "It's alright. Take a breath."

He turned away and looked out the window.

"Jesus fucking Christ," he whispered. "What a mess."

He sat for a couple of minutes, his finger tapping the steering wheel, while Robin's little sobs filled the quiet as the horizon grayed with the budding dawn.

"Listen," he said at last. "You gotta go. You have to run. It's the only fucking way."

She looked up and wiped her eyes.

"What?"

He shrugged.

"If you stay here, you're dead or worse. If it were me, I'd run. It ain't pretty, but it's all you got. Take your chances somewhere else. Run. Tonight. Right now." He made a gesture with his hand like a car zooming away. "Just go."

Robin started crying again.

"How?" she asked.

Jimmy looked at her face, red and scratched and totally free of makeup.

"Here," he said. "Take this."

He passed over his black bag, and her arms sank against the weight of it.

"It ain't much," he said. "Not really. But it's a start. It'll get you from here to there. Wherever that is."

She took the bag and opened it.

"What is this?"

He scratched the back of his neck and raised his eyebrows.

"Fifty grand, more or less. I wish it were more, but it is what it is."

She looked at the money, tightly wound into little bricks of paper.

"I can't take your money, Jimmy."

He shook his head.

"Yes, you can, and, yes, you'd better," he said. "Your money's all gone now, Robin. You can bet on that. That Guild of yours will see to it. And if they don't, the cops will when they start hunting you for what happened with your husband."

He looked away out the window and nodded as if to agree with himself.

"It's better this way," he said. "I got business here, and I probably won't walk away from it. Business that's a long time coming. I made mistakes. Too many to count. And it's time for me to face my sins."

He swallowed and looked out at the brightening night, birds already chirping as they celebrated the promise of a new day.

"At least this way, someone gets a chance," he said. "You deserve another chance, Robin. Everyone does."

Tears burst from her eyes as she considered his words, the sorry past and the frightening present. All the uncertain days to come.

"I can't," she said. "I just can't."

Jimmy pursed his lips and shook his head.

"You have to, Robin," he said. "It's survival now. You don't think. You just do it."

She firmed her mouth and looked down at the bag of money, her tears darkening the paper as they rained down from her eyes.

"I can't, Jimmy," she whispered. "I'm not like you. I'm not strong."

Jimmy turned and squared his shoulders, so they were face to face.

"Nobody's strong until they have to be," he said. "You are strong. You'll see that in time."

She looked up at him.

"What if I turned myself in? What if I went to the police?"

He frowned down at her, his face filled with genuine pity.

"If there's one thing I know, it's that prisons don't keep you safe. If someone wants you and they have the means, they'll get you in there. Hell, in some ways, it's easier for them."

Her shoulders shook as she started to weep again. He raised his hand out of instinct, and somehow it ended up on her bare shoulder. He patted her awkwardly and shushed her cries.

"Alright now," he said. "This isn't the way."

She wept a while longer, her eyes bleeding dryly now as her dehydrated body gave up the last of its moisture. Finally, she rubbed the heels of her hands against her face and sat back in her seat. Her body shuddered as she sucked in a deep breath of air.

"I'm sorry, Jimmy," she said. "You're so kind to me. Why are you so kind to me?"

He watched as she stared forward at the reddening dawn, her body growing more rigid as she tried to gather her strength.

"I don't deserve it," she said without looking at him. "I've been selfish. I've been a fool. There was always this voice in my head. All these years, this voice yelling at me, telling me to stop. Just stop and get out. To run. To run until my legs collapsed beneath me."

She stared forward, her face oranging in the fresh sunlight.

"But I couldn't act on it," she said. "Not until it was too late. I was always a coward."

She snorted the air a couple times and looked at him.

"I deserve every bit of this."

He shook his head.

"No," he whispered.

She looked up at him, her red-rimmed eyes spidered with little veins.

"Yes, I do," she said. "And I'd only hate myself more if I took your money. I can't take it. I won't. And I won't drag you any deeper into this mess."

She looked up into his eyes and firmed her mouth.

"I'm going to turn myself in," she said. "I'll take whatever comes. I'll find a way to bear it." She shrugged. "Or I won't. Either way, I won't drag you down with me, Jimmy. Don't ask me to. Please don't. Just let me have this one thing. Let me pretend to be good this once."

He looked down at her small hand on his arm, the knuckles red and bloody, one of them clearly broken. He frowned and thought for a moment, his mind playing out every eventuality. The angles so limited. Few cards left to play.

Then, he turned away and looked out the window, where the city grew red before the eager dawn. He squinted into the sun and chewed at his lip. He filled his lungs with air and frowned.

"Maybe there's another way."

They sat in the car without talking while he wove the flimsiest of plans within his sleep-starved mind.

Chapter 20

Benjamin stared into the blaring red sunrise and yawned, his bloodshot eyes squinting through the glare as the morning traffic whirred past. In each vehicle, the drivers gripped their steering wheels robotically, each well trained by years of routine.

From the passenger seat of the windowless van, he watched them with a cold curiosity, like a scientist assessing mold spores pressed between glass slides, men and women on their way to their everyday endeavors, lawyers and doctors and subway toll takers, construction workers and fast-food people, bankers and secretaries, firemen and cops.

Grubby ants marching to a tune of futility, chasing a few dollars on their way to early graves. He imagined it like gameshow contestants trapped in glass containers, each one furiously grasping at cash as it whipped all about in a vortex of artificial wind, the audience watching with big grinning faces, their eyes wide with sick delight. His lips curled up over his teeth, and he shook his head with disgust.

"We need gas," said the bald man.

Benjamin turned and showed his teeth.

"Why, may I ask, Mr. Grant, did you not fill up the tank before our little errand?"

His slow, jagged words sent a chill up the bald man's spine, and he struggled to choke out a reply.

"Well?" barked Benjamin

"I'm sorry," he answered.

Benjamin's frown cut all the way down to his jawline.

"Mr. Grant, I want to point out that we have a butchered corpse in the cooler behind us."

The bald man swallowed, his knuckles turning white as he strangled the wheel.

"Normally," Benjamin continued, "in these circumstances, it is best to avoid unnecessary diversions. Can you guess why?"

The bald man swallowed again.

"I'm sorry," he repeated.

Benjamin sighed and looked outside his window. In the neighboring car, a small child looked up at him from the backseat, his happy little face offering the rosiest of toothless smiles.

Benjamin sneered.

"Very well, Mr. Grant," he said. "Let's make it quick."

They drove a couple of miles before exiting the highway, the bald man eyeing a neighboring burger joint as they pulled into a small gas station. Benjamin watched him with disdain, his piercing eyes looking inhumanly green in the warming dawn.

"Hungry?" he asked.

The bald man glanced at him for only the briefest of moments.

"A little," he said.

He felt the heat of Benjamin's stare as he pulled the car up next to the pumps.

"It does smell wonderful," said Benjamin. "I must admit."

The bald man swallowed again before testing the air with a tentative snort. The smell of broiling meat from the restaurant's smoke stacks had penetrated the vehicle, and the bald man's empty stomach churned audibly in response.

Benjamin grinned a reptilian smile.

"Why don't you go and get you something while I pump the gas?"

The bald man turned and raised his eyebrows, his head half-cocked like a curious dog.

"Really?"

Benjamin's face darkened.

"No, Mr. Grant. Not really." He turned and shook his head with a look of pained exhaustion. "Get out and put gas in this vehicle. We cannot afford a delay. We have to get this man on ice and find his wife before the police do."

The bald man opened the door and poured his body out of the van. Benjamin watched him with contempt and then stepped out of the vehicle to stretch his own legs.

While Mr. Grant refueled the van, he took a few steps away, half to work up the circulation in his lower body, half to gain a brief respite from the bumbling idiot. He was just about to return to the vehicle when he felt the buzz in his pocket. With a hint of dread, he withdrew his phone and looked at the number. He pinched his eyebrows together and answered the call.

"Yes?"

"Is this Benjamin?"

Benjamin looked all around as if half-expecting some sort of ambush from the trees.

"It is," he said. "And who might you be?"

"I think you probably know already."

Benjamin frowned.

"Yes, I think I do, but why don't you tell me anyway?"

The line was quiet for a moment.

"It's Jimmy Hunter," the caller said at last.

Benjamin grinned.

"Ah, the famous Jimmy," he said. "I've heard so much about you. How did you get this number, may I ask?"

"You know how," said Jimmy.

"Ah, yes," said Benjamin. "From dear Robin, I suppose. Is she with you now?"

"She is," said Jimmy.

"How interesting," said Benjamin. "And do you know what she has done?"

"I do," said Jimmy.

Benjamin began pacing across the pavement, the big bald man watching him as he pumped fuel into the van.

"And now you will attempt to run, I assume," he said. "Although you have called me, which perhaps suggests another course."

The phone was silent.

"Are you still there, my friend?" asked Benjamin.

"I am," said Jimmy.

"How nice," said Benjamin. "Would you like to share your plans with me? Or do you have a request you would like to make?"

It was quiet for a few more seconds, and then Jimmy spoke.

"I'll give you the girl," he said.

Benjamin stopped pacing.

"How nice of you," he said. "And what would you like in return?"

The phone was silent again.

"Well?" asked Benjamin.

"I want Mario off me," Jimmy said at last. "And I want him off my son. I don't want him touched. You arrange that, I'll hand her over."

Benjamin started pacing again.

"Ah," he said. "Of course. These are reasonable requests. But why would you think I would have the power to help you? Mario is a powerful man, as you should know better than anyone."

"Mario's a businessman," Jimmy said. "He wants to keep doing business with your Guild. He doesn't want it jeopardized. He'll do what you ask if it will keep the money flowing."

"I see," said Benjamin.

He stopped and looked back at the bald man who was just now placing the gas pump back on its hook.

"Yes," he said. "I think we can do this for you. But I want her now. Not tomorrow. Not later this afternoon. Right now. Any further delay will cause me difficulties. This must happen immediately or not at all."

The phone was silent.

"Are you still there, Mr. Hunter?" asked Benjamin.

"Not now," said Jimmy. "Tonight."

Benjamin thought for a moment.

"Why tonight?" he asked.

The phone was silent a while longer.

"Mr. Hunter?"

"Tonight," said Jimmy.

Benjamin stared at the reddening horizon, his green eyes sparkling in the new dawn.

"Fine," he said. "Name the place."

Jimmy gave him the details and ended the call. Then, he sat back in his seat and sighed as he watched Robin exit the tiny convenience store with two large plastic bags. His eyes tracked her as she approached the car, her head whipping all about as if she'd just robbed the store.

"Take it easy," said Jimmy as she slipped into the passenger seat. "You're not chipped anymore. They can't track you."

She tossed one of the bags onto his lap and sat down beside him.

"I can't help it," she said, as she pulled a bottle of water from her own bag. She twisted away the cap and sucked the bottle dry in a few large gulps.

Jimmy looked into his bag, which held three more bottles of water and a very old-looking ham sandwich wrapped in cellophane. Robin shrugged.

"They didn't have much of a selection."

Jimmy nodded.

"This'll do fine."

He withdrew his own bottle of water and drank it halfway down while Robin watched him through a pair of wide, worried eyes.

"Well?" she asked.

Jimmy stopped drinking and ran a sleeve over his lips.

"It's all set," he said.

Robin turned away and rubbed her head like it hurt.

"I don't know about this," she said.

Jimmy frowned at his limp, wet-looking sandwich.

"They didn't have mayo?"

Robin looked at him, her face all twisted up with consternation.

"I don't know, Jimmy. I didn't look. I was a little distracted by the thought of being killed and eaten."

Jimmy's frown deepened.

"I can't eat this without mayo."

Robin started to speak, but he was already struggling to get out of the car. She watched him with disbelief as he staggered toward the gas station, her mind filling with anger and then fear as she considered his limp.

She shooed the thoughts away and started looking around again, her eyes inspecting the faces and subtle mannerisms of every passerby.

A bald man watched her from the other side of the lot, his small eyes studying her from behind his thickly framed glasses. Immediately, she looked away, and then, half-heartedly, she let her eyes drift back to see that he was already driving away. She sighed and rubbed her head as Jimmy opened the door.

"Well," he said. "They had mustard. That'll have to do."

He sat down and looked at her.

"What's the matter?" he asked.

She looked at him, her eyes filling with tears.

"How can you ask me that?" she said.

Jimmy put a hand on her shoulder.

"You need to relax."

She turned her palms upward.

"How?"

Jimmy shrugged.

"This thing is gonna play out the same way, whether you approach it with confidence or fear. You're not going to solve anything by worrying. We're doing what we can. That's all we can do. When things get like this, you roll the dice and take your chances."

She started to say something, but he shushed her.

"Don't worry," he said. "I'll be there every step of the way."

She firmed her mouth, and a tear rolled down her cheek.

"Thank you, Jimmy."

He squeezed her shoulder.

"Now, let's find a place to hide out. I've got to get a couple hours of shut-eye, or I won't be worth much tonight."

Robin nodded.

"I'm tired enough to fall asleep right here in this seat."

Jimmy started the engine.

"Good," he said. "Because we'll probably have to sleep in the car."

Chapter 21

Darkness seemed to come on fast that night, the afternoon sun putting up little resistance in its descent, as if it were eager to avoid playing witness to the night's looming events. Downward it fell and promptly slipped behind the horizon, its light reduced to a skinny hint of orange, which flared weakly along the rim of the world in a way that seemed anemic and sickly almost, at least to Robin's eyes. She watched it vanish with fear and sorrow, as if a cherished friend were abandoning her in the most desperate of hours.

Amid the quickening twilight, the city streets were nearly barren in this part of town, most of the old bars and shops shuttered years ago amid the local economic collapse.

Jimmy pointed over the steering wheel at two of the buildings.

"When I was a kid, that place was busy as hell," he said. "Now, the only places that do business are underground. Gambling, prostitution, weapons, drugs. All that stuff."

Robin looked around and shivered as a homeless man pushed a cart along the crumbling street, his pale, emaciated form almost glowing amid the low light and then vanishing entirely into the blackness of a narrow alleyway.

"Why are we doing this here?" she asked.

Jimmy frowned.

"No cops," he said. "They're one of our biggest concerns right now. And they don't come around here because Mario pays them not to."

He looked around and frowned at the decaying cityscape.

"Yeah," he said. "This place was way different when I was a kid."

Robin watched him from the passenger seat, her eyes narrow as she studied his hard face for any signs of fear or doubt. But all she saw was a tired-looking man with a heavily whiskered jaw.

She swallowed and finally said the words she'd been thinking since this morning.

"Can I trust you, Jimmy?"

He stared out the window where the last of the failing light winked out on the blackening horizon.

"What choice do you have?" he asked.

She swallowed again and rubbed her injured arm.

"Good point."

Jimmy glanced at her from the side of his eye.

"Don't worry. We just need them for the plan. When they get here, I'll apprehend them."

He pointed toward the back of the two buildings, where a wide alley cut deep and long between a pair of three-story structures.

"You won't have to worry," he said. "I'll stash you in that alley behind a dumpster. They won't even see you. Not until it's too late."

Robin looked at the alley, already growing too faint to see in the darkening gloom. Her body broke out with goose flesh, and she shuddered.

"I'm worried," she said.

Jimmy shrugged.

"I'd be worried if you weren't."

She shook her head.

"No, I mean it. You shouldn't underestimate Benjamin. He's a dangerous man."

Jimmy stared through the windshield, an almost disinterested look on his face, as if he were merely waiting on a tedious task offering little else but boredom.

"I don't underestimate any man," he said. "A child can slip a knife between your ribs. The smallest things can kill you."

He scanned the area for at least the hundredth time. Then, he looked at Robin and raised his eyebrows.

"You ready?"

Robin swallowed.

"Yeah."

They exited the car and hurried across the dark road, Jimmy's hip afire as he struggled to keep up with her nimble little steps. When they reached the other side, he glanced around and took out his pistol.

"Wait here."

She pushed her back up against one of the old buildings and vanished as the shadows absorbed her body. Jimmy disappeared into an alleyway, the sound of his footsteps growing faint as he probed the depths of the passage.

Robin pressed her palms against the rough brick wall, her heart thundering within her chest. A foul medley of odors swam through the thick, humid air, the scent of burning petroleum from a nearby refinery competing with the smell of dumpster refuse wafting out from the alley.

"Hey, girl," said a raspy voice.

She turned to see a shadowed figure standing on the sidewalk a few feet away.

"Leave me alone," Robin said, her voice cracking as she scrunched up against the building.

The thin silhouette of a man watched her, his head acrook atop his skeletal shoulders.

"Come over here," he whispered.

Robin inched away from him toward the alley, her back sliding against the brick.

"Stay away from me," she whimpered.

The spindly figure staggered forward, his hands reaching out in a terrible embrace.

"Beat it," said Jimmy as he rounded the corner.

The thin man stopped and looked at Jimmy's gun.

"I said, beat it."

Without speaking, the man retreated and rushed away down the street.

"Jesus Christ," said Robin.

Jimmy took her by the arm.

"Come on. I found a place for you."

He led her into the alley, her shoes tripping over garbage and potholes filled with rancid water and old yellow cigarette butts. One weak, orange bulb set the long corridor alight in an ominous glow, which diminished to nothing at the end of the alley, where it yawned black in the distance like a giant open mouth.

"Fuck this," said Robin.

Jimmy tugged her along.

"Don't worry," he said. "I checked it out. It ends in a chain-link fence. Nice and tall. There's nobody here except you and me."

She looked at all the old doors next to the dumpsters.

"What if someone comes out of those doors?"

Jimmy shook his head.

"That's unlikely."

Robin pulled her arm away and stopped.

"But it's possible."

Jimmy looked at her.

"We don't have time for this," he said. "They'll be here soon. Now, you can take your chances here, or you can take your chances with Benjamin. Which is it?"

She rubbed her head and sighed.

"Alright," she said with a squeaky little voice.

Jimmy pointed to one of the dumpsters.

"Squat down there," he said. "Don't come out until you hear me call."

She looked at the soiled space and cringed at the garbage and rat droppings.

"I know it's not ideal," said Jimmy. "But we don't have time to discuss it."

She swallowed and kicked away some of the filth. Then, she squatted down and shrunk back against the wall. Jimmy watched her wrap her arms around her knees and shiver.

"Hang in there," he said. "It won't take me long."

He turned and left her there with the rodents and roaches and stinking air.

When he exited the alley, Jimmy withdrew his pistol and levered a bullet into the chamber. He slipped it behind his back and into his waistband. Then, he leaned against the wall and rubbed his sore leg.

Less than an hour passed before the van rolled up next to Jimmy's car. Before the vehicle came to a full stop, Benjamin already had the door open.

"Mr. Hunter," he said as he jumped out and rushed across the street.

Jimmy lowered his eyebrows and looked past the man toward the bald driver who was fleeing the vehicle and hurrying to catch up with his over-enthusiastic employer.

"Benjamin, I take it," said Jimmy as the man approached.

"Yes," said Benjamin with a rat-like smile.

He looked at Jimmy with his sparkling green eyes, but whether it was the low light or the man on the other side of the gaze, they didn't have their usual effect.

"Who's this guy?" asked Jimmy as the bald man approached.

Benjamin looked back at the man.

"This is Mr. Grant," he said. "He's of no concern."

Jimmy looked at the pistol in the bald man's hand.

"Alright," he said.

Benjamin looked around.

"Well," he said. "Do you have the woman?"

Jimmy nodded.

"Yep."

Benjamin held his hands out to his sides.

"Well?" he said.

Jimmy looked at him.

"Well, what?"

Benjamin looked ready to explode.

"Where is she?"

Jimmy pointed toward the alley.

"Down in the alley behind a dumpster."

Both men turned to look, and when they did, Jimmy reached for the pistol in his waistband, stopping abruptly when he saw two more headlights appear next to his car.

Benjamin turned back and smiled.

"Ah," he said. "The rest of our party has arrived."

Jimmy narrowed his eyes as the doors of the car opened.

"Shit," he whispered as Marcus and Hiroto stepped out.

Benjamin glanced at Jimmy.

"Don't worry. They're only here to complete our deal."

Jimmy looked at him.

"What?"

Benjamin shrugged.

"Would you accept the terms any other way?" he asked. "How else shall I prove my end of the bargain?"

Jimmy turned and watched the two men approach, their faces pinched with the look of seriously inconvenienced men.

"The fuck is this?" asked Marcus.

Benjamin stepped forward and put his hands up, while the bald man held his pistol at his side.

"Gentlemen," he said. "Thank you for coming."

Hiroto stared at Jimmy, his eyes narrowed into slots of glowing hate.

"Why the fuck are we here?" asked Marcus. "And why the fuck are you here with him?"

Benjamin flashed his teeth.

"How dare you speak to me in that manner," he said, and something in those startling green eyes made Marcus take a step backward. "Do you know who I represent?"

Marcus glanced at Hiroto, but he was fully fixated on Jimmy.

"Yeah," said Marcus. "I know who you are."

Benjamin nodded with smug satisfaction.

"Good."

He gestured toward Jimmy.

"This man and I have come to an agreement," he said. "He will surrender Robin Patterson into my custody, and we will regard this matter closed. Business will continue. Our Guild will hold no ill will toward your employer. In return, you and your employer will cease your actions against Mr. Hunter here. Do you have any questions?"

Marcus and Hiroto looked at each other, their faces advertising confusion.

"What?" asked Marcus.

Benjamin shook his head and put his hands on his hips.

"It means you don't kill him," he said. "Him or his son. Once he satisfies his obligations with me and our Guild."

Hiroto's upper lip raised into a sneer. Marcus shook his head and spat.

"Fuck that," he said.

Benjamin looked at the man as if he'd just spoken Latin.

"Did you not hear me?" he asked. "I said business will return to normal."

He took a step toward Marcus and lifted his arms out to his sides.

"Do you think your employer prioritizes vengeance over money?" he asked. "I don't have time for this. I need to get this woman back to my superior before the morning. My reputation depends on it."

He turned back toward Jimmy, who watched Marcus and Hiroto with a wary gaze.

"You see what you've done?" said Benjamin as he spun back toward Marcus. "You've instilled doubt in this man and compromised my transaction."

He turned away and shook his head. Then, he turned back toward Marcus and snapped his fingers.

"I need this matter finished right now," he said. "Get your employer on the phone and let me discuss this with him directly."

He had more to say, but Marcus interrupted his rambling with a fist to the jaw. As his boss fell backward onto the pavement, the bald man lifted his pistol, but Hiroto's bullets were already tearing through his torso.

Jimmy watched the man fall dead.

Marcus towered over Benjamin, his eyes aflame with reckless rage.

"You think you can tell me what to do?" he shouted.

Benjamin pushed himself up onto all fours and looked at his subordinate. The bald man's eyes were open and lifeless, and his dark blood crept over the pavement toward Benjamin's fingertips.

"What have you done?" asked the green-eyed man, his face showing the indignance of someone too long under the illusion of control. "What have you done?"

He turned and looked up at Marcus, his eyes glowing like emeralds within his bleeding face.

"You'll be disciplined for this."

Marcus took out his pistol.

"Shut up, you pompous piece of shit."

He fired off two rounds into Benjamin's forehead, and, at last, his fiery eyes went dull.

Marcus looked at Jimmy, who stared back with his usual maddening blank face.

"Well," he said. "There goes that little plan."

Hiroto took his partner by the arm.

"No good," he hissed.

Marcus ripped his arm away.

"Relax," he said. "The boss won't know. We can pin everything on this stupid fucker here." He gestured toward Jimmy, who was looking down at Benjamin's shattered head.

"Now, get his gun," said Marcus, "and go find that fucking girl."

Hiroto looked all around.

"Where?"

Marcus looked at Jimmy and smiled.

"Where'd you put her, Jimmy?" he asked.

Jimmy inhaled and stood as before.

"Try the alley," said Marcus.

Minutes later, Hiroto dragged Robin from the alley, her shoes skidding on the concrete as she bent to increase her weight. Still, she came along, the Japanese man yanking her with shocking strength, as if his tall, thin body were constructed of tightly wound wire.

Jimmy watched as she passed by, her eyes stricken with bone-deep fear, a pleading within, as if she believed a man like him would always have another card to play.

"Throw her in the trunk," said Marcus.

Hiroto dragged the shrieking woman to the back of the car, and her screams went dull with the thud of the trunk door.

Marcus grinned at Jimmy.

"Well," he said. "I told you this day would come." He scratched his temple with the tip of his pistol. "Do you remember?"

Jimmy shrugged.

"Can't say I do."

Marcus laughed a little.

"Sure, you do," he said. "When I was first starting out. When Mario first opened his club."

Jimmy shrugged.

"Don't," said Marcus. "Don't even try it, Jimmy. You know what I'm talking about."

Jimmy shrugged again.

"When you slapped me," Marcus hissed. "When he slapped me, and all of them other guys laughed. I told you I'd get you someday. I said so, and now it's here."

Jimmy scratched his jaw.

"Sorry, kid," he said. "I've slapped a lot of young punks in my life. A few stick out in my memory. You ain't one of them."

Marcus's eyes lit up with rage, a flicker of embarrassment within. And then, like a flame extinguished by cool water, his face went flat.

"Well, it ain't just about me, Jim."

He gestured back at Hiroto, who was just now falling in behind him.

"You got a debt with him too."

Jimmy glanced at the Asian, who looked like a dog at the end of his leash.

"You don't say?" said Jimmy.

Marcus nodded.

"That's right," he said. "That night in the alley, when you cheap-shotted him."

Jimmy raised his eyebrows.

"Seemed fair to me."

Marcus shook his head.

"He don't see it that way. And his people, well, they're all about honor and such." Marcus raised his own eyebrows and looked at Jimmy thoughtfully. "So, here's the deal. I'm gonna let him have the first crack at you."

Jimmy's eyes flicked over to Hiroto, who looked back with a hungry glare.

"That so?" he asked.

Marcus smiled.

"Yeah, Jimmy," he said. "That is so."

Jimmy raised his eyebrows.

"What do you have in mind?"

Marcus raised his eyebrows and pursed his lips.

"Well," he said. "You're pretty good with a blade, aren't you, Jim?"

Jimmy said nothing.

"Hiroto here," said Marcus. "Well, he's pretty good with a blade, too. Some would say he's the best. I know I ain't seen better."

Jimmy and the Asian stared at each other as if to set the other afire with their eyes.

"Sure," said Jimmy. "Let's give it a go."

Marcus grinned.

"That a boy!" he said.

He raised his pistol and gestured toward the alley.

"Let's move this party over there. Less conspicuous that way."

Without another word, Jimmy turned and walked toward the alley, his limp showing as he moved across the poorly lit pavement.

Marcus looked over at Hiroto.

"Let me know if you need me to put him down," he said.

The Japanese man pinned him with a sharp glare.

"No interfere."

Marcus put a hand up.

"It's your party," he said. "I'm content to watch."

The two men followed Jimmy into the alley, their bootsteps clicking the pavement with every patient step. The harsh scent of spoilage welcomed them as they entered the passage, Marcus waving a hand before his nose as he found a seat on a short stack of crumbling concrete steps.

"Jesus," he said. "I hope you two can focus on each other with this fucking stench."

Hiroto marched right into the center of the alley and stood, his breathing steady, despite the eagerness in his eyes. Jimmy watched him with his dead-eye stare, but the skin on his face tightened as he clenched his jaw.

Above their heads, stars dotted the sky, like cleanly struck pinpricks in a dark, colorless fabric. Below their feet, dozens of potholes dotted the blacktop, each holding water from a prior rain, the stars reflecting in the tiny wells, like flawless black mirrors in a weather-torn world.

"Do you mind if I smoke?" asked Marcus as he withdrew a pack of cigarettes from his pocket. "It's a disgusting habit, I admit. But moments like this, well, I just can't help myself."

He fingered loose a cigarette and pushed it between his lips. He took out a lighter and set the thing aflame, his face silhouetted by the weak light as smoke swelled around him.

"Well," he said as he exhaled. "Let's get on with it."

Jimmy dusted his hands as if preparing to lift an immense amount of weight. Then, he moved out to the center of the alley and stood waiting, his hands hanging loosely at his sides.

He watched as the Japanese man shadowed him, his tall, slender body moving amid the alley on nimble, cat-like feet. He settled near a puddle about 20 feet away, eyes narrowing as he looked Jimmy up and down.

In his long, almost delicate fingers, he held a narrow switchblade knife, which he handled with an impressive, artistic sort of ease, as if it weren't a hunk of razor-sharp metal at all, but a sixth finger on his hand.

There was a sharp, almost noiseless click and a glint of light off the blade. And then another glint and another, as if he were flipping it over and over in his hand.

"Ah," said Marcus. "The anticipation is almost better than the actual thing."

Jimmy removed his coat and wrapped it around his forearm. Then he reached into his pants pocket and withdrew his own knife, a beaten-looking thing that looked almost as old as him.

The Asian's gold tooth caught the low light as he grinned at Jimmy's blade.

Marcus whistled.

"Jesus, Jimmy. How long you had that thing?"

Jimmy watched the Asian with his usual dead-eye stare, eyelids low, emotionless and calm. Hiroto's eyes glistened in the moonlight, and the two began to circle, eyes flicking from their faces to their hands.

Around and around, they went, shoes shuffling the ground as they searched blindly for good footing on the pitted alley floor.

"Get on with it," said Marcus. "I'd like to catch a late dinner before everything closes."

They circled as if he'd never spoken, each waiting for the other to show something. A weakness. A tell. The slightest sign of doubt.

When the Japanese man finally moved, he came low, just beneath Jimmy's naval, his knife sweeping side to side in a blur that made Jimmy stumble backward over the wet blacktop.

Even as Jimmy recovered, Hiroto kept circling, his eyes two slits of hatred, mouth stretched into a wolf-like grin.

Jimmy gathered himself and grimaced as hot pain radiated within his hip. As if sensing his disability, Hiroto stopped and crouched and feinted, forcing Jimmy to reset again. Then the Asian laughed and moved on, circling, his eyes studying Jimmy with contempt.

Jimmy squeezed the knife in his hand and tried to shadow Hiroto's movements, his limp impossible to hide as he tripped over the loose gravel and alley filth.

Marcus sat watching, his big body a featureless silhouette on the steps.

"Oh, Jimmy," he said. "I told you to get that leg checked out."

Hiroto moved in again, his knife hand almost invisible, like a blur in the night, and when he stepped back, Jimmy's forearm was cut below the elbow, and his jacket was wet with blood.

Marcus slipped the cigarette between his lips and lay the gun over his lap. He gave a slow clap as if he sat witness to some sort of play, the actors wholly committed to their dangerous roles.

"Bravo," he said as he pulled the cigarette from his mouth. He exhaled a white plume of smoke and sighed. "I told you he was the best, didn't I, Jimmy?"

Hiroto stopped and started back the other way, forcing Jimmy to do the same. Then he stopped and reversed his course, eyebrows arched up, wolfish grin wider than ever.

"Oh, shit," chuckled Marcus. "Now, he's toying with you."

Blood gushed from Jimmy's sleeve, and the trash-filled puddles drank in the splashing gouts, their waters reddening in the weak light.

Suddenly, the Asian was very close and low, and when he stepped away, Jimmy's leg was flayed open, blood warming his skin as it trickled within his pants down to his ankle.

Hiroto stood tall and swung the knife back and forth like Zorro, while Marcus laughed and clapped his hands.

Already, Jimmy's mind had begun to swim, his mouth growing thirsty as the fluid leaked out from his open veins.

Marcus's shadowed face watched him and sighed.

"Maybe you should take a second," he said. "Hiroto's a sporting man. I'm sure he'll let you take a break."

As the Asian reset, Jimmy darted forward, his knife sweeping side to side like a wild man slashing at overgrown brush.

Like a dancer, Hiroto lifted up on his toes and bent his stomach inward, Jimmy's blade coming within a whisper of his belly flesh. Then the Asian flipped around and found fresh footing several feet away.

Jimmy spun around and crouched, his lungs burning as he sucked in the air.

Marcus clicked his tongue against the roof of his mouth.

"Be careful," he said. "You almost lost everything right there."

Even as he said the words, Jimmy felt the fresh cut on his arm, this one even deeper than the first, his coat now heavy with blood. Jimmy shook it from his forearm and let it fall to the ground.

Marcus whistled at his wounds.

"You've lost a lot of blood," he said. "I hope you have enough to keep going. I really am enjoying the show."

Hiroto feinted again, and Jimmy warded him off with a quick jab of his knife.

The Asian stepped back and circled, his eyes searching Jimmy's body, like a surgeon deciding where to place his scalpel.

They circled each other, Hiroto grinning at Jimmy's mangled arm, slick with blood and trembling as he held the blade out like a torch in a dark cave.

Jimmy lunged with his knife, but Hiroto stepped aside like a bullfighter and walked away with a look of scorn, as if his opponent's very existence offended his sensibilities.

Jimmy turned and watched him, his face looking pallid, almost glowing in the light-starved gloom. Blood had trickled down over his wrist and onto his hand. He passed the knife to his other hand and wiped his sticky red palm against his shirt. He flexed his cold, numbing fingers until they began to prickle with needle-like sensations. Then he returned the knife to his dominant hand and breathed in the foul air.

Marcus smoked while they circled each other, his presence nearly imperceivable save for the burning ember of his cigarette, which flared and dimmed as he sucked and exhaled.

"I must admit," he said. "It saddens me somewhat to see you like this, Jimmy."

The two men continued circling, their feet stepping sideways, eyes watching for weakness, an opening for a fruitful strike.

"You were something back in your day," said Marcus. "No one can doubt that. But this business, it's a young man's game. And you ain't young no more. You're finished. You've been finished for a while. Walking around like you're still someone. Like you still matter."

He shook his head in the dark.

"You don't."

Jimmy shot forward and slashed twice with his knife. Hiroto twisted away from the blade, his instincts breathtaking, like a performer having already learned every step over weeks of rehearsal.

He stepped back and smiled. He passed the blade from one hand to the other.

Marcus laughed and smoked, the cigarette competing with the scent of decaying food in the dumpsters.

The two fighters moved toward each other almost simultaneously, each taking the wrist of the other's knife hand and holding on for precious life.

They grappled, their teeth flashing white, muscles straining as they twisted for leverage.

Marcus watched with mute fascination.

After several seconds, Hiroto shoved Jimmy away and retreated, his shirt flapping open above a shallow red line that ran diagonally across his stomach.

The Asian's hand drifted down and fingered the gape in his clothing.

Blood dripped from Jimmy's knife.

"Alright," said Marcus. "That's a point for you, Jimmy."

Jimmy gripped his knife and watched as Hiroto raised his head. Now, the Asian's eyes were wide, and within them swirled a fury that seemed almost to set the darkness alight.

As if to parlay his success, Jimmy rushed forward, his teeth clenched as his blade darted out.

The Asian feinted to his left and spun back the other way. As Jimmy's blade missed the mark, Hiroto passed his own knife twice across the older man's belly. Then he skipped away to the other side of the alley.

Jimmy fell to one knee and gasped. He held a trembling hand to his belly and felt the oozing blood.

His flesh was laid open down to the muscle, and he began to feel very faint.

"Bravo!" Marcus shouted as he threw his hands together.

While Hiroto gave a bow, Jimmy blinked at the pavement. Everything felt distant and dreamlike, the sound of Marcus clapping, hollow and far away, like a television murmuring words in another room.

While the two men watched, Jimmy struggled to his feet and turned around.

Marcus whistled.

"Damn," he said. "You look like shit."

He burst into laughter while the Asian eyed him with his hungry, gold-tinged grin.

Jimmy swayed back and forth like a baby deer taking his first steps. His throat buckled as he swallowed, eyes looking gray as he lifted his knife and staggered forward.

Marcus shook his head.

"You really don't know when to quit."

Hiroto raised his own knife and turned his head to the side, an expression of false pity on his face as the two commenced circling again.

Around and around, they went, the Asian darting in now and then to feint a killing blow. Then, having forced Jimmy to put up a defense, he would recede back into position and continue circling, his face split wide by the same mocking grin.

Like a great wheel, they turned, each man passing before Marcus for the briefest of moments and temporarily obstructing his view.

All the while, Hiroto's face glowed with satisfaction as Jimmy wobbled before him, like a stack of crates piled overhigh, teetering with promises of an inevitable fall.

"You'd better make your move, old man," Marcus cackled, "before you bleed out."

Still, the two fighters circled, Hiroto staring into Jimmy's eyes, which looked pale and empty, as if windowing into something already dead.

At last, Jimmy stopped with his back to Marcus. There, he stood wobbling, his dry mouth panting, shoulders weak and hunched low. He steadied himself and held up his knife, his tongue licking dryly at his pale, bloodless lips.

While the Asian searched for an opening, Marcus leaned left and right to see around Jimmy, his face contorted with frustration as he struggled to find a clear view.

While Jimmy and Hiroto stared at each other, Marcus began to speak but stopped in mid-sentence as he lost his train of thought.

What was he going to say? Something witty, he remembered. One last dagger before the final blow. He tried to form the words, but his mouth felt detached from his mind. And then he realized, only in that instant, that Jimmy had turned and slipped the knife into his eye.

As drool poured from his open mouth, Marcus brought his hand to his face and fingered the handle of the weapon. A low cry slipped from between his lips as his one remaining eye flicked up at Jimmy's face. Then, his body convulsed and slumped back against the steps.

Hiroto froze as he watched his partner fall. Without pausing, Jimmy plucked the pistol from the dead man's lap and leveled it at the Asian.

Hiroto looked at Marcus with confusion, as if his brain were straining to make sense of something beyond his comprehension. His eyes flicked over to Jimmy, and he swallowed.

Jimmy looked at the Japanese man and shrugged. Then, he cocked the gun and shot him between the eyes.

Even before Hiroto's body splashed backward into a puddle, Jimmy had turned back toward Marcus. He set the gun aside and rifled through his pockets.

His hand gathered around the car keys, so cold in his blood-starved fingers. He withdrew them and staggered out of the alley toward the car, his mind swimming as the world blurred before his eyes.

"Robin," he said as he struggled to insert the key into the trunk.

"Jimmy?" said a muffled voice that sounded as if it came from a small, whimpering child.

The hatch gave, and he threw the trunk upward. Robin lay curled inside.

"It's ok," he said as he reached for her. "They're dead."

She looked up at him, and he could tell his condition by her face.

"Oh, Jimmy," she said as she crawled out of the trunk. "We've got to get you to a hospital."

Jimmy shook his head and sat down on the concrete.

"No," he said. "We're dead if we go that route."

She dropped to her knees and started searching through his wounds.

"Jimmy, you've lost a lot of blood. You need help."

He shook his head.

"I'll be alright."

She swallowed and looked back at the dead men.

"We need to leave."

Jimmy nodded.

"Let's take their car," he said. "It might buy us some time."

He licked his lips and swallowed the void in his throat.

"Help me up."

She struggled to get him onto his feet and guided him to the passenger side of the car. When she had him safely inside, she rushed to the driver's side and got inside.

"Where do we go?" she asked, her voice cracking with panic.

Jimmy pressed his hand against the wound in his stomach and grimaced.

"We need to stop by my house," he said.

Robin jammed the key into the ignition and brought the engine to life.

"Why?" she asked.

Jimmy inhaled sharply as pain knifed through his midsection.

"We still have a card to play," he said weakly.

The vehicle lurched forward, and they sped down the road.

"What card?" said Robin. "I thought you said we needed Benjamin."

Jimmy frowned into the depthless night, breathing labored as he wrestled with his pain.

"I didn't say it was a good card."

Robin looked at his hand, dark blood seeping between his fingers as he pressed against his gut.

"Are you sure this is a good idea?"

Jimmy bit his lip and shrugged.

"No," he said. "But choices are easy when you've got nothing left to lose."

He closed his eyes and leaned back in his seat.

"Wake me up when we get close."

She started to say something, but he was already unconscious.

Chapter 22

Jean Paul awoke with a grunt, his mind working back slowly from the murk of a pleasant dream. A little hazy already. Something with a girl. A very young girl. Beautiful in the body. Lean and underdeveloped. Metal braces on her teeth and soft, supple skin.

That's all he could remember now, and he cursed at the premature culmination of such a wonderful escape.

The pressure on his bladder was unbearable. He pulled away the covers to see a mustard-color spot of urine on his pajamas and sheets. He inhaled the sharp ammonia scent and nearly retched.

He reached across the silk sheets of his oversized bed and collected the bedpan. He leveraged his rotund body over to one side and draped his flaccid penis over the edge. He waited and waited, but nothing came. At last, he cursed aloud and tossed the thing away.

With great effort, he heaved his fleshy body up and let his legs dangle over the side of the bed. He reached over to his nightstand and tapped a button.

"Yes, sir?" said a weaselly-sounding male voice.

"I need you, Thomas."

In seconds, the great door to the bedroom creaked open, and a thin man entered. He wore a tailored butler suit, and his face was decorated with a thin waxed mustache. He greeted his master with a pleasant smile that was warm and gentle and a million times refined.

"How may I assist?" he said as he stood with his hands behind his back.

"I need to piss," said Jean Paul.

Thomas gave a sharp nod.

"Shall I get your chair?" he asked.

Jean Paul shooed his words away with a flip of the hand.

"I'll walk," he said.

"Of course, sir."

Thomas hurried over and put an arm out.

"Ready?" he asked as Jean Paul took hold of it.

"Yes," said the old fat man.

"And one, and two," the servant said as he leveraged his master up and onto his feet.

With a practiced patience, the servant led Jean Paul across the room, big purple varicose veins bulging like snakes on the old man's calves as he shuffled toward the bathroom.

The servant's back screamed with pain as he helped the obese man onto the toilet. Then he stood up and rubbed the buttons of his lower spine.

"Shall I wait outside?" he asked.

Jean Paul shifted on the toilet seat as he passed gas.

"I may be here some time," he said. "Bring me something to eat."

Thomas offered a polite smile as if this were the most ordinary of requests.

"What would you like?"

Jean Paul tipped his chin up thoughtfully, his mind appearing to play out possibilities, flabby wet lips smacking at the flavor of imagined treats.

"The dancer," he said at last. "The one from the ballet."

Thomas nodded.

"Very good, sir."

He turned and walked away, pausing for a moment at the door.

"Will you be alright here, sir?"

Jean Paul sneered up at him, an especially thick glob of yellow crust beneath his one cloudy eye.

"Go," he said with a snarl.

Thomas swallowed and turned away.

"Yes, sir," he said as he rushed from the bathroom.

Jean Paul farted into the toilet and groaned. Then he grimaced as urine began to drip from his shrunken manhood, the splashes audible in the still, quiet night.

The drips increased to a slow drizzle and then stopped entirely when he heard the little explosion outside. With a sharp sting, he cut his efforts short and strained to listen.

Another little explosion detonated in the courtyard outside the mansion. A rifle, he surmised, as he perked an ear up into the air.

With a hurried hand, he reached toward another button, this one positioned next to him on the wall. But before he could press it, Thomas stepped into the room.

"My apologies, sir," he said. "There is a disturbance outside."

Jean Paul frowned up at him.

"What is it?" he asked.

Thomas shrugged.

"Someone on the grounds, perhaps? Security has assured me that everything is under control."

Jean Paul flinched as another shot popped off outside.

"It doesn't sound under control," he hissed.

Thomas stood erect, his hands clasped behind his back.

"Shall I call the authorities?"

Jean Paul looked up at him.

"Don't be absurd," he said. "Just let me know when they have the situation under control and tell them to take the perpetrators down into the understructure. Or whatever is left of them anyway."

Thomas raised his eyebrows.

"Yes, sir," he said.

"Now, bring me my meal," he said as he readjusted himself on the toilet.

Outside, men scurried around in the darkness, their automatic weapons darting all about, aiming at the trees in the darkness.

"You and you," said a short, muscular man all dressed in black. "Take two men and get up in there. Root that son of a bitch out!"

The man nodded and hurried away.

"What the hell is going on?" asked the security team point man, his blonde hair mussed, eyes looking wired from interrupted sleep. "The client is trying to sleep."

The short man pointed up into the trees.

"A sniper, we think," he said. "Somewhere up on the hill, moving around in the trees."

The blonde man squinted into the darkness.

"Just one?"

The short man shrugged.

"There might be more," he said. "Or it could be one man moving around. It's hard to tell at this point."

A shot popped off, and the dirt puffed up at their feet.

"Jesus Christ," said the blonde man as they both scurried behind one of the cars. "Why are you fucking around? Turn on the goddamned floodlights."

The short man shook his head.

"They are on," he said. "The bastard shot them out."

"All of them?" asked the blonde man.

"He's a dead shot and very well supplied," said the short man.

The blonde man started to say something, but his open mouth filled with blood and brain as a bullet sheared through the window glass and cleaved the short man's head in two.

With shrieking gags, the blonde man collapsed onto his stomach and spat the other man's brain matter onto the grass, his face contorted in a look of abject horror and disbelief.

He vomited out a late supper and sucked in deep lungfuls of air. Then he pulled out his radio and started barking orders.

"Get everyone into those woods!" he yelled. "I want every last one—"

He cut off his words, as teakettle screams bellowed from the woodlands, the shrill cries of agony knifing through the darkness and then cutting off in abrupt silence.

He lifted his radio and repeated his demands, but he heard only static when he waited for replies.

Upstairs, from his luxurious bedroom, Jean Paul peered out the window, a silk sheet held up over his chin, his bad eyes struggling to make sense of the tiny world beneath him.

There was a shuffling outside his door, and he turned his body, the sheet pushed out like a makeshift shield against whatever evil lurked on the other side.

"Go away!" he yelled as he stumbled backward on his trembling legs.

"Sir!" yelled Thomas.

Jean Paul dropped the sheet and clutched a hand over his chest. "Thomas?"

"Yes, sir," he yelled. "Please open the door."

Jean Paul eyed his wheelchair a moment and then staggered across the room toward the door. With a trembling hand, he unlatched lock after lock.

"Thomas?" he said as he opened the door.

The servant rushed in and slammed the door behind him, his face pale, hair a mess.

"What's happening?" asked Jean Paul, his eyes wide, big wet mouth agape.

"He's inside the mansion," said the servant.

Jean Paul swallowed.

"Who?"

Thomas looked down at the fat old man, his face pale, eyes wide with fright.

"The gunman, sir."

Jean Paul put a hand over his forehead.

"Oh, dear," he said.

Thomas swallowed and looked around the room.

"Have you a weapon, sir?"

Jean Paul nodded.

"In the drawer of my nightstand."

Thomas rushed across the spacious bedroom and ripped the drawer open. He rifled through its contents, the denture cream, the antacids, a purple vibrator with a barbed tip.

When he found the pistol, he yanked it out and looked it over, the black metal dull and flat in the low light.

"You must take me to the panic room," said Jean Paul. "We must lock ourselves inside."

The servant looked at the gun a second longer, his eyes transfixed on the weapon, heavy in his pale white hands, hypnotic.

"Thomas!" yelled Jean Paul.

The servant blinked and looked at the old man.

"Yes," he said. "Yes, of course."

He swallowed and licked his lips.

"You stay here. I will check to see if it's clear."

Jean Paul nodded.

"Please hurry," he said.

Thomas nodded and rushed out the door, the pistol pointed forward, his eyes darting this way and that, the whites glowing in the darkness as he inched away from the room.

Jean Paul slammed the door behind him and re-fastened all five locks. Then he stumbled away, his body falling backward as his feet lost their purchase on the floor.

With a crash, he met the hardwood surface, a cold streak of pain radiating up his spine. He cried out as if expecting a team of servants to rush into the room. Then he blinked up at the ceiling and struggled up onto his feet.

Shots fired downstairs, and he held his fat hands over his ears.

"Oh, no," he muttered as he retreated from the door. "Oh, no,"

He turned and rushed toward the window, his feet slipping on the silk sheet as he steadied his ill-used legs before the glass.

Outside, low below, bodies peppered the manicured lawn, a half-dozen security men looking like action figure toys, with their arms and legs bent away from their lifeless bodies.

"Oh, dear," Jean Paul whispered to himself.

The faintest sound of a car engine burbled, and Jean Paul squinted down as a triangular swath of headlights painted the grotesque landscape.

"Oh, no," he said. "Oh, no."

"He watched from high above as Thomas' car lurch forward and sped away from the property, its carriage jostling as it crunched over corpse after corpse.

Jean Paul pushed open the window and screamed into the night.

"Thomas!"

The car sped away from the mansion and grew small as it crested the hill.

"Thomas!"

The old man flinched as footsteps creaked outside his bedroom door.

"Oh, no," he whispered almost inaudibly.

He turned and stumbled backward, his fat hands folded in front of his mouth, like a desperate secular man resorting finally to prayer.

Chapter 23

There were fields on the outskirts of the city. Undeveloped land bought at a premium, back before the economic collapse. Long before the drug rings and weapon rackets. The human trafficking and police corruption. Back when order presided, and the cancer hadn't yet sunk its roots. Back when things were better, and life made more sense. Now, these lands lay fallow, every acre pregnant with possibilities but lacking any meaningful investment dollars.

So, it had been for at least two decades, and now the grasses stretched high into the air, their long wispy strands lashing in the wind below the light of a pale moon. Beautiful yet haunting, at least to Jimmy, as he drank in the landscape with half-open eyes.

Robin watched him with growing concern. In the past couple hours, his breathing had grown labored, and his skin had turned frighteningly pale.

"Jimmy," she whispered.

He shook his head.

"Not now. We have to finish this."

She sat back in her seat and stared through the windshield at the sprawling expanse of waving grass, which tumbled like an infinite sea into the visible horizon. An ocean at sway glowing almost white beneath the lunar-lit heavens.

"Jimmy," said Robin. "I want to tell you something."

Jimmy blinked at the field, his eyelids looking heavier than ever.

"However this ends," she said. "However things turn out, I want to thank you."

He shook his head.

"It's going to work."

Robin looked out her window and took in a shuddering breath.

"But if you're wrong?" she said. "I mean, if it doesn't work out like you think, I wanted to say thank you. I didn't deserve your help. But you gave it anyway. Because you're a good man, Jimmy."

His jaw flexed as a feather of light reflected on his face through the rearview mirror.

"They're here," he said.

Robin turned around into a pair of beaming headlights.

"You stay in the car," said Jimmy.

Robin shook her head.

"No," she said. "We'll finish this together."

She waited for him to complain, but he only shrugged.

"I'll do the talking."

He opened the door and threw a leg out onto the dusty dirt road. He held a hand over his bandaged stomach and sucked in a great breath, like a man preparing to do a great acrobatic feat. Then, he gave a little squeak and forced his beaten body onto its feet.

Robin stepped out on the other side of the vehicle, and they both squinted into the headlights, the blinding white light cut black by the silhouettes of three figures.

"You look like shit," said the woman as she stepped forward.

Jimmy clutched his stomach and shrugged.

"It's been that kind of night."

He looked past the woman toward the whispering man, his face concealed as always by a black ski mask. To his left, there was another man, his shoulders broad, jaw thick and square. Each man held automatic rifles, but they seemed benign compared to the heat of the woman's gaze.

The woman looked at Robin.

"She doesn't look much better."

Robin tried to meet the woman's gaze but quickly found herself studying the ground.

The woman turned toward Jimmy and frowned.

"Well," she said. "Where is the husband?"

Jimmy looked back over his shoulder at Robin, her slight body wrapped in his oversized coat, giving her the appearance of a rescued child. He turned his eyes back toward the woman and frowned.

"Dead," he said.

The woman's face turned dark, and a hint of teeth flashed from between her lips.

"That's too bad."

She gave a nod to the whispering man, and all three turned to walk away.

"Wait," said Jimmy.

The woman stopped and looked back.

"Yes?"

Jimmy bit his lip and took a step forward. The whispering man raised his weapon, but the woman stayed his hand.

"What is it?" she asked.

Jimmy shrugged.

"We're not quite done yet."

The woman raised her eyebrows.

"No?"

Jimmy shook his head.

"Nope."

The woman stepped forward, her shoulders back, bold eyes wide.

"How so?" she asked. "We had a deal, Jimmy. I help her, she convinces the husband to help me." She shrugged. "The husband can't help me now." She looked at Robin. "Nor can she."

She flashed her teeth again as she stared up at Jimmy.

"If anything, you've only made my work harder. What other business do we have? What can you offer me?"

Jimmy looked down at the ground and frowned.

"No," he said. "No, everything you say is correct. We fucked things up in a pretty spectacular way."

The woman looked him up and down.

"But?" she asked.

He looked at her, his eyelids low, always low.

"We have something else," he said. "Something I'm hoping will even the scales."

The woman rubbed her forehead as if exhausted by the ramblings of a wordy child.

"Alright," she said. "Let's see this something else. Make it fast."

Jimmy looked at the whispering man.

"Take it easy there, buddy," he said. "I gotta get something from the trunk."

The whispering man said nothing, his gun pointed toward the ground.

"Hurry," said the woman. "I have mistakes to mend and new plans to make."

Jimmy nodded.

"Alright."

They all watched as he staggered across the dirt road, his limp more noticeable than ever as his boots stumbled over the uneven terrain.

He approached the rear of his car and slid his key into the lock. He turned it over, and the hatch gave way with a gentle pop.

The woman watched as the trunk bounced open, half rising on her toes to get a better look. Jimmy bent and wrestled with something in the darkness. Then he slammed the trunk shut, and the woman's eyes narrowed.

"What have you got there?" she asked as she took a step forward.

The whispering man gripped his weapon as Jimmy kicked someone forward, the person's head concealed by a wet paper bag, sniffling sounds audible in the quiet, uncaring night.

The figure limped forward, its robust body trembling as it moved blindly ahead. After a few feet, Jimmy kicked the figure in the back of the knees, and they all watched it collapse to the ground.

"That's our offer," said Jimmy as he looked down at the sobbing heap. "Best we got."

The woman stepped forward, her eyes flaring with bright curiosity. She bent and took hold of the paper bag. She ripped it away, and her eyes grew round.

"Hello, there," she said.

Jean Paul blinked up, his nose bleeding snot, eyes leaking tears.

"You," he whispered sharply, his words accusing, eyes wide with terror, floppy jowls trembling around his jittering jaws.

"Yes," the woman said as her eyes flickered with internal delight. "Me."

The whispering man watched the scene unfold with quiet confusion. Jimmy cleared his throat and frowned.

"Will that do?"

The woman's eyes smiled down on Jean Paul, who had pissed himself for at least the third time.

"Oh, yes," she said. "This will do nicely."

She stepped back from Jean Paul and gestured toward her silent partner.

"Load him into the van," she said. "We have much to discuss."

The whispering man stepped forward and took hold of Jean Paul, who wept like a broken child as he was dragged away over the bumpy ground.

The woman looked up at Jimmy and smiled.

"This is sweet, I must admit," she said as she stepped forward. "But my plans are still altered. I have no way inside Viox Genomics. All I have is a fat old man with peculiar dietary habits."

Jimmy watched her approach, his face showing signs of fatigue.

"I know," he said.

The woman shrugged.

"But?" she said.

Jimmy raised his eyebrows.

"But I'm going to help make that right," he said. "If you help her." He gestured toward Robin, who stood quietly several yards behind him. "If you hold up your end of the bargain, then I'm your man."

The woman looked at Robin and then back at Jimmy, a little smirk on her face as she approached within a few inches.

"Alright," she said. "I can use a man like you."

Jimmy breathed in through his nose and nodded.

"So, we have a deal?"

The woman stuck her hand out.

"We do."

Jimmy reached out and took her hand, the feminine fingers like wire as they curled around his.

"There is the matter of Mario," he said as they shook. "He'll keep coming for me. And anyone who's on my side."

The woman smiled.

"You leave all that to me," she said. "I protect what's mine."

He released her hand and tried to look into her eyes.

"If I'm your man now," he said. "Maybe I should know your name."

The woman smiled up at him, her dark eyes like boiling wells of oil in the lightless night.

"Claire Foley," she said. "Nice to meet you."

Chapter 24

Mario stomped across the parking lot, the gravel crunching beneath the immense weight of every pounding step. Behind him, a pair of well-dressed men hurried to keep up, their black hair oiled and slicked back and reflecting the moonlight as they approached the front door of the club.

A thickly framed bouncer straightened when he saw them, his Adam's apple buckling as he swallowed the void in his throat.

"Hey, boss," he said with a squeaky little voice.

Mario stopped before him and listened to the music pounding at the walls from inside.

"You asleep out here?"

The bouncer swallowed again and shook his head.

"No, boss," he said.

Mario frowned.

"I want everyone out," he said.

The bouncer looked past Mario, and the other two men shrugged.

"Everyone?"

Mario's face darkened.

"The girls and customers," he said. "All the civilians."

Mario stepped past him without another word. The bouncer looked at the other two men.

"He serious?"

"He sounds serious to me," said one of the men as they pushed past.

Inside the club, a sparse crowd was loosely dispersed amid the strobing lights, their eyes tracking the movements of a bare-breasted dancer who jiggled and bounced upon the stage. The two men peered into the tobacco haze and saw that Mario was already halfway to his office, his girth carving space like a falling building as people rushed to get out of his way.

They hurried to catch up while the bouncer followed them inside and made his way to the DJ. He whispered something in the DJ's ear, and the man looked at him with obvious confusion. The bouncer barked something else and pointed at Mario's office. Without another word, the DJ reached for his keyboard, silencing the music with a tap of a button.

With a jarring suddenness, the club fell silent, the dancer covering her breasts as if noticing her nudity for the first time. The guests groaned as the DJ pulled the microphone up to his mouth.

"May I have your attention?" he muttered. "I'm afraid we'll be closing early this evening."

The guests groaned again, and the DJ looked back at the bouncer, who pushed him aside and put his lips to the microphone.

"Everybody out," he said. "Right fucking now."

Mario glanced back over his shoulder as he neared his office, the two men following with their heads pointed down.

"How many men we got here right now?" he asked.

One of the men pushed his lower lip out and looked around.

"Eight," he said. "Nine, maybe."

Mario looked at the other man.

"Get on the phone," he said. "I want everyone here, right now. Armed to the teeth. Everyone."

The man nodded and rushed away.

"You," Mario said to the other man. "Follow me."

They entered Mario's office and shut the door. Mario approached his desk and ripped open a drawer. He withdrew a half-empty bottle of scotch, the amber fluid sloshing within the glass as he slammed it down hard on the desk.

"Fuckin Christ," he said with a soft voice more frightening than his thunderous roars.

The man jerked his chin up and swallowed as he shifted his stance before Mario's desk.

"Any news?" he asked.

Mario plopped down in his chair, and it complained with a sharp strain. Without speaking, he gathered up the bottle, a large thing that looked strangely small within the curl of his meaty fingers. He slid two glasses onto the desk and filled each one halfway, the glug of the fluid deafening in the awkward silence, which hung in the air like the thick humidity before a storm.

"The news is I can't reach nobody," he said as he pushed the glass toward the man. "Not the client. Not Marcus. Not that Asian sumbitch. Not no fuckin body."

The man licked his lips and reached for the glass as if he were taking an eyelash from the bait pan of a trembling bear trap.

"You think it's turned bad?" he asked as he gathered up the glass.

Mario's heavy lids slid up over his egg-like eyes.

"What the fuck do you think?" he asked as he frowned up at the man.

The man shrugged.

"Whatever you say, boss."

Mario shook his head and wrapped his hand around his glass.

"Fuckin Christ," he whispered again as he brought the glass to his lips.

He downed the entirety with two big swallows, and the man sucked down his glass in turn, his inferior gullet requiring double the swallows.

"Motherfucker," said Mario as he tossed the glass across his office.

The man flinched as glass exploded against the wall.

"Here's what I want," said Mario as he pointed a big fat finger toward the man. "I want Jimmy Hunter dead. I want his kid found. And I want him dead. I want his great fucking uncle dead. I want his wife dug up from the cemetery just to make double fuckin sure she's dead."

The man's face pinched together as if he were trying to solve a tricky math equation.

"For real, boss?"

Mario's big fleshy face turned red.

"No, not really, you fucking moron," he said. "I mean, yeah, really about Jimmy and his son. Not really about the great uncle and dead wife."

The man tilted his head like a flummoxed dog.

"Fuckin Christ," said Mario as he leaned back in his chair.

A gun went off outside the office.

"What the fuck?" yelped the man as he scurried away from the door.

Mario straightened in his seat and listened, his hand already wrist-deep in another drawer, fingers gathering up his .45 pistol.

There was a second gunshot, this one just outside the door. Someone screamed. Glass shattered. Men barked orders and then fell silent, their voices diminished into choking grunts.

The man withdrew his own pistol and backed his ass against Mario's desk.

"What in Christ?" he said.

Mario stood up and levered a bullet into the gun's chamber.

"Lock the door," he said.

The man didn't move.

"Now!" said Mario, the thunder of his voice spurring the man forward.

He swallowed and approached the door, his trembling hand reaching out slowly, hand taking the doorknob in a delicate grasp, as if testing the metal for proof of fire on the other side.

"Hurry up," said Mario as he rushed over to a large steel door on the far side of the room.

Automatic weapons went off like fireworks, and both men cringed downward as two bullet holes appeared in the door. More screams pierced the air, and then everything went quiet.

"Jesus fucking Christ!" said the man.

He straightened and reached toward the door, his fingers shaking as he turned the lock.

"Leave off that shit," said Mario as he shoved a key into the big steel door.

With a click, the lock gave way, and he yanked it open with a hollow bong.

Inside, there were weapons of every sort. Military-grade rifles, incendiary grenades, things he'd never used, things he didn't know how to use.

He withdrew a pair of machine guns and tossed one to the man, who snagged it from the air and hurried away from the door.

They both crept backward and knelt, the wall surprising them as their feet crept backward involuntarily.

Amid the silence, shoes crunched outside the door, glass breaking beneath a pair of small, almost gentle footsteps.

The man pulled the trigger and shot wildly, the door splintering under a shower of gunfire, as he screamed mutely into the bullet-torn air.

He stopped firing and waited, both men staring into a haze of smoke as the scent of gunpowder fingered its way up their nostrils, familiar in its way, like the 4th of July.

And that's the way they stood for seconds that stretched into minutes and minutes that would not stretch at all. For, try as they had to restrain them, and struggle as they might to deny them, days of reckoning, like all things inevitable, without exception, ultimately arrive.

Chapter 25

Jimmy sat in his underwear upon the hotel bed, a bad spring digging into the small of his back with every labored breath. He gave a grunt and shifted his weight, the ice pack stinging his flesh as it shifted over his bad hip.

The joint ached worse than ever, but it was nothing next to the pain from the stitched wound in his gut.

Every minor movement brought searing little agonies, as if a fresh, invisible blade lashed in and out of his abdomen. It hurt to cough. It hurt to cry. He figured it would probably hurt to laugh, but life hadn't given him reason to test that theory for a long, gray while.

Things were bad and bound to get worse if they didn't get moving. The cops would be searching for Robin over her husband. They'd also be looking to question him about Howard. Then there was this Guild and its remaining members.

And above all else, there was Mario. His connections spidered throughout the entire east coast, and his reach was long. They really couldn't wait another day. If they were going to last, they'd have to get out on the road.

He ran a gentle hand over the blood-crusted bandage on his stomach and winced. Then he held up the remote control and tapped buttons in search of some kind of news.

"Protecting the well-being of a nation," said a soft female voice on the television over video of a family embracing. "Leading at the forefront of innovation," the voice purred as a scientist peered into a microscope. "Viox Genomics helps ensure the health of our families with leading-edge technologies that protect our present and pave a path toward a brighter tomorrow."

Jimmy narrowed his eyes at the television, where a smiling doctor chatted with an equally beaming patient.

"With support from America's leaders and a diverse team of compassionate experts, we continue our mission to advance the human impact on the world in positive ways that reach far and wide into a bright future for all."

A line of children held hands amid a golden field, their hair flowing in the wind as they walked toward a vivid sunrise.

"Viox Genomics," the voice said, "the future of medicine, today."

Jimmy shook his head and raised the remote but froze as the commercial yielded to a news report. He bit his lip and sat up a little as a big red graphic shot across the screen.

"Breaking news!" said a deep, echoing, almost-robotic voice. "From KFIE, your most trusted news source."

The graphic gave way to a middle-aged newsman in a stiff-looking suit.

"Good morning," he said as he stared into a teleprompter. "We have breaking news from David Barker, who's joining us live from the downtown sector. David?"

"Yes, Tom, I'm here live in the southwest side of the downtown area, where violence and fire have cut a fresh wound into a city that was already deeply scarred."

The reporter gestured over his shoulder at the smoking remains of a structure, where police and firemen picked through a mass of blackened rubble.

Jimmy jerked up with recognition and cried out as hot pain radiated through his gut.

"We have limited information right now," the reporter continued. "But what we do know is shocking and disturbing. According to police, late last night, gunfire erupted at this location behind me, which was formerly an exclusive gentlemen's club. The exchange of bullets resulted in numerous fatalities, including the business owner, Mario Casella, who had been the subject of several investigations relating to numerous alleged criminal activities."

The door to Jimmy's hotel room opened, and Claire Foley entered.

"It's time," she said.

She watched him for a moment and then followed his eyes to the TV.

"Ah," she said. "Catching up on the news?"

Jimmy swallowed and gestured toward the screen.

"Is this your work?" he asked.

The woman looked at him and frowned, her face stony and closed. But her eyes, those dark, depthless eyes, they smiled.

"You know," she said as she approached the television. "You really shouldn't watch the news." She flipped it off, and the screen winked black. "It's just so damned depressing."

Outside in the parking lot, Robin stood watching as Jimmy staggered from the hotel room, his weathered face pinching against the glare of a bright new day.

As the woman followed, Jimmy limped across the parking lot, his eyes trained on Robin, who looked pale and ragged and long without sleep. Behind her, a short man stood next to a sedan, his arms crossed, eyes concealed behind a pair of dark sunglasses.

"This is John," said Claire Foley as they approached Robin. "He'll be relocating Robin. She'll have a new identity, enough money to get started. You know the drill."

Jimmy looked the man up and down.

"Is he good?"

"Of course," said the woman. "I only deal with the best." She looked from Jimmy to Robin. "I'll give you two a minute."

They watched her walk away, and Robin seemed to relax once she'd gone.

"Is this what you want?" she asked Jimmy. "To work for her?"

Jimmy shrugged.

"Gotta pay the bills somehow."

Robin looked him over and frowned at his bruise-blushed face.

"I'm sorry, Jimmy," she said. "This is my fault."

Jimmy shook his head.

"It was my choice," he said. "It's what I decided."

She swallowed and looked past him.

"Be careful," she said. "That woman is very, very dangerous."

Jimmy glanced back over his shoulder and nodded.

"Yeah," he said. "I'm getting that."

He turned back toward her and took a deep breath.

"Well," he said. "This is it."

"Yeah," she said. "I guess so."

She took in a deep breath, and he put a hand on her shoulder.

"Don't worry," he said. "You're free now. You have a second chance,"

She looked up at him, her eyes glistening with fresh tears.

"It's just," she said, "I don't think I deserve it."

Jimmy looked back at her and shrugged.

"Sometimes life gives you a second chance," he said. "It doesn't matter why. It doesn't even matter if you really deserve it. What matters is what you do now that you got it."

Her chin dipped downward, and he squeezed her shoulder.

"The past is gone," he said. "It doesn't matter anymore. What you did, what you didn't do. It's all irrelevant now. You don't earn second chances before you get them, Robin. You earn them after you get them. Not in the past, but in the future. Don't ask if you deserve it because you probably don't. You have to go earn it."

He squeezed her shoulder again.

"Start now."

Tears trickled down her cheek, and she threw her arms around him, his stomach wound burning as she gave him a tight squeeze.

"Thank you, Jimmy," she said.

Then, without saying another word, she released him and turned toward the sedan, where the short man was waiting with the door open.

Jimmy watched her through the window glass as the car drove away, but she didn't look back, and something inside him felt glad about it. He took in a shallow breath and turned away.

The woman watched Jimmy approach, his pistol hanging loosely from her hand.

"You left this in the hotel room," she said as she held it out.

Jimmy took it and slipped it into his waistband behind his back.

"Thanks."

He turned, and they both watched the car diminish as it sped toward the horizon.

"She'll be alright," said the woman.

Jimmy nodded.

"Yeah."

She turned toward him and looked him up and down.

"You ready to get your hands dirty?"
Jimmy looked back toward the car, but it was already gone.
"Yeah," he said.
The woman smiled.
"Then let's get started."

THE END

WHAT TO READ NEXT:

The **five-book Claire Foley thriller series**, available at AMAZON.

Who is Claire Foley? What's the secret behind Viox Genomics? Find out in the five-book thriller series. Start with book one, GIRL IN A RABBIT HOLE, at Amazon.

Also available:

JIMMY HUNTER and Tracy Sterling in

LIES AND BONES (BOOK 1)
CAPITOL KILLER (BOOK 2)
DROWNED AT DAWN (BOOK 3)
STEW OF BONES (BOOK 4)

Each title available at AMAZON.

Also by RJ Law:

THE HELL THAT FOLLOWED

A Request from the Author:

Dear friend,

I rely on reviews to get the word out about my books. If you enjoyed this book, can I ask you to take a moment to leave a brief review on Amazon?

You can leave a quick customer review at the bottom of the page at https://www.amazon.com/dp/B0B1RWTZYS

Also, to make sure you never miss a new release, please visit my website www.booksbyrjlaw.com to join my email list, so I can alert you when I publish my next book. I promise I only send messages when I have a new release. You can also follow on Amazon, at Bookbub and on Twitter at @RJLaw3,

Thank you so much for reading. I hope you enjoyed this book as much as I enjoyed writing it. Readers like you are what keeps me writing and I thank you for your support.

All the best to you and yours.

RJ LAW

This is a work of fiction. Any names or characters, businesses or places, events or incidents, are fictitious. Any resemblance to actual persons, living or dead, or actual events is purely coincidental. No part of this eBook may be reproduced or transmitted in any form or by any means, electronic or mechanical, including photocopying, recording or by any information storage and retrieval system, without written permission from the author.

Copyright 2022 RJ Law All rights reserved.